THE PRETTY BEACH LIFE

POLLY BABBINGTON

PollyBabbington.com

Want more from Polly's world?

For sneak peeks into new settings, early chapters, downloadable Pretty Beach and Darling Island freebies and bits and bobs from Polly's writing days sign up for Babbington Letters.

1

The aroma of cinnamon buns just out of the oven drifted through the house as Lotta cradled a cup of tea in her hands. She strolled into the library room, taking it all in with a smile on her face. The room warmed the cockles of her heart as her books looked back at her from the floor-to-ceiling shelves, from her desk, and in stacks here, there, and everywhere. Neat piles of well-organised, colour-coordinated books also peered up at her from the coffee table, together with a wicker tray displaying layers of enormous creamy-white pillar candles and a small vase of flowers. A little side table also made her smile, adorned as it was with picture frames and a glass vase filled with flotsam and jetsam from her walks by the sea. This was Lotta's happy place. A room full of books that made her heart sing.

With her feet tucked up under her, she settled onto the plush, blue velvet sofa, sipped her tea, and let the cushions envelop her. The velvet fabric reminded her of the day she'd dragged the sofa into the house and started the transformation of the place into what was now her very own library room. Along with the transformation of the room and the transformation of her house, Pretty Beach to the Breakers, *she* had been transformed too, and she adored how that made her feel. She'd gone from jobless, and more or less homeless, to successfully employed, slowly doing up her old home, and setting up a business as a second income. Life was pretty darn good from her side of the fence. And she'd like it to stay that way thank you very much.

Musing over her life and sipping her tea, Lotta's gaze landed on the blue curtains, also velvet, that she'd rescued along with the sofa from the garage. The memory of her hard work and scrambling to get the room sorted and Jack's help with it, made her smile. Her attention shifted to her Kindle, neatly lined up on the coffee table, and the notebook alongside it, and she thought about her reading influencer work where she was slowly getting more and more business. She shook her head at the irony of it all. Year after disappointing year of trying to make her mark in the cut-throat world of publishing had got her nowhere. And now here she was actually getting paid work as a book influencer. Her world had turned in its own very mysterious way. Who would have thought her voracious reading habit would have turned into a job? No one, least of all her. But that it had, and she was more than pleased about it.

As she sat on the sofa, lost in thought, her mind drifted between the past, present, and future. Despite an up-and-down few months, where she'd wondered if Jack really did like her, here she was now, standing at the threshold of creating new memories. Almost at the start of a new journey in what had been a tumultuous few years. It was astounding how her existence had turned on its head since the fateful day when she'd first bumped into Jack at the bar in a country house hotel. Then, she'd been lonely and at the bottom of the ladder of life. Now, she was so far from that perched on the top rung of the ladder that it made her feel almost giddy.

Cradling her steaming tea, the warmth spreading through

her fingers as she glanced out the window, she took in the garden and blue skies with glimpses of the sea just visible in the distance. Pretty Beach had been another transformation in her life. She adored living in the little town with its gorgeous old lighthouse, picturesque views, and friendly locals. The thought of capitalising on that, putting roots down, building a life and a business in Pretty Beach surrounded by her books and love, brought a smile to her face.

With her tea finished, Lotta gently placed the cup on the coffee table, feeling a deep sense of gratitude for the path her life had taken. Her past with her ex Dan and the disaster of his startup business with his app had been a horrible time in her life with more downs than ups, but in its own funny way, it had led her to where she found herself now. A place brimming with new and nice beginnings – a good job, a lovely house, and a new partner. Life was on the up. Her phone pinged, jolting her out of her thoughts.

Jack: *Hey, how are you?*

Lotta: *Good. I was just thinking about you.*

Jack: *Thinking how lucky you are?*

Lotta raised her eyebrows and chuckled to herself. If only he knew.

Lotta: *Of course.*

Jack: *Ready for the weekend?*

Lotta: *Do you mean am I ready for more work?*

Jack: *I do. After the garden working bee, we need to get on and swiftly.*

Lotta: *Yep, I know. Yes. I'm ready.*

Jack: *Good. By this time next week, you're going to have the first Pretty Beach reading retreat locked and loaded.*

Lotta gulped. She tried to smile, but her stomach churned with uncertainty. Had she made the right decision with the reading retreat? She bit her lower lip and crossed her fingers, hoping that it would be a success. She was gambling money on it. Only time would tell.

Lotta: *Yes, exciting – I think.*

Jack: *You'll be fine. Ok, spk later. Love you.*

Lotta sent back a love heart and then sat staring out the window, contemplating Jack's words. She then pondered the old building beside the boathouse; it had almost been on the same journey as her…in a state of neglect, sad and unloved, but now was slowly but surely coming back to life. She couldn't wait to see how it turned out. Hopefully it would be the final part of the puzzle in her new life by the sea.

2

With a strong sea breeze coming in off the water, Lotta stood looking at the woodwork on the old building next to the boathouse. When she'd first contemplated its renovation, everything had been weathered by time and seaside living. Its paint had been peeling, the old climbers over the door gnarly and overgrown, and a couple of panes in the dirty windows cracked. Now it stood proudly in its little spot at the end of the garden, ready to embrace a new repurposed life.

When she and Jack had first considered the building, Lotta had been doubtful and not quite full of enthusiasm that it could be turned around. But once it had been cleared of junk and given a coat of paint, potential had poured from every orifice. Lotta had taken the bull by the horns and ran with it. She'd spent days creating Pinterest boards, hours scouring house renovation stories, and way too much brain power gathering inspiration to fill the place with the sorts of things that would bring her vision of comfort-reading to life.

Inching past the bay trees in dolly planters she'd strategically placed on either side of the heavy old door, she strolled in and looked around. It was so different to how it had looked before –

almost as if it was an entirely different building altogether. The walls now wore a soft colour palette, the wide-plank floorboards had been sanded back to the natural wood, and the brickwork by the fireplace, without its harsh coat of paint, had softened. Lotta walked around nodding and mentally noting the things she had left to do to add the finishing touches to the reading retreat of dreams.

Everything was so nice, it was as if she herself wanted to move in. In the small bathroom with its exposed timber ceiling, she wanted to run the bath, get a book, seep down low into the water and have a soak. She stared up at the natural timber, remembering wobbling on the top of a ladder with a sander, erasing years of grime and layers of brightly coloured paint. Now the timber, with its splits, knocks, and marks, looked as if it had come from a different world and smiled down at anyone below.

The brief in Lotta's head and the result of her Pinterest surfing had been simple; to create an easy, relaxing environment which would invite one to sit and not do much at all – a place to lounge on a sofa with a Kindle or sink into a tub full of bubbles with a good book. The vision in front of her was doing a good job of fulfilling what she'd been thinking in her head. An old re-enamelled freestanding tub she'd found on eBay stood in front of panelled walls, and a vintage glass medicine cabinet by way of someone on the Pretty Beach community page hung over the sink. A long, antique black pendant light was tucked in the corner, and a skinny rustic timber bench weathered by time stood in front of a Victorian column radiator, ready and waiting for stacks of fluffy towels. All of it crying out for someone with nothing to do but have a stash of books to read, to come and stay.

Back in the kitchen, Lotta nodded to herself. It also fulfilled her vision. When she'd first walked into the tiny room, her heart had sunk. She'd known then that, to her mind, any sort of reading retreat worth its salt would need a welcoming, heart-warming kitchen, and when she'd first seen it, it was so far from that it wasn't funny. As she'd planned the retreat, she'd ascertained that if her guests were anything like her, the kitchen would need to be a place to read at the same time as cooking, pottering and drinking. On her Pinterest boards, she'd pinned away to her heart's content, envisioning a kitchen bathed in gorgeous Pretty Beach natural light, large windows offering glimpses of the sea, cabinets painted in soft, muted tones filling the space with calm and warmth. Now those actual ideas stood before her, tall and proud. A round scrubbed pine table surrounded by mismatched chairs held a glass vase with a single stem of dried flowers, and a deep butler's sink with a gooseneck tap nestled beneath the old sash window. Along the facing wall, open shelves displayed an eclectic collection of cookware, mixing bowls, and dishes, and hanging from hooks above the hues of copper pots contrasted against the whites of the walls and cabinets.

As Lotta stood in the kitchen, her thoughts brimmed with ideas and inspiration. The reading retreat was so close to being done that she could almost smell it. The last push to making everything a reading dream was the courtyard, a water feature and the soft furnishings. Once those were sorted, she'd be finally taking the plunge and making it available to rent out.

Just as she was standing with the back door open, pondering the last few touches, she heard Jack coming across the garden with a large box in his arms.

'Lotta as in hotter.' Jack beamed.

'Just Jack. How's your morning been so far?'

'Not bad. I need a coffee though, that I can tell you for free.' Jack laughed as he kissed Lotta and then followed her through to the tiny kitchen, his frame seeming to fill the whole room.

Jack put the huge box he was carrying down on the table and patted the top of it. 'The water feature of your dreams.'

'Thank you,' Lotta said, peering at the pictures on the side of the box. 'You think it will work in the space? I hope so.'

'I can't see why not. I had a look at the instructions earlier… Put it this way, it may take us a while. They are complicated.'

'Oh. Gosh, you know me and instructions too,' Lotta stated with raised eyebrows.

'Hmm. Well, we'll see how we go. Teamwork.'

Lotta nodded as she squinted at the water feature, pulled the instructions from inside the box and flipped through the booklet. Her eyes widened. 'Err, yep, we're going to need a coffee before we get into this.'

'I know.'

'I'll go and make some.'

Ten minutes later, Lotta walked into the courtyard with a timber tray holding a cafetière, mugs, and a slab of organic dark chocolate. Jack sat with a frown on his face, the booklet in one hand and his phone playing a video in the other, as Lotta poured the coffee. 'Yeah, this is written for engineers.' Jack chuckled. 'I'll be doing this all day by the looks of it. So much for it being quick and easy to install. It actually says that on the side of the box. I don't know who could do this quickly or easily.'

Lotta looked from him to the courtyard garden. 'It really will make it,' she said as she looked at the jumble of pots adjacent to the old copper outdoor shower, remembering how she'd scoured Marketplace for pots and plants. Then she'd not really been sure about her gardening skills, but now somehow she'd ended up with a lovely mix of thriving beauties.

Her eyes scanned the small, enclosed space. She'd envisioned a haven filled with a jumble of plants nestled in vintage pots of varying shapes and sizes, the brick walls providing a warm suntrap backdrop, and dappled shadows on the brick terrace underfoot. Now with a fair bit of backbreaking work behind them, it was looking back at her.

'How strange to have an outdoor shower,' Lotta mused, her gaze drifting towards the sunny little corner and the shower. 'Imagine stepping out of that when it's really warm.'

Jack smiled at the thought. 'It does sound rather idyllic.'

'Yep, and lovely with the water feature too.'

'I think installing it just there might be good. If we can actually get it to work,' Jack said, pointing beside the spot with the outdoor shower Lotta had been admiring.

As she followed his gaze and surveyed the courtyard, Lotta nodded. 'Yeah. I reckon.' She stood up and started to dive into the water feature pulling out polystyrene and plastic bags one after the other. Spreading out the various components, she picked up the assembly instructions Jack had been studying with a frown. 'Alright, let's see... step one,' she read aloud, squinting at the small print and the diagrams. 'Attach the part marked A to support B... Where on earth is the part marked A?'

Jack rifled through the assortment of pieces, eventually holding up a small, curved bracket. 'I think this might be it.' He squinted as he turned it over and shook his head. 'I don't see an A, but it does look like the diagram.'

Lotta rolled her eyes. 'I don't think this job is my skill set. Not at all.'

'Whose *is* this skill set?' Jack bantered. 'Not mine either.'

'I don't know, but I think I'm much better suited to bedlinen and collecting pots and pans for the kitchen than trying to work this out. In fact, I'm better horizontal on the sofa in the library room with a book.'

For the next hour or so, they fumbled through the instructions, laughing back and forth in amusement at the conundrum of the water feature. Once they were what they assumed was nearly at the end, Lotta frowned at a pipe coming out of the copper feature bowl filled with pebbles. 'You've attached that the wrong way round!' she chided gently, pointing at a misaligned pipe.

Jack feigned indignation and winked. 'I think that bit was your job.'

Lotta rolled her eyes, grinning. 'How do they reckon this is easy to install? It's taken us longer to put this together than it did to put an actual bath in! All this just to hear a few trickles.'

'I know. Too funny.'

A long time later and finally with the water feature installed, Lotta stood back as the sound of trickling water filled the air. The shallow bowl filled with pebbles and topped up with shells and stones from Lotta's walks on the beach was nestled into the jumble of pots and planters in the corner. She had to admit that it might have taken a long time, but it was more than worth it.

'A job well done if not taking a very long time and a lot of effort,' Jack joked, slipping an arm around Lotta's waist.

'Yep, thank you,' Lotta agreed, leaning into his shoulder with a smile on her face. She pointed to the timber outdoor table in the corner, basking in flecked sunshine. 'It really is a nice place to sit and lose yourself in a book, isn't it?'

'It is, and coming from a non-reader, that says a lot,' Jack agreed.

Lotta felt ridiculously and immensely pleased with herself as they both stood watching and listening to the water feature. With its installation, everything had finally slotted into place. She rubbed her hands together and smiled. Now all she had to do was see if anyone would be half as enthusiastic about reading in a little retreat by the sea as she was.

3

The next morning, in a loose linen top and ripped jeans, her hair pulled up in a casual bun, Lotta stood in front of Pretty Beach to the Breakers with a cup of tea in her hand, looking up at the sky. It was as if someone had washed the world above her in a kaleidoscope of colours. As she stood on the driveway, she couldn't help but feel a flutter of excitement in her stomach as she waited for the arrival of the furniture for the reading retreat. Everything about the renovation had been done on a tight budget and a wing and a prayer, but she'd made the executive decision that the sofa and the bed needed to have no expense spared. So she'd plunged a lot of money she didn't really have into goods from the Cotswolds and hoped they'd recoup their cost in guests having lovely stays. Who really knew if it would work? Least of all her.

She stood looking out for the delivery van and drinking in the colours in the sky until she heard it rumble into view. Lotta smiled as the van beeped and reversed onto the drive, and she recognised the same portly man who had delivered her bed climb out of the cab. He beamed, squinted down at his phone, and then looked up with an enquiring look on his face. 'Two sofas, one king bed, one small, limited access?'

'Yes.' Lotta smiled. 'Hi.'

He frowned and looked up towards the first floor of the house. 'Didn't I deliver a sleigh bed here a while ago? Turning stairs?'

'Yes, you did.' Lotta laughed. 'No stairs for this lot. We're going through the garden and in the back there.'

'No steps or tight corners?' he asked.

'Nope, it's just a bit narrow through the doorways which is why I ticked limited access.'

'No worries. Just what I like to hear.'

Lotta held up her mug. 'Cup of tea for any of you?'

The man grinned and looked over to his team, who were unlocking the back doors of the van. 'I reckon we'd all love one. One with two sugars, the rest without.'

'I'll be back.'

Twenty minutes later, after the delivery men had downed the tea, Lotta watched as the sofas, a pair of sumptuous linen beauties, were carefully manoeuvred through the door. Once they were in place, Lotta was absurdly pleased with herself for ploughing most of her budget into them. Their soft, inviting cushions and thick arms made the whole place sing and notched it up a level. She could already imagine her future guests curled up with a good book, losing themselves in the pages with the sounds of the sea in the background.

Next came the beds, their luxurious mattresses destined for the retreat's bedrooms. She stood back, watching as the delivery team assembled the frames and swallowed a little lump as it all came together. She couldn't quite believe it. She, Lotta Button, who had not that long before been jobless and hopeless, was looking at the embodiment of not just her hard work but a whole new life. She wasn't going to argue with that.

Once the delivery men had finished up, Lotta stood in the

utility room in Pretty Beach to the Breakers and finished ironing gorgeous washed linen sheets and duvet covers for the new beds. As she spritzed the covers with linen spray and pushed the button on the steam iron, the air filled with the scent of sheets dried in the Pretty Beach elements; she wanted to bottle it and put it beside her bed.

Piling the linen into her arms, she strolled across the garden, pushed the retreat door open with her foot, made her way through and walked into the bedroom. Even though, with Jack's help, she'd done the majority of the work herself, Lotta was still surprised at what greeted her; the funny old building, which had previously been filled with years of old junk, grime, and dust, had gradually morphed into a charming, cosy haven by the sea. It was exactly as she'd hoped it would be; a place where visitors could lose themselves in the pages of a book whilst being very comfortable and, at the same time, enjoying the fresh coastal air of Pretty Beach. After initially wondering whether or not she was doing the right thing, she had poured her heart and soul into every little detail, making sure the retreat was perfect, and now it was showing every which way she turned. She wanted to give herself a big old pat on the back, her accomplishment felt that good.

As she began to make up the bed, she flung open the windows and smiled; it was the kind of day where the sea shimmered and sparkled, and the salty breeze blasted through the windows. She looked around as she finally smoothed the covers on the bed. Everything had come together beautifully. The scent of lavender from a little bedside diffuser wafted through the air, and soft pastel linen curtains swayed in the breeze. In the corner, the reading nook she'd created, complete with an overstuffed armchair, a stack of books, and a table lamp, was ready and waiting to illuminate late-night reading sessions, and the dress cushions on the bed invited sinking back and getting lost in the pages of a book.

Lotta finished the beds and then walked around the freshly renovated retreat, taking in the results of her and Jack's hard work. The once neglected, in-need-of-love building now exuded an inviting atmosphere. With its whitewashed walls, large windows framing picturesque views, and timber floors, it truly had come up trumps.

As she made her way through the building, she couldn't help but be pleased with herself. The sitting room, with its puffy linen sofas, a vintage coffee table adorned with a stack of carefully selected books, and an antique hurricane lamp, suggested a sit-down and a pause from the world outside. The soft glow of floor lamps added warmth to the room, and an oversized sisal rug underfoot provided a cosy spot for guests to curl up with a book.

The kitchen, once a cramped and dingy space, was now a bright, welcoming corner of the retreat. A sturdy butler sink, flanked by two wooden worktops, took pride of place beneath a window that offered views of the courtyard garden. Warm sunlight streamed in, catching the timeworn copper pots and pans hanging above the sink. Lotta ran her fingers over the open shelves that displayed an array of mismatched crockery, a vast collection of cookbooks, and jars filled with herbs and spices. All of it showed her hard work and effusive Pinterest diving.

A quick glance at the bathroom brought a smile to Lotta's face. The clawfoot bathtub, with its gracefully curved feet, sat ready for an indulgent soak. Lotta could already imagine her guests unwinding in the tub, a glass of wine in hand and a book propped on the bath tray. A candle would be lit on the side, a stack of fluffy towels would be ready to go, and getting lost in someone else's world would be the order of the day.

Standing back and surveying the transformed retreat, Lotta almost hummed in anticipation. It had been hard work, sometimes backbreaking, true, but she had sucked it up and breathed new life into the once-dusty and sad place. It was now as she'd hoped it would be – a sanctuary in Pretty Beach for book lovers to escape the chaos of the world.

Nodding to herself, immensely satisfied, it wasn't lost on her that in Lotta's *actual* life, she had done precisely the same thing. The trajectory of all of it was a one way street. One which pointed in one direction only; up.

4

A few days later, on her way to work, Lotta was swamped with tasks, what with the reading retreat, her book reviews and that thing that paid the bills – her actual job. She was feeling far too uppity to go straight to the arcade, so she'd hustled for the early ferry so she could have a read in the bandstand to try and calm down and set herself up for her day. Her nerves were because of a plethora of small, inconsequential, but at the same time somehow exceedingly busy events in her life. She ducked into the coffee kiosk and stood in the queue.

'Morning, Lotta. How was your commute? That wind coming in is a bit biting considering the time of year,' the woman behind the counter said with a smile.

It still made Lotta smile that her ferry ride was considered a commute. It had to be one of the better commutes in the world. She'd take sitting on the top of a ferry bobbing up the coast over a smelly, dirty old train under the ground any day of the week. 'Yep. I was glad I had a jacket this morning. I was sitting up the top, and the views were gorgeous, but it was definitely chilly.'

'I bet. A clear sky means good views and sometimes a cold wind out on the coast there.'

'I'm beginning to realise that,' Lotta agreed with a nod.

'Usual?'

'Yes, please.'

'How are things with you?'

Instead of continuing with her usual socially acceptable 'Fine, thank you,' Lotta paused. 'I've got quite a lot on my mind.'

'Ahh, yes, same here.'

And then she heard herself embellishing further. 'I have a huge week coming up here at work. A load of politicians are in, and the schedule is daunting, to say the least. I'm also posting my reading retreat online for the first time. I told you all about that, remember?'

'You have a job and half there if you've got politicians in.'

'I know.'

'Ooh, so you must have made good progress with your renovations, have you?'

'Yes, it's all done and ready to go.'

'Well done. Go for it. I'm sure, from what you've told me, it will go down a storm.'

'Hope so,' Lotta replied as she took the coffee. 'We can but try.'

'Yes indeed.'

As Lotta got to the bandstand, she tucked her cream silky V-neck blouse into her high-waisted belted trousers and took off her jacket. Despite the cold, chilly breeze, the bandstand in its position sheltered her from the wind. She sat down and opened her Kindle, but unable to concentrate, she let it rest in her lap, got out her phone, pulled up Google Docs, and reread the description of the reading retreat.

Welcome to Pretty Beach Reader's Retreat. If you've always dreamt of a holiday tucked up in a little house with all the joys of the quintessentially English seaside on your doorstep, you're in the right place.

Come and stay in our beautiful old seaside abode. Nestled at the end of our garden with views looking out over the sea, you'll find yourself in a haven of books and coastal delights.

With a lovely kitchen in a soft natural colour palette, rustic details, and direct access to a gorgeous, dappled light pebble garden, with a bubbling water feature surrounded by ferns, you'll switch off almost from moment one.

Access to the house is completely separate, and you'll enter via a cosy & beautifully arranged sun-facing ground floor reception room with a relaxed three-seater sofa, comfortable armchair, & floor-to-ceiling shelving jam-packed full of books. And yes, there's a book ladder on wheels.

With space to sit and read in every room, complete with a gorgeous old wood burner and views over the courtyard garden, you'll have nothing much to do but sit and lose yourself in a book.

For your soaking whilst reading pleasure, a simple, relaxing, panelled bathroom comes complete with a freestanding bath, basin, and toilet. With its huge floor-to-ceiling sash window, you'll love a long bath with a view.

The two bedrooms are furnished with gorgeous Edwardian-style beds with new, top-of-the-range sumptuous mattresses, where you'll want to do nothing but stay under the covers and read all day long. Both bedrooms sport washed linen bedding handmade in Portugal, sweet breakfast tables, reading lamps, & sumptuous throws to cosy under and get lost in the pages of your favourite read.

Our little abode has some of the best seascape and old town views, and the pebble garden, with various little reading nooks and seats, offers plenty of places to catch both the morning & afternoon sun. A luscious green area with a timber outdoor table includes comfy chairs, a vintage umbrella, and a beautiful water feature trickling over pebbles from the beach.

Just a short stroll from the house, you'll find the calm waters of Pretty Beach and the rugged coastal walk up to the lighthouse.

We guarantee you'll utterly love it.

Lotta nodded to herself. She wanted to move in. Shuddering at the thought of the cost of not only the sofas and mattresses but the Portuguese linen, she reminded herself that buying fewer, nicer, high-quality things had been her philosophy for the reading retreat, meaning that, hopefully, they would last a long time. She only hoped the time and money showed.

Copying the text, she pasted it into a message and, together with her latest photos, sent a text to her cousin Liv, asking her to have a read. A message fired back straight away.

Liv: *When can I move in?*

Lotta: *Anytime. Ha!*

Liv: *Seriously, it sounds amazing.*

Lotta: *I hope so.*

Liv: *The pictures are lovely. I'd book it, that's for sure.*

Lotta: *I really need this to go well with all the money I've spent on it.*

Liv: *You spent your money on the things that mattered.*

Lotta: *Yes, and everything else was pre-loved and recycled.*

Liv: *You've got a sustainable holiday home. On trend, Lott. ;)*

Lotta: *I'll add that to the list of benefits, shall I?*

Liv: *It's very imp. Maybe you should.*

Lotta: *Ha ha. I've done my bit for the planet.*

Liv: *Send me a text when it's live and I'll book lol.*

Lotta: *Will do.*

Once Lotta had finished in the bandstand, she'd stopped on the corner, changed into her power heels, and then stepped through the black doors of the old arcade where she worked. As she walked in, she wondered what the day would bring. The more she got to know her job, the more she loved it with every day throwing up new things. She looked around at the lobby of the beautiful, historic building feeling very grateful and very lucky to call it her place of work. She really had gone way up in the world of employment. She couldn't quite believe that she was *actually* proud of where she worked and how it made her feel. It had been a long time coming. Her days of answering Facebook messages disguised as publisher marketing whilst sitting in a grotty damp office were long gone. With her heels clipping on the shiny floor, she no longer had to try to appear confident and battle with imposter syndrome as she first had when she'd started the job. Now she felt confident and comfortable in just being herself. It was the best feeling *ever*.

With a little bit of a hustle in her step, she passed the walls tastefully displaying pictures in thick black frames showing scenes from Newport Reef's past. She scooted under the long line of pendant lights and past the ginormous pots full of lush palms, and after keying in a code, the door to the inner lobby clicked open, and Lotta made her way to the office. She beamed as she saw Marie perched on the edge of the sofa, tapping away at an iPad.

'Morning!' Lotta said cheerily.

Marie beamed. 'Here she is. Ms Button has arrived. Do you want the bad news or the bad news?' Marie said with a little bit of an eye roll at the end of her question.

Lotta matched the eye roll and chuckled. 'Oh god, not already. I was snowed under before I even arrived this morning.

At least problems here will take my mind off other stuff in that thing they call my brain.'

'Yep. I'm glad I'm supporting you today and not leading.' Marie laughed.

Lotta remembered the first time there'd been a major problem at one of her events. She'd been convinced she'd get the sack, but what, in actual fact, had happened was the opposite. Now she wasn't daunted by work problems. The one thing she'd learnt is that they happened as a regularity in her workday, and sometimes came thick and fast. 'What's happened?'

'One of the politicians has asked if the sandwiches are sustainably produced. Apparently it's in their manifesto and is taken to the letter.' Marie paused and tapped the iPad. 'Another one is stuck in Birmingham because of a broken down train and is asking to be Zoomed in. Umm, what else?' She looked down again. 'The one who RSVP'd as a no is now a yes, and there's a power outage on the sockets and switches in the conference room.'

'Okay. I can deal with all of that apart from the broken down train.' Lotta laughed.

'Yeah. I've phoned the emergency electrician and he's on his way.'

'Good. Thank you. So I just need to set up another seat and pack for the extra attendee and find out what's in the sandwiches. Correct?'

'Yep, you do.'

'I think I might do myself a coffee before I get going. I've already had one this morning, but I feel it's going to be needed.'

'How's the divine and gorgeous, Jack?' Marie asked as she got up from the sofa, picked up the iPad, and followed Lotta into the kitchen.

'He's good. He's off to Germany on business this week. Just a quick there and back.'

'Gosh, he gets around! Weren't you going to the States with him for a weekend?' Marie said with a frown.

'I was, but we've had a rethink on that.' Lotta lowered her voice. 'It would use up a few days of my holiday, and I think I'd rather go somewhere else.'

'Hmm. I get you. Where was it again he was going?'

'Texas.'

'Hmm, yeah, right.'

'I think I'd rather have a week in Greece, if I'm honest,' Lotta said with a nod of her head.

'Don't blame you one iota.'

'So, yes, I'm just going to wait and see,' Lotta said as she poured out a black coffee. 'I also have to keep my mum in mind. You never know when I might have to go back to Singapore.'

'How is she?'

'Okay, but quite frail. So we'll see what happens.'

'Hmm. You just have to wait and see, I suppose, yes. There's not a lot more you *can* do.'

'I do. Right, okay, let's get going.' Lotta took a deep breath and sipped her coffee, steeling herself for the inevitable chaos that was about to unfold. She loved her new job and found she almost thrived on it. She was now able to predict a day of problems ahead, and she could see one coming up. She exchanged a quick nod with Marie, and they set off towards the lobby.

As they walked across the tiled floor, Lotta couldn't help but thank her lucky stars that the job had found her. Everything about it was just lovely – the fast pace, the good people, plus the classic English decor, the rich panelling adorning the walls, and the plants made for a very nice place to spend one's working day. As they scooted around to the welcome area, plush armchairs upholstered in deep green velvet were clustered around low, gleaming coffee tables, and the scent of fresh flowers and polished wood filled the air. Low rent it was not.

As they approached, Lotta could see the area was already

beginning to fill up, the attendees helping themselves to coffee and a low buzz of conversation reverberated around the room. Lotta swallowed at the knowledge that, as it stood, there was no power in the conference room.

'Alright, let's get to work,' Lotta whispered to Marie. 'I'll deal with the extra guest and the sandwich situation, you keep an eye out for the electrician.'

Marie nodded, her expression matching Lotta's. 'Sounds like a plan.'

With a wink from Marie, Lotta spoke to a few attendees and then stepped outside, where she phoned the catering company and spoke to the owner about the sustainability of the sandwich ingredients. After a brief conversation, she was relieved to learn that the sandwich platters were indeed sustainably produced, and everything, including the bread and all the fillings, was locally sourced. Food miles were not part of the equation. She chuckled to herself as she copied the text sent to her, popped it into an email, and sent it to the attendee.

Next, she dashed back to the conference room, setting up an additional seat for the unexpected attendee, prepared a small welcome pack, and ensured the iPad was set up and ready to go. As the clock ticked closer to the event's start time, Lotta began to feel the pressure mounting. The electrician had yet to arrive, and she'd taken a call from the speaker, who was stuck in traffic. She exchanged a worried glance with Marie, who had been anxiously hovering by the door awaiting the electrician's arrival.

'We're being tested this morning,' Marie hissed, beckoning Lotta over. 'The electrician just called. He's minutes away, but we're cutting it fine.'

'We have another problem, too,' Lotta said with wide eyes. 'The speaker is now stuck in traffic over at those lights on the one-way system. We have a while to go, but it's getting close.'

'When it rains, it pours.' Marie chuckled. 'Why does it always seem to happen like that? What do we do about the speaker?'

Lotta's mind raced as she considered their options. 'I have no idea, other than possibly dialling her in from her car. That won't go down well, though. I don't know why people just don't leave enough time so that if things like this happen, which they invariably do, it's not a problem.'

Marie nodded just as the electrician bustled in, toolbox in hand. He smiled at Marie and Lotta. 'Morning, ladies. No sockets or switches this morning! Not a good way to start the day.'

Lotta chuckled back. 'We need you to work your magic.' She turned her right wrist over and looked at her watch. 'And fast.'

He made a beeline for the problematic sockets. 'I'll see what I can do.'

'Coffee while you work?' Lotta asked.

'Love one, please.'

When Lotta was back with a coffee, Marie was outside with the attendees. Lotta held her breath as the electrician worked and she spoke to the speaker on the phone. The minutes ticked by, and the room filled with palpable tension. Just as Lotta was beginning to lose hope and was trying to think of a way she was going to solve the problem of not only no speaker but no presentation either, the electrician triumphantly declared the sockets fixed.

Lotta breathed a sigh of relief as she turned to Marie. 'Thank goodness. That's one thing sorted.' She pulled her phone out as it pinged. Reading the text, she looked up and smiled. 'And the speaker is going to be here on time after all. The jam cleared.'

Marie's eyes sparkled. 'Lotta Button does it again.' Marie grinned. 'Just another day in the life of event organisers, I suppose.'

Lotta nodded. It was indeed, but she, for one, wasn't going to start complaining anytime soon about the problems her job threw up. For Lotta, a nice, stable income and a good job had more or less changed the trajectory of her life. No one could argue with that. She smiled. 'Phew. I'm shattered already.'

'Yep, and we've hardly even started the week yet,' Marie acknowledged.

'Yeah, and I'm busy with second and third incomes this week too.' Lotta laughed. 'My plate is full.'

Marie looked interested as they strolled away from the conference room. She tapped Lotta on the arm. 'Oh, I meant to say to you, I mentioned the retreat to my cousin. Remember I told you about her?'

Lotta's mind was blank. She vaguely recalled Marie telling her something about a cousin of hers when they were working on one of Marie's events, but she couldn't quite remember what. 'Sorry, I can't remember exactly what you said.'

'The one with the book club.'

'Run it past me again.'

'You know, she's the CEO of that football club in Birmingham.'

'Oh yes, yes, sorry, I do remember.'

'Well, yeah, I told her about your place, and she asked for first dibs.'

'What, without seeing it?' Lotta clarified, screwing up her nose in question.

Marie laughed. 'I showed her your social media account and the library room, and she said by the looks of that, the retreat would be the same and she'd book it right away. She treats herself to what she calls "recharges" every few months. It's how she manages to do her fourteen-hour days, seven days a week.'

'Right. So, hang on. You're telling me she wants to book it as in, like, now?'

'I am. She asked me to ask you when it will be ready.'

'It's ready now. I'm putting it live in the next few days.'

'Have you got the pictures?'

'Yeah.' Lotta slipped her phone out of her pocket, tapped on her photos, selected the ones of the reading retreat, and sent them to Marie's phone.

Marie opened the message and then stopped in the middle of the lobby as her chin dropped to her chest. 'Goodness. Leave alone her coming for the weekend, she needs to get in line behind me. What the…'

'You like it?'

'Lotta, you seriously played this down. How on earth did you do this?'

'A tonne of work and a *lot* of thought. Plus, I had the amazing graft and help of the lovely Jack.'

'Oh my gosh, look at the kitchen! It's like something out of a movie. I love it! Those copper pans!'

Lotta scrolled through her phone, selected a few more pictures, and sent them to Marie.

Marie gasped as the pictures arrived. 'Oh my, it's lovely! It looks like the quintessential English cottage kitchen, but with books everywhere,' she said.

Lotta nodded. 'Good. That's the look I was going for. Soft neutral palette walls and white wooden cabinets. Lots of fresh flowers and herbs.' She trailed off as Marie expanded a picture and squinted. 'Books of all shapes and sizes in little nooks and crannies everywhere.'

Marie nodded in agreement. 'Ooh, the table in the corner, the farmhouse sink, all of it! I can just picture myself standing there, looking out the window at the sea with a cup of tea. It's a shame I don't have time for a retreat. This sitting room looks so cosy! The perfect place to unwind with a good book. Look at that ladder on wheels! Well done, you. Absolutely good job. Although I don't know why I expected anything less.'

Lotta nodded in agreement. 'I really thought about what I would want it to be like, you know? The kind of space that feels like home, but at the same time is really special. All the things I used to dream about when I was stuck in a grotty hovel of a flat, wondering where my life was going to end up.'

Marie's eyes widened. 'You certainly achieved it. Ooh, look at that little nook in the corner. The armchair and cushions. I could just curl up with a good book and a cup of tea on a rainy afternoon and not emerge for days. Weeks even.'

Lotta grinned. 'That's exactly the reaction I was hoping for.'

Marie laughed. 'Wait until I send her these. I can guarantee you, you just got your first guest. She'll be all over this like a rash.'

Lotta gulped, but she was secretly over the moon with Marie's reaction. Was it really all going to be as simple as that? She hoped so; she really did.

5

Lotta sat in the library room surrounded by the books she loved, and stared at her phone. She was about to go live on her account to talk about her latest venture – her new reading retreat at the bottom of the garden. She took repeated deep breaths, trying to calm herself as she felt a mixture of nerves and excitement coursing through her veins.

Fiddling with the decor behind her, she made sure the vase of flowers on the shelf was perfectly aligned with the camera on her phone. She then lit the oversized three-wick candle on the coffee table, straightened a pile of books, and switched on the lamp on her desk. Looking at her notes in front of her, she swallowed with nerves and shuddered as she went through the listing for the reading retreat on Airbnb.

She wasn't sure what she was feeling or how it was going to go, but she did know that she was quite far out of her comfort zone with a churning stomach and fizzing veins. She really had no clue how her retreat was going to be received. Her followers had been more than encouraging and enthusiastic about her transformation of the library room, and they'd followed along with the retreat renovations with a lot of gushing, but when the exchange of money was involved, things changed. As she waited for the time for the live to click over, she couldn't sit still and fidgeted by plumping the cushions on the sofa and redoing her hair.

Once it was time to get going, she tried to cast her nerves aside, tapped the button, and was off. She tried to relax as she looked into the screen and saw the shelves laden with books and fairy lights behind her. She peered into the dot at the top of the screen, forced herself to beam, cracked a joke, and hoped for the best. 'Hello, everyone!' Lotta said as she started the live stream. 'I'm thrilled to be here today to talk to you about the thing you've heard me going on about for ages – my very own reading retreat! You've seen it and me at our worst, but now we've got our bling on and we're ready to rumble.' She smiled widely, hoping that her followers could sense her enthusiasm and crossed her fingers tightly on her lap.

As she talked about her vision for the retreat, her followers began to ask questions. 'Will there be a mini version of the library room?' one asked.

'Already done and dusted,' Lotta replied, thanking her lucky stars that she'd decided to fill the sitting room in the retreat with books. 'It's all there in the photos now on my stories.'

She continued to enthuse about the retreat – the cosy bedroom with its window seat overlooking the pebbled courtyard and glimpses of the sea, the beautiful kitchen, and the little area with the outdoor table and water feature, which now also came with the added pleasure of a hammock strung between the trees.

As she chatted, the hearts up the side of her phone screen went ballistic, and her feed was filled with questions. Lotta felt her nerves start to dissipate – not much but ever-so-slightly. She heard herself talking almost as if it was somebody else. 'I wanted to create a space where people could escape from the world, curl up with a good book, and just relax,' she said. 'It's something I've always looked for but never really come across. At least not in the way I wanted to do it.'

Her followers seemed to be excited, and the questions kept coming. 'Will there be book clubs?' someone asked.

'Absolutely,' Lotta replied. 'I'm planning on hosting book clubs, workshops, and other events that celebrate the love of reading. I have heaps of things in the pipeline.'

As the live stream came to an end, Lotta felt her shoulders sag. Relief washed over her as she pushed the end button on her phone. There was one thing she knew for a fact – the live streams, with their constant questions and needing to be on the ball and keep the interest going, were nowhere near as easy as they looked. It was both exhausting and draining trying to be so upbeat.

Pushing herself up from the sofa, she went straight upstairs, stripped off her clothes, dropped them to the floor, and stepped into the shower. As she rubbed balm all over her face and scrubbed off her makeup, thoughts about the live raced through her head as she replayed her words over and over again on repeat.

As she analysed it all, Lotta couldn't believe a few things; firstly, that she'd actually got the whole thing up and running, secondly, that she'd had the nerve to do it at all, and thirdly, that if her followers' reaction was anything to go by, it looked as if it was going to go well. Very, very well indeed.

As she dried, put on her dressing gown, and walked through the house and into the kitchen, she felt, for once in her life, proud of herself. She had taken her love of books and turned it into a tangible project that would help her to pay off the debt on her credit card from her ex-partner, Dan. It felt so very good to finally be in charge.

Pouring herself a glass of white wine, Lotta smiled as she looked around and through to the conservatory. It, and she, had come a long way since the days when she was struggling to make ends meet. Now, thanks to encouragement and help from Jack and Liv, a lot of hard work and sheer grit, she had turned her passion for books into what was not quite a total game changer for her life but definitely the beginnings of what *could* be a thriving business.

Cutting herself off a hunk of French stick, she took some cheese out of the fridge and went and sat down in the conservatory. With only the faint sound of the sea in the distance and the rustling of the vine beside her, she couldn't help but reflect on how far she'd come. From the days when she'd first arrived in Pretty Beach and was struggling in almost all areas of her life, to now, turning her reading passion into a successful venture. Her life had been transformed. It felt amazing.

She took a sip of her wine and looked out into the garden, and the reading retreat nestled beside the boathouse at the end. She knew it was the sort of place she'd love to stay at and get lost in the world of books. Filled with gorgeous linens, lovely homewares, luxurious sofas, and the special little touches here and there, she'd thought of every detail and ticked every box.

As she savoured her cheese and wine, Lotta felt grateful for so much in her life – for the house, for Jack, having Liv. But more than anything, she was grateful for the opportunity to turn her hobby into a successful business. Top of it all, though, was finally getting rid of the noose named Dan that had been around her neck for a very long time and paying off his debt. That felt all sorts of delicious rolled into one.

She raised her glass to the reading retreat and to the future, feeling optimistic and excited about what was to come. Life was looking up for Lotta Button, better than it had for a long, long time, if ever. She just hoped that it wasn't going to change anytime soon.

6

A couple of days later, Lotta had just come off the phone with Jack, who was staying in a business hotel for the night. She was getting ready for Liv to come over for dinner and pottering around in the kitchen. Listening to an audiobook playing from her propped-up phone, she peeled potatoes for cottage pie, the skin coming off in long strips. As she chopped up onions and carrots, her mind felt like a whirlwind, spinning around and around like the potato peeler as she thought about the reading retreat and tried to concentrate on the audiobook. Taking a bottle of white wine out of the fridge, she poured herself a glass and took a big swig as she set about making the meat base. Adding mince, bouillon, garlic, and herbs to a pan, she stirred it all together, and as she waited for it to brown, she continued to tidy up and listen to the audiobook.

Once the meat was done and the kitchen tidy, she mashed the potatoes, spooned them over the meat in a big ceramic dish, and then layered grated cheese over the top. After grinding on copious amounts of salt and pepper, she slid it into the oven and nodded. Pottering around in the kitchen, and listening to a book, always had a way of calming her down, even when everything else in her life was spinning what sometimes felt like out of control.

As the house filled with the smell of the pie, Lotta wandered into the conservatory as soft evening light filtered through the glass roof. Plumping the cushions on the wicker chairs, she then flicked a white tablecloth into place, arranged plates carefully on top of rush placemats, added cutlery to each place setting, and then placed a wine and water glass at the head of each plate. Putting a jug full of freshly picked greenery onto the middle of the table, she opened the conservatory door, snipped a few extra sprigs of lavender and rosemary from the bed by the terrace, and shoved them into the jug.

As she pottered around, she wallowed in the simple domesticity of getting a meal ready and setting the table. Looking around at the conservatory, she almost purred in pleasure; living in Pretty Beach to the Breakers wasn't anywhere near getting old. The conservatory was one of her favourite rooms in the house – with its climbing vine, beautiful old glass and warmth, and now thanks to her piles of books absolutely everywhere, it felt like a sanctuary. She loved how the little changes she'd made had made *so* much difference. The fact that the old vine had come back to life, the now sparkling glass panes, and the way the fresh coastal air breezed in through the door.

With a smile on her face, Lotta turned to head back to the kitchen and recalled her conversation with Liv from earlier in the day. She squinted her eyes in thought. Something was going on with Liv, but she was yet to know what. When Liv had requested cottage pie, she had moved swiftly from thinking that Liv wasn't quite right to being sure of it. Certain more like. Just as Lotta was checking on the oven, she heard Liv in the hallway, and then she saw her appear in the breakfast room.

'Hello!' Liv said. 'How are you?'

Lotta ignored the sound in Liv's voice and stopped herself from saying anything. 'Good. How are you?'

'Yep, yep, fine. It smells so good. I could smell it on the driveway.'

'You requested cottage pie, meaning you get cottage pie,' Lotta joked.

Liv trailed into the kitchen behind Lotta and plonked her bag on a chair. 'Good, I'm starving.'

'You okay? You don't sound yourself.'

'I'm fine,' Liv replied, dismissing Lotta's concern with a shake of her head.

'It won't be long,' Lotta said, gesturing to the oven. 'Drink?'

'Large one,' Liv replied. 'Also, I'm staying.'

'Right, all good,' Lotta replied, now absolutely convinced there was something wrong with Liv.

Lotta tried to ignore the nagging voice in her head telling her that everything wasn't right as she poured Liv a glass of wine. She knew Liv, though. She'd tell her in her own time.

With her hands in oven gloves and the cottage pie held out in front of her, Lotta headed into the conservatory, where Liv was already at the table. Liv was circling her finger around and around the top of her wine glass and gazing out towards the garden. As Lotta put the cottage pie in the centre of the table, she noticed that Liv's eyes were slightly red and puffy, and she kept fidgeting in her seat, indicating that something was definitely off.

'Are you feeling okay?' Lotta asked, sitting down opposite Liv.

Liv let out a small sigh. 'Just a bit under the weather. You know how busy my life has been lately.'

Lotta nodded, but she didn't quite believe that was the whole story. 'Is everything okay at work? You seem a bit…off.'

Liv let out a small, tight laugh. 'You know me too well, Lott.

It's been really stressful lately. I'll be fine, though. Don't worry about me.'

Lotta smiled, taking Liv's words as a cue not to ask any more questions. They tucked into the cottage pie, and she topped up their glasses from the wine bottle. With candlelight from tiny little votive holders flickering all around them, Liv talked more about work as Lotta listened attentively, but as Liv explained in detail about a woman at work who wasn't at all nice, Lotta couldn't shake the feeling that there was still something more that Liv wasn't telling her.

She didn't push it, though, and continued to listen and chat. After they'd finished eating, Lotta cleared the plates and poured them each another glass of wine. Liv more or less sank the lot in one. Lotta couldn't stop herself from raising her eyebrows in surprise. 'Okay, spill it. What's *really* going on with you?'

Liv hesitated for a moment before letting out a deep sigh. 'I'm just so tired, Lott.'

'Maybe you need a bit of a break.'

Liv joked, 'What, at the end of your garden? Surrounded by Portuguese linens?'

'Feel free, but no, you haven't had a holiday for a long time, what with that new job and everything.'

'I know,' Liv said with a small smile. 'I was so desperate to do well. I think I've burnt the candle at both ends.' She shook her head. 'I don't *think* I've done that; I *know* I've done that.'

They sat in silence for a moment, the only sound coming from the crackling of the tealight candles on the table. Lotta knew how serious and committed Liv was to her job, so she wasn't sure what to say for the best. 'You need to get away for a bit perhaps,' Lotta said.

'I'll be fine.'

'You've already said that. Maybe you should go to the doctor and have some tests done or something if you're that tired?'

'Nah, it's just the really long days and working on the weekend that's doing it.'

Lotta leaned forward, reaching across the table to squeeze Liv's hand. 'You really aren't yourself.'

Liv gave Lotta's hand a grateful squeeze in return. 'Maybe you're right. Look, anyway, let's not dwell on me.'

'We're fine to dwell on you. It's been me since Dan left, so I think I owe you a spot of friend therapy.'

Liv laughed. 'I thought it was called cousin counselling.'

'Yeah, whatever we're calling it, I'm glad we've got it.' Lotta smiled. 'You're stuck with me whether you like it or not, Liv. Blood is thicker than water and all that.'

They clinked their wine glasses together in a toast, but there was a niggle in the back of Lotta's mind that Liv, underneath it all, wasn't quite right. But if she knew anything about Liv, it was that it would take a while for what was bothering her to come to the surface.

7

'Ready for drinks on the pier?' Jack asked as he stood on the driveway to Pretty Beach to the Breakers and looked over the bonnet of his car. 'Apparently, it's a Pretty Beach right of passage.'

'Oh, yes. I certainly am.' Lotta nodded with a huge smile on her face. 'I'm so ready. Bring it on.'

'At least I got an invite this time. Last time you went to a Locals Only event in Pretty Beach, you didn't take me,' Jack joked. 'You were thinking too much about a pink jacket, if I remember rightly.' Jack laughed, referring to Lotta mistakenly thinking that a jacket she'd seen on the back of Jack's office door was another woman's and not his sister's.

'You were actually attending a family thing,' Lotta shot back. 'That's why you couldn't come.'

'I was, true. Righto, okay, got everything?' Jack asked. 'Is your Kindle coming with us for a little trip out?'

Lotta tapped her bag and chuckled. 'It is. I never leave home without it. It's my best friend.'

Jack rolled his eyes. 'It is. How's your day been?'

Lotta also rolled her eyes briefly. 'It's been manic at work this week. Glad to see the back of it, if truth be told.'

'Same on my end. I'll be glad to sit down and have a drink,' Jack agreed with a nod.

'Yeah, I've been focusing on this to get me through the week. What time does it say that we need to be at the pier?' Lotta asked as she checked in her bag for her keys.

Jack looked down at his phone. 'It starts from six. We've got plenty of time to stroll.'

Lotta pulled the front door shut behind her. 'Right, let's go.'

They ambled along, chatting and wandering through the back streets of Pretty Beach on the way to Princess Pier. Jack looked up at the sky and then down at the weather app on his phone. 'The weather is going to stay dry by the looks of this,' Jack noted.

'Always good for an outdoor event,' Lotta remarked jokingly.

'It's been touch and go all week,' Jack said. 'Let's hope it stays mild.'

Fifteen minutes later, Lotta and Jack had walked through Pretty Beach and made their way to the pier at the end. As they stood in the queue to get in, Lotta gazed along the length of the pier snaking into the sea. 'This is lovely. Actually, why am I surprised? Everything in this little town is lovely.'

Jack read from the information board they were queueing up in front of. 'It's heritage-listed, too.'

'Heritage-listed and gorgeous,' Lotta said.

'It *is* lovely,' Jack replied, squinting down the length of the pier. 'It makes you wonder who came up with the idea of putting a building like this into the sea. On stilts too. Weird, really.'

'Whoever it was, right now I'm thanking them.' Lotta smiled.

'Yeah. Looks like we're in for a good time.'

Lotta put her hand on Jack's arm. 'Thanks so much. This is going to be wonderful.'

Jack lowered his voice. 'I think we're very lucky to get these tickets, seeing as I don't even officially live here. We'd better keep that quiet.'

'We are.' Lotta chuckled. 'Xian in the bakery said these tickets are like gold dust.'

They continued in the queue until they got to the entrance to the pier, the waves gently lapping below them, the breeze around them ruffling their hair. A man dressed in a smart pressed shirt, smiled as he scanned Jack's phone. 'Welcome, welcome, welcome. I'm Dimitri. Okay, been here before?'

'Nope,' Jack replied with a smile.

'Well, you're lucky ducks then. You need to stroll thataway,' he said, pointing to the end of the pier. 'Once you get there, you'll find your reserved place with a little number on a chalkboard tied to the railings. Director's chairs looking out to sea, and drinks will be arriving once the lights come on. That's more or less the nuts and bolts of it.

A few minutes later, they were sitting in the chairs. Lotta let out a gigantic sigh as she looked over towards the horizon. 'I love this place. I really do.'

As Jack followed her gaze, he shifted in his chair. 'Yeah, same.' He then turned to her, coughed a little bit, and then put his hand on her leg.

Lotta frowned at his change in body language. 'Err, you okay?'

'More than okay. Which is my point.'

'Sorry, you have a point? About what? Has that craft beer you had earlier gone to your head?'

'I, umm, have something for you.'

'Like what?' Lotta said, giggling at Jack's serious face as he leant forward in his seat.

Jack fiddled with his jacket pocket. 'I've got, err, yeah, I wanted to get you something.'

Lotta shook her head. 'Why? I think a bed, curtains,

bedroom furniture, and all your help was enough for me for a while.'

'Yeah, but that was because I couldn't stand sleeping in the alcove in a tiny bed any longer. It wasn't really a gift for *you*. Plus, who wants a bed as a present? Said no one ever.'

'I don't know; it's a very, very nice bed. Very nice things have happened there too.' Lotta chuckled. 'Ooh, so you've bought me a present, have you? This date just keeps getting better and better.' Lotta smiled.

Jack pulled a small box out of his jacket pocket.

'What? I didn't expect anything like this!' Lotta almost squealed as she took a small velvet-covered box from Jack. As she lifted the lid, she gasped at the sight of a gold bracelet. She picked it up and realised there was a tiny sparkling charm hanging from it. She turned the charm over and over in her fingers, beamed, and couldn't stop shaking her head. 'A charm in the shape of a book... wow, this is so beautiful. Thank you. I don't know what to say, Jack,' Lotta said, smiling.

Jack coughed again, a frown on his face. 'You like it?'

'Do I like it? I love it!' Lotta smiled, attaching the bracelet to her wrist. 'Where on earth did you find the charm? It's so pretty.'

'I had it made.'

Lotta felt her voice catch as she looked at Jack. A very nice man was having jewellery made for her. She had come a long way. A long way indeed. The road had been drawn-out, windy and, quite frankly, full of horrible bumps. She lifted her wrist and watched as the charm caught the light and smiled. Life had never been quite as good.

8

Lotta was sitting at her desk in the library room after having spent hours working from home and finalising a sponsored live reading review for a client. She could hear Jack in the kitchen and the sound of the kettle as it came to a rolling boil. Running her fingers over her eyebrows and sighing out of her nose, she pushed her chair back and stalked through the house into the kitchen. Jack was sitting at the breakfast table working at his laptop. He looked up and smiled. 'How are you getting on?' he asked.

'Hmm, well, I have about seventy thousand architects to email about the change of date in their event. I have two sponsored reading posts to detail and send to the client. Umm, and the new training document on the changes in the health and safety guidelines to be familiar with before Monday. And because I have a life and loads of other things going on, namely the reading retreat I've sunk money into, well, my mind is kind of saturated. That's about the long and the short of how I'm getting on.'

Jack didn't miss a beat. 'Is that the long and complicated way of saying that you need a cup of tea?'

Lotta chuckled. 'You nailed it in one.'

'Do you need some of Xian's Special Drink in it?' Jack joked. 'Sounds like it might help you out.'

'Tempting, but I need to actually continue doing all of the above for the rest of the day.' Lotta gestured towards the library room. 'I've just remembered something. I'll be back for tea.'

Ten minutes later, she came back in. Jack was standing in the kitchen pouring the tea from the pot. She took a mug and stood beside him, leaning on the worktop. 'So, anyway, how important is this reading retreat anyway?'

Jack frowned. 'What?'

'I like my job, I like, you know, all of this, I like you, so what if the retreat fails? It doesn't matter, does it?'

'Lott, it's been like a week or so, and you've had so many enquiries, it's not even funny, and yes, it is important.'

'You think? I'm trying to tell myself it doesn't matter because I'm not exactly having people lining up to rent it. I may have had a lot of interest, but that doesn't and *hasn't* translated to money in the bank.'

'Patience. You can't expect something like this to happen overnight.'

Lotta started to ramble and pace up and down. 'I mean, why did I plunge all that money into the bed and the sofa and all that stuff in there if it's going to sit there unused? I should have just been content to pay the credit card bill slowly. Why did I do this? Why?'

Jack looked at her blankly. 'You had a plan. You are now *executing* the plan. This is how it works. Like turning the pages of a book. Think of it like that.'

Lotta continued to pace and catastrophise. 'But, ahh, what was I thinking? It's been so expensive, and now it's empty! What the actual? I must have been stark raving to take this on.'

'You were thinking it's a very good idea. It has a completely separate entrance to the house, and everyone around here has evidence that it will not only work, but work well. All you need to do is wait. Rome wasn't built in a day.'

Lotta tutted and sighed. 'I'm just having wobbles. Life wobbles. Everything wobbles.'

'Right. Not sure how much I can help with those. At least they're not pink jacket wobbles,' Jack deadpanned.

'Do I sound as if I've lost it?'

'Yes.'

Lotta huffed. 'I have. I actually have. I'm going back to the library to work. I can't even settle until I get more stuff done. It's doing my head in.'

'You do that, Lott,' Jack said with a smile and then slid a bar of chocolate across the worktop. 'Here, this might help.'

As a million things went around her mind at once and regret was zipping around her body about the money she'd sunk into the retreat, Lotta snatched up the chocolate. Going back into the library room, she ripped it open and, one by one, began to shovel squares into her mouth as she sat down at her desk.

A couple of hours and two more cups of tea later, she was still sitting at her desk when her phone pinged with a new message. Frowning at an unknown number, she opened it and then ascertained that it was from Marie at work's cousin, Emily, who was interested in renting out the retreat for a long weekend. In the text, Emily was asking for a few clarification details. Excited at the prospect of getting her first booking and sharing her little slice of paradise, Lotta started typing out a message.

Lotta: *Hi Emily, great to hear from you. Yep, there's everything you need for a peaceful weekend away here.*

Emily: *It looks lovely on the website.*

Lotta: *Thanks.*

Emily: *It says there are loads of walks around???*

Lotta: *Yes, so many. The walk up to the lighthouse is phenomenal. You can also go up to the hills, and there's a funicular railway. If you just want to hibernate though, everything is set up – cosy throws and luxurious bedding, so you can sleep all day if you want. It's very quiet here.*

Emily: *So it sounds like I don't really need to bring anything.*

Lotta: *Correct. Not even a book. There is a selection of books and cosy reading nooks where you can curl up with a cup of tea. Plus, we're just steps away from the beach, so you can take a stroll along the sand whenever you like. It really is glorious here.*

Emily: *Great. Okay then, if you can squeeze me in, I'd love to book for a long weekend next week if it's free. Marie said you'd had loads of enquiries already.*

Lotta: *I have, but it's free, yes.*

Emily: *Great. How do you want me to book?*

Lotta: *It's probably easier if you do it on the website, and then you'll automatically get all the details sent to you.*

Emily: *Fab. Thanks, I'm so excited!*

Lotta nodded and let out a sigh of relief. Not nearly as much as she was. She was jigging up and down as she raced into the kitchen to tell Jack. She had her first booking! She was on the way to making a dent in her debt. She really hoped that Emily's booking would start the ball rolling and the reading retreat would be a success. She wasn't sure, though, if she should hold her breath.

9

In jeans, a white t-shirt, oversized sunglasses, and with her book bag over her shoulder, Lotta strolled down the laneway in Pretty Beach, drinking in the delightful pastel hues of the shops. With a smile on her face and a spring in her step, she pushed open the door to Pretty Beach bakery. Inhaling the smell of freshly baked bread, cinnamon buns, coffee, and the general buzz of happy locals. She felt as if she'd just landed in bakery heaven.

Standing in the queue, she smiled as Suntanned Pete, wearing his usual metallic wraparound sunglasses, flip-flops, and shorts, turned from the counter and, recognising Lotta, his very weathered face broke into a grin. 'Ahh, lovely Lotta! How are things with you? How's the garden after the working bee?' Pete beamed.

'Very good, thanks. The garden is doing well. Thanks again for all your help.' Lotta smiled.

'Not a problem.' Pete swept his hand around the bakery. 'It's how we do it around here.'

'Yes, I'm getting used to it, slowly but surely.'

'How did you get on at the pier the other night?'

Lotta shook her head. 'Love, love, *loved* it.'

'Sounds like we have your approval. I'm on the committee…,' Pete explained.

'Ahh, yes, you certainly do have my approval. It was fabulous,' Lotta replied.

'And the love life?' Pete asked, chuckling.

'Yep, that's good too.' Lotta reached out and touched the timber on the side of the counter. 'Touch wood, everything in my life is good at the moment. Long may it last.'

'Ahh, just what we like to hear,' Pete said. 'And what about your mum? You were telling me she wasn't well when we were working on the garden.'

Lotta squidged her lips together. 'Not much change there. It is what it is.'

'It must be hard having her so far away.'

'Yes, it is.' Lotta wasn't even going to contemplate explaining the complex situation with her mum to Pete. She swiftly changed the subject, moving the conversation onto something else. 'Anyway, what are you up to today?' Lotta asked.

'I'm off out on my boat.' Pete held a white paper bag up in between them. 'I have my supplies, and I won't be back for hours. Just how I like it. Getting a bit of sea and sun in.'

'Sounds good to me,' Lotta remarked. 'I might have to join you one day.'

As they continued to chat, Holly, the bakery owner, came bustling out from behind the counter with her mum, Xian, behind her, who was shouting into her phone in Vietnamese. Holly tutted towards her mum and rolled her eyes. 'Morning, Lotta, how are you?'

'I was just saying to Pete that I'm doing really well, thanks.'

'Good to hear. How's the house and the retreat? Are you ready to go on that yet? I hear you might have had a nice wee delivery from the Cotswolds the other week.'

Lotta nodded and chuckled. 'Yes, the mattress is worth more

than the house, ha ha. I've put the retreat live on the website now, and I've had a lot of messages and enquiries, but so far only one booking via someone at work. My followers on my reading account seemed to love it when I did a tour, but they haven't booked.'

'Don't worry, it'll come,' Holly said, patting Lotta on the hand.

Suntanned Pete nodded in agreement. 'Yup, once the word gets out. I could rent my places six times over in July and August.'

'Same,' Holly agreed. 'Once the ball is rolling, you'll be fine.'

'I hope so. I need it to work now,' Lotta stated.

'And how is the lovely Jack?' Holly asked.

'The lovely Jack is well.' Lotta held up her wrist, and the diamonds on the little book charm caught the light. 'He gave me this. I know you like sparkles, so you might approve.'

Xian broke off from her phone for a second. 'Lovely! It's fabulous.'

Holly tried to raise her eyebrows as she examined the little book charm. 'Those are my kind of diamonds. Wow! That's so pretty and *so* you.'

'They're gorgeous, aren't they? Do they meet with your twinkle approval?' Lotta joked.

'And then some.' Holly nodded enthusiastically.

'Well, I owe you a loan of jewellery,' Lotta said, referring to when she had been fake dating Jack and Holly had loaned her a necklace and earrings.

'Ahh, I won't be taking a love token from you.' Holly chortled.

Pete chuckled and raised his eyebrows at Holly. 'You need to find a love interest of your own to give you diamonds. I should say *more* diamonds.'

Xian nodded, moved her mouth away from her phone for a second and interrupted, 'I've been telling her that for years.'

Holly shook her head. 'No time for all that in my life, Pete. You know that. Once bitten, twice shy.'

Pete inclined his chin towards the door. 'You never know what's around the corner.'

Holly nodded. 'I know a love interest isn't on the cards. I'm more than happy with my lot in life, thank you very much.'

Xian finished her phone call, took a swig from a flask she'd pulled from her pocket and peered at Lotta's bracelet. 'That really is very pretty.'

'I'm lucky,' Lotta said.

Xian chuckled. 'Now, didn't I tell you he was a keeper? I know these things. I should do it for a living. I need to start charging for my advice.'

Lotta giggled. 'You did indeed. I now know that you were right.'

Xian smiled as Holly rolled her eyes. 'I always am, Lotta. Me, I was born to be right.'

Lotta ambled away from the bakery with a bag of cinnamon buns and a smile, almost as if she was on cloud nine. The weather was warm, the sun was shining, and things in her world were more or less going to plan. As her phone buzzed and she looked down, her euphoria changed in a split second, and her heart plummeted as she saw her mum's partner, Dave's name flashing across the top of her phone. This was not going to be nice news. She knew if he was calling, it probably meant that things were not good. Lotta sighed and shook her head. As had happened many times in her life, her mother and her behaviour had an uncanny knack for bursting any, if not all, of the bubbles in Lotta's life. Lotta answered the call with a heavy heart.

'Hi, Dave,' Lotta said, trying to keep her voice steady. 'Is everything okay?'

'Hi, yeah, not too bad. Look, I'll get straight to the point. I'm sorry to have to tell you this, but your mum, well, she's been drinking a *lot* again. I'm, yeah, I'm quite worried this time,' Dave said, his voice full of concern.

'Oh dear,' Lotta said, feeling a lump form in her throat, but she was not surprised. Unlike Dave, she'd been on the end of such news or in the thick of it many times before. 'How is she?'

'Not good, I'm afraid. She's really struggling, if I'm honest. Not that it's all out in the open,' Dave replied.

Lotta felt a pang of sadness in the pit of her stomach. She hadn't spoken to her mum in a while because her mum would never answer her calls, but she'd had a feeling the big drinking might have started again. She swallowed as the familiar mix of guilt and sadness ran through her veins. 'I'm sorry, Dave. I don't really know what to say,' Lotta said, trying to stop her voice from breaking.

'There's not much you *can* say,' Dave replied, his tone sounding defeated. 'I just wanted to keep you in the picture.'

Lotta wiped at the corner of her left eye. 'Do you think I should come over?'

'That's really up to you. I know it's a big deal to get here. You have to weigh up the practicalities, I suppose. It's a long way, and you know what happened last time,' Dave replied. 'I wasn't calling to say you should come, I was just phoning so that you were in the know, as it were.' He paused for a second. 'If it gets worse and anything happens, I don't want it to be a shock. This way you're in the loop.'

Lotta went cold. Dave was clearly very worried. 'I know, thanks... I know it's not about me, but I don't think I'm going to put myself through that again. She didn't want me there when I came, so there's really not much point,' Lotta said, feeling hopeless.

'No, of course. I just wanted you to be up to speed on it,' Dave stated.

'Yes. Thanks for letting me know, Dave,' Lotta said, her voice heavy with sadness.

'No problem. Take care of yourself,' Dave said before ending the call.

Lotta stood on the side of the road staring out at the busy street, feeling lost and helpless. Her brain played the call over and over again in her head. She wished she had a better relationship with her mum, but it was never going to be. Her mum was drinking heavily again. No surprise there. She wondered if she should go to Singapore, but all of it seemed totally overwhelming. She glanced back towards the bakery with a heavy heart. A mere minute ago she'd been saying how good her life was, and now, as always where her mum was concerned, news from the other side of the world had changed that in one fell swoop. She sighed as worry, thoughts, and a dull, sad ache in her stomach accompanied her on the pavement, and a strange kind of foreboding made her feel as if the worst with her mum was yet to come. It did not feel good.

10

It was a few weeks after the news about Lotta's mum via Dave. Lotta had spoken to him a couple of times, and from what she could ascertain and by the radio silence from her mum herself, Lotta knew things were not great. She'd been in the cycle way too many times before. There wasn't much she could do about it though, so she'd spent her time concentrating on everything else going on in her life.

She was sitting behind the reception desk at work with the log book in front of her, a little vase of bright flowers to her left, a coffee in her hand, and the computer screen facing her. She was covering for someone who'd called in sick and had barely stopped since she'd first walked through the door. Marie came out from the office behind her with a frown on her face and her iPad in her hand. 'Yeah, so you're meant to be supporting me, which you can't do because you're on the desk, and by the looks of that rain, water is going to start coming in through the door and people will be late.'

'Yep.' Lotta nodded. 'Is there wiggle room in the schedule?'

'There certainly is.'

'Good.'

'John isn't here yet, either,' Marie noted.

Lotta chuckled. 'It looks like I'm getting a mop and bucket and doing that by the front door then.'

Marie laughed. 'You see, this is why I love you.'

'Not many people say that.' Lotta winked.

'Okay, I'll be back shortly.'

Lotta continued on the reception and looked out at the weather. The grey sky seemed to merge with the pavement, the wind whistled around, and the rain did not look as if it was going to stop anytime soon. Ten or so minutes later, the rain had turned from pouring down to coming down in sheets, hammering against the windows, and it sounded as if elephants were landing on the roof. The sound was deafening, drowning out anything else at all. Seeing what Marie was talking about as water gathered by the front lobby doors, Lotta grabbed a mop and a bucket and headed towards the front door as the rain continued to pour down. In sky-high heels, she chuckled to herself as she mopped, as she remembered mopping the toilets in offices when she'd worked through the night to make extra money. As she mopped back and forth, she realised how far she'd come from those days. Her mental health was in a completely different place now. So obvious it was almost blinding.

After continuously mopping and then wiping the floor to dry it, she stood by the door, watching the rain and looking out for conference attendees. The first one, a woman without a coat and a huge bag trotted along the pavement, looking harried and drenched. As the woman ran in, Marie hurried over, offering a stack of plush white towels and apologised for the weather. Lotta meanwhile continued to mop up the rainwater and placed a sign warning people to be careful of the slippery floor. As the attendees slowly trickled in, wet and stressed, Lotta took their coats and umbrellas as Marie directed them to the coffee and tea.

'It's insane out there,' Marie muttered as she helped Lotta shake out a couple of umbrellas.

'Absolutely is,' Lotta agreed as she watched a group of late-comers rush along the pavement, water splashing up around their ankles.

'I'm going to need a hot bath after this,' Marie said with a grimace.

'You and me both,' Lotta replied, adjusting her jacket as she looked around at the soggy attendees. 'At least they are all here now. I can't believe how many people have made it through this weather. I thought we'd have half the numbers we were expecting.'

'I know, right? You never can tell. It just goes to show...'

As the event got underway, Lotta kept an eye on the door, ready to clean up any more rainwater that might come in. Marie was busy dealing with attendees and speakers, trying to make up for the late start and the chaotic arrival of everyone. Despite the rain, everything was going well, and Lotta breathed a sigh of relief and was back sitting behind the reception desk. Marie came up to her, her iPad still in her hand, a smile on her face. 'Thanks for all that. You didn't know that mopping was going to be one of your duties.'

'All in a day's work,' Lotta replied.

'It's so nice to work with someone who just rolls their sleeves up and gets on with it.'

'Ditto.'

'Right, I'll go and get us a coffee, then we'll sit down for a second and catch our breath before it all starts again with the lot who arrive this afternoon.'

Ten minutes later, Marie was also sitting behind the desk, and both of them had steaming coffee in their hands. They chatted away as they sipped their coffee, and Marie leaned forward, excitement in her voice. 'Right, now that is all over we can actually chat. Emily is going to be your first guest at the reading retreat, right?'

Lotta nodded. 'Yes. She messaged me, and I sent her more details, and she booked. So that's good. Thanks for mentioning it to her. I'm really grateful.'

Marie grinned. 'I'm sure she's going to love it. When I passed on your pics, she was gushing.'

'Good. I think it was the clifftop walk to the lighthouse that swung it. Ha ha.'

Marie laughed. 'Or the linen sheets, clawfoot bathtub, and copper pans in the kitchen. I think that might have had something to do with it. Or the books...'

'That was the aim. I thought about everything down to the last nitty-gritty detail.'

Marie nodded approvingly. 'It's the little things that really make the difference, you know?' Marie swung her arm around to encompass the lobby. 'It's why this place is so successful. People appreciate all the thoughtful touches around.'

'I hope so,' Lotta said, smiling. 'I just want her to have a really special experience while she's there.'

'I'm sure she will,' Marie said. 'She's quite easy to please. She just goes away to do nothing but recharge, so she won't be up to much.'

'Well, she'll be in the right place.'

'I can't wait to hear all about it when she gets back. Who knows, maybe she'll get you some more bookings and spread the word. She's got quite a few in her book club too.'

Lotta laughed. 'Let's not get ahead of ourselves, but I hope so.'

'I have no doubt about it,' Marie said, patting Lotta's arm. 'You've put so much time and effort into it already, and it shows.'

Lotta swallowed at the thought of all the money she'd spent and that she had one lone booking for one lone weekend. Part of her was wondering if the whole thing had been a very big, very costly mistake, and with a past chock-full of mistakes, she wasn't very happy about how that made her feel at all. Lotta had thought she'd left a past of mistakes behind her in a cloud of dust. But with a severe lack of bookings for the retreat, maybe she wasn't quite so sure of herself after all.

11

A week or so later, Lotta hadn't heard much else about her mum. She'd had a couple of texts from Dave to say there was no change, and she'd tried, mostly, to put it to the back of her mind. As she walked down the laneway, she strolled past a gorgeous white building next to a seaplane workshop and made her way to the ferry, where she was meeting Jack before they went to the pub. Looking out to sea, dark rain clouds were rolling in, and the weather was looking dubious. Lotta's mood was as clouded as the purple sky, and she couldn't stop thinking about the reading retreat. Despite the fact that she'd done a live tour on her socials, and having had a lot of interest, she still had only one booking – the one via Marie. She tried to stop thinking about it and accept that it would take time as she pulled her jacket tighter whilst watching the Pretty Beach ferry chugging into the bay. It bobbed precariously left and right and dipped up and down over a huge swell. At some points, it appeared to go under – it did not look like her sort of fun.

As she got to the wharf and watched the ferry come safely in, she smiled as she caught Jack's eye as he stood waiting in the queue to get off. He strolled up, kissed her and then gestured back to the ferry. 'That was a bit of a ride.'

'It looked like it was going to go under at one point.'

'You should have seen us in the Middles. I was holding on for dear life.'

'I would have been petrified.' Lotta laughed.

Jack squinted towards the coast. 'Looks like it might rain. What do you think?' He pointed up to the dark clouds rolling in from the sea. 'Do you want to walk back to the house and then drive to the pub?'

Lotta shook her head and wrinkled up her nose. 'I wanted some fresh air and thought the walk home later would be nice. I've been stuck in the library room all day. I've hardly moved from my desk. My spine is feeling it.'

With a dubious look on his face, Jack peered up at the clouds. 'Okay, but don't say I didn't warn you. It's been threatening to rain on and off all day, and the weather forecast says it's coming tonight.'

'We'll be fine,' Lotta replied.

'I'll blame you if we get soaked,' Jack said, and as he grabbed Lotta's hand, he kissed her, and they strolled away from the ferry towards the laneway. 'Thank goodness it's the end of the week. I'm looking forward to a nice, easy night in the pub.'

'Me too,' Lotta replied, trying not to think about the fact that the retreat still had a big fat zero number of bookings and her mum was drinking heavily again.

They were chatting away and ambling through the back streets of Pretty Beach when there was a rumble from above. The rumble was followed by a clap, which was followed by a flash of lightning. Jack looked upwards. 'This does not look good.' His face wrinkled into a frown. 'The whole sky has gone dark. I hope you're ready to get wet.'

In a flash, the heavens opened, and gigantic plops of rain began to land on the pavement. Chuckling, they quickened their pace, both wedged into the side of the street as the rain got heavier and soaked them. 'Ahh, this is nuts! We're getting soaked!'

'This is what you get for wanting some fresh air,' Jack teased as they scooted along.

Lotta giggled. 'I do actually love the feeling of rain on my face.'

'That's lucky then,' Jack deadpanned.

Lotta struggled to keep her umbrella from turning inside out as they hurried along, laughing at the absurdity of it all. In the end, she gave up and stuffed it in her bag. By the time they arrived at the pub, they were both soggy. As they approached the door, Lotta paused to wipe her feet on the doormat, watching as the rain continued to pour down outside. Jack held the door open, and they stepped inside, greeted by the warm, dry air. Lotta pulled her umbrella back out of her bag, lodged it in a bucket in the porch, and peered out at the rain as it seemed to come down even harder. 'It's coming thick and fast. We'll be flooded!'

'And you wanted to walk home,' Jack deadpanned as he shrugged off his sopping-wet jacket.

'Hopefully, it'll ease up,' Lotta said as she pulled her arms out of her coat and added it on top of a jumble of coats hanging to their right.

As they pushed their way through the inner door to The Pretty Smugglers, lovely cosy old pub smells and sounds hit them all at once. The scent of hops, beer and whatever was cooking in the kitchen wafted in the air. The cosy glow of the pub was a relief after the rain outside, and a buzz of conversation and laughter filled the room.

Lotta's eyes darted around – as with the other times she'd been in the pub, she loved all the details. The walls were adorned with vintage photographs of the town and its people, while old-fashioned lamps and flickering lanterns bathed the room in soft light. Wooden beams and exposed brick lent a rustic charm to the place, and the beautiful polished bar held happy locals sitting with pints. Jackets and coats hung on the backs of chairs, groups of friends huddled around their drinks, and a gaggle of men were gathered around a corner table enjoying a game of cards.

As they approached the bar, Lotta wondered if the barman, James, with his friendly smile and jovial manner, who was pouring pints for the regulars, would remember her. She shouldn't even have doubted it. Not only did he beam in recognition, he remembered her name. 'Evening, Lotta, Jack.'

'Evening.'

Lotta smiled as she looked around the room, taking in the scene. The pub was just as lovely as the rest of the town. She felt lucky to be a part of it, and even more, felt grateful to be there with Jack. As she stood smiling at the banter between James and Jack, she inhaled the scent of freshly poured ale, and as she sat down on a stool, she forgot about the rain and her mum and the retreat and could feel herself beginning to relax.

James leant on the end of the bar and lowered his voice. 'Locals Only is fish and chips. Cod by name. Cod by nature.'

Jack turned to Lotta with an enquiring look on his face. 'Good for you?'

'Done,' she said with a quick nod of her head.

'Too easy,' James replied. 'I'll put your order in, shouldn't take too long, though we're packed this evening.'

'I thought the rain normally keeps people indoors,' Lotta said.

'Not when we have fish and chips on.' James chuckled in reply.

As they made their way to the table, Lotta smiled at a group huddled around a chessboard in the corner, their faces creased with concentration, pints in front of them. Jack pulled out a chair for Lotta; she made herself comfortable and he took the seat opposite her. She smiled at him and at the surroundings, and as they waited for their food, they chatted about their day, about the rain, and about their work weeks. Lotta told him how she'd spent a lot of the week sorting out problems because of the rain and covering for Marie.

Jack squeezed her hand. 'Is there something else on your mind?'

Lotta smiled at him, wondering how he'd read between the lines so deftly. 'Ahh, I don't know. If I'm honest, I'm fed up with the retreat bookings. The lack of them, I should say. It all looked so good on paper. I can't believe it's not going well.'

Jack nodded and smiled, his eyes meeting hers. 'At least it's not a pink jacket and a bottle of perfume in my drawer that's on your mind.'

Lotta giggled. 'How could you tell something was wrong?'

'You're doing that weird, chirpy voice.'

'Right. I didn't realise.'

'Look, don't worry about the retreat. It *will* take off. I have no doubt about that.'

Lotta felt grateful for Jack's confidence but not quite convinced. 'I just feel a bit stupid. I, I mean we, have put all that effort into it. My eyes water at the cost of the mattress and the sofa, and it's sitting there empty.'

'Give it a chance!'

Lotta shook her head and blinked rapidly. 'I'm just worried about the credit card debt. Really worried.'

'I've already told you I can help out with that.'

'And I've already told you thanks, but no way.' Lotta changed the subject, not wanting to think too much about the retreat. 'So, what's been going on at work for you?'

'Nice change of subject, but I'll go with it.' Jack contemplated for a second. 'Just the next deal with the Americans. You know how the last one went. There's a lot of toing and froing. A lot of smooching and sucking up. They do love a bit of dallying around and brown-nosing. It is what it is.'

'When are you going over there again? I've forgotten the actual date.' Lotta asked with her nose wrinkled in question.

'A few weekends' time. You're still sure you don't want to come?'

Lotta shook her head. 'It's not that I don't *want* to. It's just work, really. I'd need to take the Friday and the Monday off, and both of those days are big days. If I hadn't had the Singapore thing, it would have been fine. I mean, it's not like I've been there years either.'

'I thought you said they were okay with Singapore?' Jack asked.

'Well, technically, they are, but I've only been there a short amount of time, and it's going so well. I'm the lead on both of those days. Yeah, no, I think I'm going to leave it.'

'Yep, not a problem. You have to do what's best for you.'

'I love my new job, I really do. I can't quite believe I've got it, and I want to keep it.'

'They want to keep you, more like. They're getting their pound of flesh from what I've seen.' Jack noted.

Lotta considered some of the truly awful jobs she'd had, including one where she'd more or less been sitting in a cupboard answering customer service calls all day long, getting abuse from irate customers. Shuddering at the thought, she didn't want to do anything to jeopardise working in the arcade. 'No, you'll be back in a jiffy anyway.'

'I will, and to be quite honest, it's not going to be much fun.'

'I don't really want to get food poisoning from prawns, anyway,' Lotta joked, referring to her fake date with Jack where she'd ended up with food poisoning.

Jack nodded, and just as he did so, their food arrived, steam rising from the plates and the smell of fish and chips filling the air. Lotta picked up her knife and fork, cut the batter on the cod, and popped it into her mouth. She raised her eyebrows and lowered her voice, 'This Locals Only thing gets better, and better the more I have it.'

Jack followed suit. 'It's so fresh.' He looked around the pub. 'What a place. What a town.'

'I know. How lucky are we?'

'Yep, very. All we need now are some bookings for the retreat and for me to get this next America trip out of the way, and we'll be laughing.'

'Yes,' Lotta replied. 'I know I've got the thing with my mum, but life has been a lot worse.'

Jack tipped his glass to Lotta's. 'Long may it last. We're on a roll Lotta Button. On a roll.'

12

The roll hadn't lasted long. Lotta had had another call from Dave, and things had not improved where her mum was concerned. Lotta had also then spoken to her mum, not that her mum had been very enamoured by it. Lotta had known *instantly* that the drinking had grabbed hold. She could tell from the sound of her mum's voice. From years of experience, Lotta knew that things had gone from bad to worse.

Lotta felt a knot form in her stomach as she thought about her mum's drinking problem. She shook her head and closed her eyes. She was *so* over it, at the same time as feeling *so* guilty. The constant niggling gnawing at the back of her mind had always been there throughout her life, her whole existence. No matter what good things were going on, her mum always somehow had a way of sneaking in and ruining things. It had happened way too many times it wasn't even funny. It all felt blindingly unfair.

As she sat at her desk, supposedly working but instead scrolling mindlessly through social media, Lotta's mind wandered to the past. It wasn't pleasant wandering. Birds were not chirping and the sun did not have his hat on. Instead she felts as if she was in a black cloud. She thought about the times she'd tried to talk to her mum about her drinking, but it had always ended in an abusive argument. She shook her head and looked around at her desk in the library room and felt grateful that at least she had Pretty Beach to the Breakers. At least she now had a sanctuary and her own home. The vintage reading lamp beside her cast a warm light over the workspace, a couple of wicker baskets held her neatly sorted papers, and piles of books for her to review were arranged in perfect order, each one stacked to attention with their spines neatly aligned. A pen pot overflowing with pencils sat next to her laptop, and the soft hues of a bunch of David Austin roses from the garden set the scene. All of it perfectly nice. All of it in direct contrast to the chaos going around in her head. All of it a trillion miles away from where she'd started off in life spending her childhood teetering around on eggshells and broken glass.

Lotta sighed in a long, dramatic exhale through her nose, trying to clear her thoughts. She needed to focus on the reading retreat and not let her mum's condition worry her too much, at least for now. She'd put so much time and effort into the retreat, she needed to make sure it didn't fail. There was no time for sitting around wasting dead time, gazing and scrolling through her phone, and letting chaotic thoughts hammer around her head. Her mum didn't want to be helped, least of all by Lotta.

She grabbed her notebook and a pencil from the pot and absent-mindedly started to brainstorm ideas to publicise the retreat. She jotted things down she could try to do to get some bookings, wondering if she could contact any book clubs or maybe put a notice up in the library. Noting down every idea that came to her, she realised, as everyone had told her, that it was very early days. Maybe she was jumping the gun to be worried. But she seriously didn't want another thing in her life to fail. As she sat at her desk, her mind flitted from one thing to the next – from her next event at work, to emails, to her mum, to the reading retreat. Back and forth it clicked. Tick tock. Tick tock.

She looked over towards her shelves full of books and sighed for the millionth time. For a long time, she'd felt like she was simply juggling too many things at once. And although in her new life things were a lot better, she still had a lot going on. Her mind was constantly racing with thoughts of this, that, and the other. It was all becoming too much, and she was starting to feel overwhelmed. The only time she didn't feel it was when she had her nose nicely tucked in a book.

As she sat at her desk, staring at the long list of emails on the left-hand side of her computer screen, the retreat constantly whirred through her mind. She couldn't help but wonder if she'd completely wrongly read the room. Was the reading retreat just *her* dream? Was it a stupid, ridiculous idea? Was no one else on the planet interested in a weekend in a gorgeous little place surrounded by books? To her, it was the *epitome* of bliss and recharge. To others, maybe not so much.

Squeezing her eyes together in concentration, Lotta's brow furrowed as she leaned forward slightly, her eyes focused intently on the laptop screen in front of her. Some hair had escaped from her messy bun and was dangling in front of her face. She pushed it away and started to note down a plan. Biting her lower lip, she read down her points and nodded. She wasn't going to let a lack of bookings get her down. She would forge onwards.

Sitting there thinking about it all, she doodled all the way down the side of her notebook and then as she got up to go and make a cup of tea, she spoke to herself as she walked to the kitchen. 'I, Lotta Button, will not be discouraged. I will, rather, behave like a heroine in one of my books. I will be strong. I will be focused. I will be the master of my own destiny. I will be driven. Where there's a will, there's a way.'

She looked at herself in the mirror in the breakfast room

and raised her eyebrows. 'Or maybe I'll just get a chocolate biscuit and read a few pages of my book.'

~

After spending most of the day working from home, Lotta finally logged off and looked around at the house, and her chores looked back at her. The place *really* did need hoovering from top to bottom, the kitchen *really* did need a deep clean, and she *really* needed to do some laundry. She also *really* needed to get fully lost in a book and the housework *really* would still be waiting for her the next day. She needed to read not just a few pages but dive deep down into a proper gung-ho reading session. Her TBR pile was not small, and her brain needed to decompress in someone else's world. There was going to be next-level reading. One where the actual world faded away and took her down into a vortex via the pages of a book.

And she'd done just that for hours and hours and hours, completely ignoring housework as much as she possibly could. Accompanied by cup of tea after cup of tea, with the open door to the library room bringing in a breeze from the sea, her binge-reading had done well to take her brain away from things going on in her actual life.

Just as she finished the last page of a book, her phone pinged with a video call. Seeing that it was Liv, for a second she thought about not answering, but changed her mind. Pulling the throw beside her over her knees, she perched her phone on top of a cushion and pressed the button to accept the call. Liv's face appeared on the screen with a look of concern all over it.

'Hi. Everything okay with you?' Liv asked.

'Yes and no. You?' Lotta replied. She could see that everything was not okay with Liv.

'I got a text message from your mum,' Liv stated bluntly, concern lacing her words.

Lotta closed her eyes and winced. 'Oh dear. Things really are bad.'

'I know. I thought precisely that. What's happened?' Liv asked, her brow furrowed with worry.

'How many guesses do you want? If she's texting you, you know she's out of it. What did it say?' Lotta sighed.

'The same as before.'

'About the family shunning her.'

Liv nodded. 'Yep.'

Lotta shook her head again in quick little movements as if doing so would make the situation go away. It didn't work. In the past, Liv had been on the receiving end of some nasty texts from Lotta's mum, which had been the final nail in the coffin with their family. Both Lotta and Liv knew that the texts meant the drinking was heavy. It was like an unspoken code going back and forth between them. A code and game Lotta didn't want to play in anymore.

Lotta started to explain the latest call from Dave. She described the sadness she felt at her mum's condition, together with the overwhelm and the exhaustion of it all. 'The thing is, Liv, I'm just so tired of it. Which in turn makes the guilt ginormous. I have pro-level guilt. I shouldn't be thinking about me here.'

Liv listened intently, her eyes filled with compassion. 'Pah! Oh yes, you should! She's certainly never thought about you. Grrr! She's so selfish! Sorry, Lott!'

Lotta nodded. 'True. That doesn't help me from feeling guilty, though.'

'You've always just had to carry all of this. She's never thought about you. God, it makes me sick!' Liv almost spat.

Lotta shook her head despondently. 'There's just nothing I

can do about it. Nor can anyone else. At least nowadays, I know that.'

'Not where she's concerned,' Liv said resignedly.

'It's sad that you and I both know that,' Lotta stated. 'There is nothing you or I can do to help her. Dave, doctors, no one.'

'You need to take care of yourself in this,' Liv said gently.

Lotta nodded, the corners of her eyes pricking with tears. 'I know, Liv. I feel so helpless about it all.'

'You don't have many choices, really,' Liv acknowledged.

Lotta's heart felt heavy. 'Do you think I need to go back to Singapore? If she's texting people like you, it's bad.'

Liv raised her eyebrows and shook her head. 'Who knows? I've no idea what you should do for the best. I'll come with you if you want.'

'Thanks, but that would be pointless. Then there'd be two of us getting upset and abused.'

'Yeah, I suppose so, after what happened last time.'

Lotta nodded. 'It was awful. You know what? I'm *definitely* not going to go.'

'Nope, I don't think you should. All that way, all that money and upset, and she'll just be nasty and not be able to behave herself.'

'Yep. You don't need to tell me.'

'What do you think Jack will say?'

'I don't know, he'll probably say the opposite. He has a *normal* mother with *normal* family relationships. People just don't understand. You're about the only person who does.'

'True.'

'He'll think I should be there.'

'Well, I think you have to protect yourself. She doesn't even deserve to have you think about her, let alone board a flight, stay in a hotel, and make all that effort,' Liv said.

Lotta smiled at Liv's reaction. Liv always became very angry where Lotta's mum was concerned. 'I think I'm going to just keep abreast of it from here. There's no point in me rushing out there because Dave has finally seen the cyclical nature of how this all goes. The difference now is that she's older, and her body isn't able to deal with it any longer.'

'Precisely. I mean, Lott, this could go on for years. Who knows what's going to happen?'

'I know.'

'Yep, just sit tight and not being mean, but let Dave deal with it. He made his bed.'

Lotta nodded. 'Yes, this time I think I will. This time I'm going to put myself first.'

As Lotta hung up the call with Liv, she felt a sense of relief that at least she'd decided what to do. As she sat curled up on the sofa, she picked up a new book and tried to focus on reading, but her mind kept drifting back to her mum. She took a deep breath and tried to push her thoughts aside. She needed to focus on work and on taking care of herself. At least she had the library room – her own little haven. A place where she could escape from the stresses of the world and immerse herself in her books. A place where real life was kept at bay.

She glanced over at the nook in the corner – at the plump cushion on the wicker chair, the orderly stacks of books on the table, the vintage lamp casting a warm glow, and the jug of lavender from the garden. All of it was mostly things she'd rescued from the garage and charity shops – a really simple and really pretty space, but it was *all* hers.

With a deep breath, she snuggled down onto the sofa and pulled the throw further up until it was just about over her head. As she started to read, she felt herself drift away and began to get lost. She relished it as the words on the page started to almost dance as they worked their magic. She didn't want to come up for air.

13

With a full and busy week at work, Lotta hadn't had much time to sit around reading or, for that matter, moping or worrying. She'd been in touch with her mum via text message and was crossing her fingers that her mum would be okay. Dave hadn't called again, so she was taking that as a plus. Only time would tell.

She stood outside the boathouse building and gazed at the in bloom roses going around the door. Everything was looking lovely for her first guest, Marie's cousin Emily, but sadly, Lotta had not had another firm booking for the retreat. She'd tried to remain positive and was determined to make Emily's stay a memorable one and hoped that more bookings were around the corner.

Pulling on rubber gloves and grabbing her bucket full of cleaning supplies, she got to work with gusto on the preparations for her first guest. Starting with the bathroom, she sprayed, wiped, and scrubbed every inch of the white porcelain sink and the clawfoot bathtub until they gleamed. In the kitchen, she checked each and every piece of cutlery, wiped down the worktops, and made sure they shone. Next, she moved on to the bedroom, replacing the sheets with fresh-from-the-line ironed ones. She then plumped the pillows and smoothed out the duvet, making sure everything was just right, not a crease to be seen anywhere. Adding little ginger jar vases stuffed full of freshly cut, pale apricot roses to the bedside tables on either side of the bed, the room looked ready and waiting for its first guest.

As Lotta worked, she was more than frustrated with the lack of bookings, but at the same time, she was rather proud of what she'd achieved. The whole place was lovely; she'd put her heart and soul into it, and whatever happened, she knew that she couldn't really have worked much harder to make it work. At least in that knowledge, she was secure.

She paused for a moment, looking around the space. It was definitely small but very cosy, and the little piles of books everywhere and the reading nooks invited anyone who was a bookworm to sit and stay a while. Filled with a mix of emotions as she continued to meticulously clean every nook and cranny, she didn't hang around moping at its lack of bookings. As she crawled around on her hands and knees with a cloth wiping the skirting boards, she couldn't help but feel a sense of nervous anticipation at Emily's arrival.

As she plumped the cushions on the cosy armchair by the window, she pictured her future guests curled up with a good book and a hot cup of tea, the rain tapping against the window panes. The thought of people enjoying the space she had created brought a warm feeling to her chest. She just needed to get them over the line and through the blooming door.

But along with excitement, there was also a nagging doubt in the back of her mind. What if no one *ever* booked? What if her business failed before it even had a chance to take off? The fear of failure made her hands shake slightly as she carefully arranged flowers in a vase on the windowsill.

She tried to focus on what other people in business had said to her about their views on the place. People like Jack, Suntanned Pete, and Holly had all told her they believed the retreat would be a success. With a deep breath and a determined set to her jaw, she continued on.

Once there wasn't a speck of dust anywhere in the place, Lotta started to get the supplies ready. In the fridge, she carefully arranged locally-made cheese on a wooden board. She placed milk in an old-fashioned ceramic top glass jug in the fridge, together with honey from the hills and locally-cured bacon from the farm which had come with Suntanned Pete's seal of approval. As she stood looking at the fridge, she hoped the little touches would make all the difference. Time, and her first guest, would tell.

A few hours later, Lotta was standing chatting with Emily in the courtyard area of the reading retreat. Emily was already gushing at the place from the outside, and Lotta had to admit that in real life, it did appear as good as it did in the pictures. The little pebble water feature bubbled, the sun shone on the vintage-style sun umbrella, and everything in the pots looked healthy. Lotta herself had to do a double take at how it had all turned out as she remembered when she and Jack had first set to work, when it had been in need of a lot of love. Now it looked like the sort of place to settle down with a huge jug of cold drink and a big stack of books.

'How was the traffic?' Lotta asked as she stood next to Emily, making polite conversation.

'Not too bad. The usual spots where it gets a bit snarly weren't great. I had a lot of stuff to think about, so it actually did me good to be stuck in the car for a bit.'

'Yes, it sometimes helps,' Lotta acknowledged and then pointed to the door. 'Well, there you are. Everything is set up for you. I've messaged you details of the online pack with lots more information about the area.'

Emily nodded. 'To be honest, the only reason I'll be leaving is to go for a walk.'

'Marie was telling me you often go on these weekends away.'

'Yes. I learnt the hard way, actually. I was working big weeks, I'm talking eighty-plus hours a week, and then suddenly one day I simply lost the plot. Just like that. All of it came crashing down by my ears. Never again. Now I make sure I take care of myself. You live and learn.'

Lotta looked interested. She felt as if for a long time, in the days when she'd been with her ex-partner, she'd done the same. 'What sort of things do you do to take care of yourself?'

'Ahh, nothing fancy. Nothing fancy at all. I'm not one for treatments and all that malarkey. I'd rather poke my eyes out than lay there having a facial.'

'I totally get you,' Lotta agreed.

'When it first happened, I just went away to the lakes for a weekend and did nothing at all. I even took M&S dinners with me. I watched films and walked and that was it. I think it rained most of the weekend. Now I go away often. It's my first time in Pretty Beach, though, and from what I've seen so far, I think I'm going to love it.'

'Yes, it's lovely here,' Lotta acknowledged.

'Been here long, have you?'

Lotta shook her head. 'Actually, no, I'm new to the area. I love it. The air is amazing and the people are lovely. It's really changed my life being here.'

'Sounds good to me. I hope I get a few of the same vibes.' Emily chuckled.

Lotta turned around and pointed up in the direction of the cliffs. 'The best walk is up to the lighthouse if you want to blow away the cobwebs. It really is breathtaking. The views are amazing.'

'Right, great, I might do that this afternoon.'

Lotta wasn't really sure what she was supposed to do, whether or not Emily wanted a handhold and to be shown around. She was getting the feeling that Emily wanted to be left to it. She gestured over towards the house. 'Shout if you need anything.'

Emily picked up her bag. 'Will do, but I don't think you'll be hearing much from me. Let the recharging begin,' Emily said with a big smile.

Lotta nodded and watched as Emily let herself in. As she walked away, Lotta gulped; she really hoped that Emily was going to be happy with her stay.

Jack was sitting up in Lotta's ginormous sleigh bed, gazing at his phone. Lotta stood at the window behind the curtain, squinting down at the garden. 'What I need is binoculars. Why didn't I think about that before?'

Jack shook his head. 'You've turned into a peeping Tom. If you were a man, someone would be calling the police.'

Lotta giggled. 'I can't stop wondering what she's doing. Do you think she's okay?'

'She told you what she was doing. Nothing.'

'I know, but do you think she's enjoying herself?'

'How do I have any clue whether or not she's enjoying herself?' Jack replied.

'Do you think everything is okay?'

'I cannot answer that either. You have also asked me both of those questions at least ten times already this evening, possibly fifteen.'

'But what if she doesn't like it?' Lotta persisted.

Jack contemplated for a second. 'If she really hated it, she probably would have gone home. I would say that is a logical conclusion to make.'

'True.'

'And if she hated it a bit, you might have had a message from her asking for something.'

'Right. Yes, yes. Do you think I should message her?'

'No! No way. She said she was coming here for peace and quiet.'

'Do you think I should take her something in the morning?'

'Like what?'

Lotta shrugged her shoulders. 'I have no idea. Like, I don't know, cinnamon buns or something. I could walk down to the bakery and get some fresh ones.'

'I thought you said there were some in the freezer in there.'

'There are, but they won't be as nice as getting a delivery of fresh ones. Flowers. What about flowers? That would be nice.'

'I think you should just leave it,' Jack instructed. 'Honestly, you're overthinking this.'

'Right.'

'And stop standing there at the curtain. You've been there for ages.'

'The light is still on in the sitting room.'

Jack laughed. 'She said she was watching movies. I presume she'll need a light on for that.'

'Yeah, yeah, so she'd still be up.'

'Just leave it.'

'Okay. I think I'll go down and make a hot chocolate. Do you think she might like the offer of a hot chocolate?'

Jack rolled his eyes. 'No, Lotta as in hotter, I don't.'

'I'll just leave it then, shall I?'

'Yes. I think we've already established that. Lott, just chill out! She's fine.'

'Okay, right. Yes, yes, chill out. Okay, I'll go and make a hot chocolate.'

That night, Lotta had still spent way too much time worrying about whether or not Emily was enjoying the retreat. It had whirred around her head so much so that she'd ended up with a visit from her old friend insomnia, who had come and sat on the end of the bed at about three o'clock when all in the house was quiet and dark. After spending nearly an hour laying on her back dead still so as not to wake up Jack, she'd snuck out of bed, gone down to the kitchen, and made herself a cup of tea. It hadn't helped at all.

Lotta dragged herself out of bed the next morning, leaving Jack still deep somewhere in the land of nod. Her eyes were heavy, and her head was foggy from her racing mind and lack of sleep. She stumbled into the kitchen and flicked on the kettle, rubbing her tired eyes. As she waited for the water to boil, she couldn't help but think about Emily and whether she was enjoying her stay at the reading retreat. The worry had consumed her the night before, keeping her up and filling her head with endless what-ifs, and it was just as prevalent now.

The kettle got louder as it boiled, interrupting her thoughts, and Lotta made herself a cup of tea. In her dressing gown and slippers, she shuffled into the conservatory, craned her neck to see if she could see any movement at the end of the garden, and as she sipped her tea, she ran through her day. The housework wasn't going to do itself, she had a load of work emails to follow up on, and she and Jack had a long walk planned in the Pretty Beach Hills followed by a sit on the beach. She just needed to get stuck into all that and let Emily take care of herself.

A few hours later, Jack had been down to the bakery, washed both their cars, and changed the bed. Lotta had vacuumed from top to bottom, deep cleaned the kitchen, and scrubbed the bathroom. The scrubbing and putting her house in order had calmed her mind. Just after they'd got a picnic ready and Jack was loading the car, Emily walked past the end of the drive and waved. 'Hi,' she called out.

Lotta wanted to shriek and ask her if everything was okay. She did, however, attempt to make her voice steady. 'Hi. How are you?'

Emily beamed. 'How am I? I'm brilliant, thanks. What an amazing night's sleep I had! My goodness! Could you have thought of anything else? The lavender diffuser by the bed mingled with the sea breeze. Honestly, it was so good. I want to bottle everything.'

Lotta heaved a massive inward sigh of relief. She tried to sound casual. 'Ahh, good, yes, the sea air helps. It's lovely at this time of year.'

'And all the little extra bits this morning. Thank you for those. It really does make a difference. That homemade jam was like something else,' Emily gushed.

'I'm so glad you liked it.'

'I loved it!' Emily's face screwed up into a frown. 'What were the buns? I had one with my coffee mid-morning out in the courtyard there. I've never tasted anything like it. Cinnamon, was it? I'm not usually keen on things like that, but it certainly didn't last long.'

Lotta said a silent thank you for the Locals Only cinnamon buns and Holly from the bakery. 'Yes, they're from the bakery in the laneway. You'll pass it on your walk.'

'Right, well, I think I might have to take a load of those home with me when I leave.'

Lotta smiled, not bothering to explain to her that she wasn't going to be able to get the Locals Only buns. It was far too complicated to go into for someone not from the area. 'Where are you off to?'

'I'm taking your advice and going up to the lighthouse. I have a few work things on my mind that I need to work through. I thought it might do the trick to take myself up there.'

'Lovely. Oh yes, there's nothing like a walk up to the lighthouse to take you away from it all.'

'Yes, so true. Well, thanks then.'

'Let me know if you need anything,' Lotta said.

'Will do, but I don't think so. Once I'm back from the walk, I'll be hibernating again.'

'Sounds like a plan.'

'Cheerio.'

Lotta watched Emily as she walked along the pavement, and then she got into the car. Jack smiled. 'That went well. She sounded pleased with it.'

'Thank goodness! I'm so pleased. I can breathe again.'

'Your first guest is a happy guest. She was gushing,' Jack noted.

'She was! I'm so glad I made all that extra effort.'

'Yeah, makes all the difference.'

'I hope she does a review,' Lotta stated.

'All in good time. What we really need is for her to tell her friends. Word of mouth will work wonders in this, I think.'

'Yeah. Hopefully, she'll put it on her socials and tag me. That might get the ball rolling,' Lotta replied optimistically.

'Yep.'

'I was thinking about putting a competition on my reading account for my followers for a weekend stay. What do you think? That might be a good way to drum up some interest,' Lotta said as she scrolled down through her feed as Jack reversed the car off the drive.

'Great idea,' Jack replied as he checked his mirror and indicated.

'I might just strike while the iron's hot. It's not as if I have any dates to worry about fitting it in.'

'Yep. When is your next live?'

'I haven't got one scheduled. Maybe I'll do one tonight. I don't really have much to lose.'

'Sounds like a plan.'

~

A few hours or so later, Lotta was sitting on the beach next to Jack. From the comfort of her chair, she gazed up and down the beach and sighed at the sight of the long line of beach huts snaking away into the distance. Painted in the soft, pastel regulation colours of Pretty Beach, they juxtaposed against the blue hues of the sea and sky. Lotta let her eyes wander from hut to hut, each one seemingly with its own unique character and charm. One a soft blue-grey, another a delicate mint-green and a pale oyster pink one she wanted to park herself in and have a little sleep. Then there was the soft, pastel bunting draped ceremoniously from hut to hut. It fluttered in the soft sea breeze coming in from the sea.

As she sat there and alternated between pondering what was going on in the huts with gazing out at the sea, she felt grateful for Pretty Beach. She utterly wallowed in not doing anything, in the peace and quiet, the sun warm on her skin, the sound of the waves in her ears, and sitting there next to Jack, soaking it all in. Divine.

In front of them, the water sparkled in the sunlight, and seagulls circled overhead, swooping down occasionally to peck at the shore. Lotta closed her eyes, listening to the sound of the waves and the laughter of children in the distance. This was what her new life was all about – little moments of nothing sprinkled deliciously into her weekend. Lost in a world of her own, she came to when Jack tapped on her hand. 'You okay?'

'I am. This is so nice.'

'I was just thinking the same.'

'I could sit here all day, all week, even. Maybe have a little doze. A read. Nothing.'

'Yep, me too. Shame I've got so much travelling coming up,

otherwise I would have taken a few days off to make the most of the weather.' Jack pointed to his phone. 'The weather app says we're going to have a run of sunshine.'

'No rest for the wicked, eh?'

'No. Not at all.'

'You're not looking forward to the travelling?' Lotta asked.

'No. Going over the Atlantic is getting old. It's such a long way. It's a shame you're not coming with me. That would help.'

Lotta sighed. She was half with Jack and half not, and her mind was torn in two. The thought of having to sit and make small talk with Jack's business people didn't fill her with joy. If she had time off, there was only one place she wanted to be – in the pages of a book. The mere thought of his huge journey, sitting around in airports and then having to be cordial and put on a façade to people she didn't know, wasn't ticking any of her boxes at all. 'You'll be back before you know it.'

'Yeah, I will. I'll miss you, though.'

'That's what we have our phones for.'

'True.'

'Remember when you video-called me in Singapore? It was almost like you were there with me,' Lotta noted. 'Don't you just love how we can do that from our phones?'

'I know, yup, it was.'

'Except you didn't get the heat.'

'Ha! No, I didn't. Have you heard anything else about your mum? Any updates over the last few days? Sorry, I forgot to ask what with everything going on at work.'

Lotta shook her head. 'Not really, other than a few texts from Mum. She's not exactly that communicative with me.'

'What about Liv? Do you know if she has heard any more?'

'Not as far as I know.' Lotta sighed.

'That's good then.'

'Yes, I hope it stays that way…' Lotta trailed off, but she had a feeling something was in the water.

'I feel like there's a but coming.'

'And you're right. There is. I hate to say this, but we've been here before. I don't know. We're in a cycle here and it's not a nice one. Mum messaging Liv before was *not* a good sign. I've been here many times. I just have this horrible feeling that something is going to happen…'

'Don't say that. If anything is going to happen, it needs to wait until I'm back from America. If I'm needed, I want to be in the country, at least.'

Lotta nodded. 'Yes, yes, it does indeed. Yeah, no, I'm not even tempting fate. I'm remaining positive. Everything will be fine.'

14

Lotta was sitting in the library room, setting up her phone to go live on social media. She'd decided not to worry about the reading retreat too much, and as she'd mentioned to Jack, she was going to offer a competition to her followers. As she got ready for the live, plumping cushions and tidying up, she noticed the picture frames on the shelves behind her – a photo of her and Liv on Liv's wedding day, one of her and Liv on holiday, and a black-and-white image of her and Jack taken on the ferry. The vintage reading lamp on her desk illuminated the room, casting a warm glow over the coffee table, and as she fiddled with the camera on her phone, ensuring she had the right angle, she smiled to herself and hoped that the competition might start a flurry of bookings for the retreat.

As she waited for her live to begin, she glanced out the window, taking in the view of the garden outside and crossed her fingers that the retreat would take off. Once it was time, Lotta looked at her phone and began to tell her followers about the competition.

'Hi, everyone, I've got something lovely for you today! A competition to stay in my new reading retreat. I know you've all loved following along with its makeover, so I thought someone might love a treat. A whole weekend of doing nothing but relaxing by the sea and reading is up for grabs!' she joked. 'Give me all the books.'

As Lotta continued and pointed the way to pictures of the retreat, the comments were rolling in thick and fast, and she struggled to keep up. She scrolled through them quickly, trying to respond and answer as many as possible. She couldn't help but smile as love hearts flurried up the side of her phone. Many of her regular and oldest followers had turned up. They were so supportive and enthusiastic, it meant the world to her, and she felt a strange connection and sense of comfort to be surrounded by the group of women she only knew from her little corner of the internet.

The more she got into it, the more the chat flowed easily, and Lotta found herself feeling a bit more confident that the reading retreat would be okay as the comments continued to pour in. Many of her internet friends told her they were looking at dates and planning stays, others said they couldn't wait for the book club to be announced. Lotta felt overwhelmed with gratitude for the support. It made all the hard work, elbow grease, and stress worth it.

An hour or so later, she was more or less in the same spot, but she was horizontal. Jack was at the other end of the sofa watching football on his laptop. An unfamiliar sound pinged from her laptop, which was open on the table.

She heaved herself up and squinted and couldn't believe what she was seeing – a booking confirmation for a long weekend at the reading retreat. Her heart pounded in her chest as she turned to Jack, who was completely absorbed in the football game.

'Ahhh! Yes!' she exclaimed, nudging Jack on the arm and almost bouncing with excitement and anticipation. 'Jack! We've got our next booking!' she exclaimed, waving her laptop screen in front of him.

Jack looked up from his laptop and frowned. 'What?'

Lotta gushed, still beaming from ear to ear. 'Oh my goodness! Someone has booked the retreat for a long weekend!'

A huge grin spread across Jack's face. 'No way! Who's booked it?'

Lotta quickly clicked on the notification, her eyes scanning the details of the booking. 'It's a couple from Scotland. Ahh, yes, I recognise the name. It's one of my followers. Yes!'

Jack reached over and gave her a quick hug. 'I'm so proud of you. I knew it was only a matter of time.'

Lotta couldn't stop grinning. 'Hopefully, this will get the ball rolling.'

Jack laughed. 'I think the ball is officially rolling.'

'I'm going to need to make sure it's absolutely perfect.'

'There's no doubt about that. They'll love it, just as Emily said she did.'

Lotta couldn't believe it. A mixture of relief and happiness flooded her body. It was all finally coming together. Two bookings down, hopefully, many more to go. She felt like she was buzzing with excitement and couldn't stop herself from grinning widely. 'I can't believe it, Jack! This is really happening!' she said, bouncing. 'Thank you. I couldn't have done this without you,' she said, looking up at him with tears in her eyes.

Jack smiled. 'And now you can finally start paying off the debt from that idiot and his app, and stop it from weighing you down like a ball and chain around your neck.'

Lotta laughed and hugged him tightly, feeling like everything was falling into place. This was it – her dream was coming true. She was going to be a successful business owner and get her debt paid off. She picked up her phone and opened Instagram, scrolling through the comments on her post.

'How long until you get the next one?' Jack asked, interrupting her thoughts. 'What are the comments saying?'

'People are just saying that they'd love to book it.' Lotta looked up at him, her smile widening. 'I'm just so grateful, it's unfathomable. For you, for my followers, for this moment.'

Jack grinned back at her. 'Me too, Lotta as in hotter. Me too. This is the beginning of many more good things.'

Lotta nodded. She really hoped that Jack was right.

15

Lotta and Jack sat in a corner of the bustling coffee shop in the airport, surrounded by people with luggage, the smell of freshly brewed coffee, and the sound of chatter and clinking cutlery. Lotta sipped a hot chocolate and fidgeted with her phone, trying to delay the inevitable goodbye as they waited for Jack to go through on his way to the States.

'You know I wish you were coming with me,' Jack said, taking a sip of his coffee. 'We should have made it happen.'

Lotta smiled weakly. She'd not been attracted to the business side of the trip, but now that he was about to go, she wished she'd sucked it up. 'I know. I wish too. Texas suddenly seems so very far away.'

Jack reached across the table and patted her hand. 'I'll be back before you know it.'

Lotta nodded. 'I know.'

'You might be pleased to get rid of me for a bit,' Jack joked.

Lotta raised an eyebrow. He couldn't have been further from the truth but she played along. 'Totally.'

They sat in silence for a few moments as Lotta glanced around the coffee shop, taking in the hustle and bustle of the busy airport. She felt a pang of envy towards the people who were jetting off to exciting destinations and a tinge of sadness that she wasn't one of them. It reminded her of the long, exhausting trip to Singapore – that had not been fun at all.

Jack squeezed her hand again. 'What's on at work this week?'

'Loads. I won't have time to miss you.' Lotta chuckled. 'Barring any disasters, it's all on schedule, though.'

'Oh dear, that sounds ominous.'

They finished their drinks and headed towards the gates to go through to immigration. Jack hugged her. 'Now you've got the drive back to do on your own. See, I should have jumped on the fast train.'

Lotta flicked her wrist to look at her watch. 'Nah, the traffic will be fine at this time of day. I'll be fine.'

Jack nodded his head as if something had just come to him. 'The penny's dropped! Now I realise why you were so keen to drive.'

Lotta chuckled. 'I just wanted to drop you off personally.'

'You have a book to listen to.'

'I do. A new book, actually.'

'That's alright then. Okay, love you, and I'll text you from the air.'

Lotta smiled and waved, but as she walked away, she felt a tiny prick of tears in the corner of her eyes. Feeling a tad lost, she made her way back to the car park and tried to push the fact that she was already missing Jack to the back of her mind, reminding herself that she had work to do and a reading retreat to run. Lotta Button didn't have time to mope around.

A couple of days later, Lotta was on her way to the pub just down the road from Liv's house. James, Liv's husband, was also away, and Liv had suggested a much-needed and long-overdue night out.

Lotta walked briskly towards the pub, her cardigan resting over her arm as the warm evening enveloped her. Passing a long row of gorgeous old coastal terraced houses with pretty doors and neatly trimmed hedges, she was very much looking forward to a night out with Liv. It had been long overdue. The sound of her footsteps echoed in the quiet street as she got to the corner where the pub sat at an intersection, its hanging baskets swaying in the breeze.

As she approached the old brick building, with its whitewashed walls and sloped roof, she smiled at the cosiness of it all. Pots overflowed with flowers, greenery adorned the windowsills, and the steps to the entrance were graced with colourful shrubs. A few round tables with pub parasols were set up outside, where people sat around with drinks, enjoying the warm summer evening. The sound of clinking glasses and soft chatter filled the air as Lotta pushed open the heavy wooden door with its brass knob, and made her way through the pub, dodging groups of people as she went. Scanning the room as she walked, the floorboards creaked under her feet, and when she finally spied Liv in a cosy corner by the fireplace, nursing a glass of wine, she broke into a huge smile.

'Hey!' Lotta smiled.

'It's so good to see you in the flesh!' Liv said, getting up to give her a hug.

After going back to the bar and getting a drink, Lotta settled into the corner and took a sip of her drink. 'It's been too long since we've caught up properly,' she said, leaning back against the soft cushions. 'Apart from the cottage pie night, I've hardly seen you.'

'I know, right? So, how's the reading retreat going?' Liv

asked. 'Anything more since that booking the other night?'

Lotta sighed. 'It's been a bit slow going, to be honest. Nothing steady yet. I wouldn't say I've got people queueing up at my door.'

'I suppose it'll take a bit of time,' Liv noted.

Lotta nodded. 'Yeah, I've been trying to get the word out on social media. Time will tell.'

'Well, I'm happy to help in any way I can. Maybe I could put a message on my work Facebook page or something,' Liv offered.

'That would be great. Every little helps, as they say.'

Liv took a sip of her drink before looking at Lotta with a raised eyebrow. 'So, what about Jack? How was it dropping him off at the airport?'

Lotta let out a sigh. 'I probably shouldn't have gone to the airport. I hate that,' she admitted. 'I miss him already. I know he goes away all the time but it's usually not too far away or Europe.'

Liv nodded sympathetically. 'I know what you mean. I hate it when James is away, although it's sort of bittersweet at the same time.' She chuckled. 'I like the peace and quiet, too.'

Lotta smiled. 'Yeah, you're right. I'm actually excited about cracking on with my TBR pile while he's gone.'

'No surprise there.' Liv laughed.

They chatted about Lotta's plans for the reading retreat, and as they ordered another round of drinks, Lotta realised how much she loved spending time with Liv. A low hum of chatter and laughter drifted through the air around them, and as Lotta took a sip of her drink, Liv leaned in, her expression growing more serious. 'How's your mum doing? Have you heard anything much?'

Lotta sighed, feeling a weight settle in her chest. 'Not great, to be honest. She's not admitted it, of course, but she's been drinking loads. Dave sent me another few texts. I just don't know what to do. I feel like I'm failing her somehow.'

Liv reached out and patted Lotta's hand. 'You and I both know there is nothing you can do when she gets like this.'

Lotta nodded, feeling grateful for Liv's understanding. 'I know. It's horrible, though.'

Liv smiled softly. 'We'll just have to wait and see what happens.'

Lotta nodded. It was good to have someone to talk to, someone who understood what she was going through. She took another lug of her drink. 'I don't know. I just thought the heart attack would change things. I guess I was stupid to think that.'

'I think most people might have come to the same conclusion,' Liv reasoned.

Lotta found herself lost in thought for a second. She couldn't help but wonder if she was doing enough where her mum was concerned. She'd always thought her whole life that there might have been something she could have done to prevent her mother's drinking. Like somehow it was all her fault. She couldn't shake the feeling of helplessness that had been gnawing underneath since she'd been to Singapore. Liv looked at her with concern etched on her face. 'Are you okay?' Liv asked.

Lotta shook her head slowly. 'I don't know, yeah, course I am. I'm only talking about it because it's you. It's just so tiring even thinking about it.'

Liv took a deep breath and looked at Lotta intently. 'Listen. You can't blame yourself for her actions. She needs to take responsibility for her own life. Steer her own boat as it were.'

Lotta nodded, taking in Liv's words. She knew Liv was right, and even though Lotta knew what was what, she still found it hard to deal with. 'It's just that I've been here before with the cycle of drinking, but this time it all feels much more serious.' She paused for a second. 'And I don't know, but I have this odd feeling of foreboding.' Lotta tried to push the feeling of unease down, but it lingered. 'I said the same thing to Jack on the beach the other day. It's not a nice feeling at all.'

'Right, I hope not.'

Lotta hesitated for a moment, trying to find the right words. 'I don't know. I just have this strange sense that bad news is coming. And with everything that's been going on with Mum…' Lotta trailed off, her thoughts scattered. 'I've tried to ignore it and not tempt fate.'

'I hope not, but I know what you mean. The message she sent to me wasn't a good sign,' Liv admitted. 'It doesn't bode well.'

Lotta felt a lump form in her throat. 'Exactly. You nailed it. It doesn't bode well at all.'

16

Lotta woke up in Liv's spare bedroom, feeling as if her mouth was the lining at the bottom of a birdcage. And not a clean one. It was not a pleasant feeling at all. Groaning as she gingerly lifted her head off the pillow, she then slowly let it sink back into the softness again. Considering shaking her head at what had happened the night before, she thought better of it. She never should have followed Liv's lead and constantly ordered more drinks. Liv had been on a mission, and Lotta had blindly followed. Now she was regretting it big time.

She winced as a beam of sunlight pierced through the gap in the curtains, her head throbbed in time with her heart, and she reached for the glass of water on the bedside table, taking a long sip before slumping back on the pillows again. With slitty eyes, she stared at the ceiling, thinking about the rest of her week, and silently said a prayer that she was so caught up at work that, in actual fact, she was ahead of herself. She'd learnt in her job that the more she was on top of things and preempting problems, the better her life would be. And now, with a raging hangover, that was going to put her in good stead.

Checking the time on her phone and hearing nothing but

silence in the house, she decided to let her pounding head stay in bed for a bit. Sliding her hand out from under the covers, she rooted around in her overnight bag for her Kindle, pulled it out, flipped it open, and pressed to turn it on. Half an hour later, she was lost in a world where the protagonist had just been on a dream trip around the world. The escapism enveloped her from deep down inside her Kindle screen and had helped to ease her pounding head as she'd travelled from LA to Bali from the comfort of Liv's spare room.

Finally, hearing Liv shuffling down the stairs, she pulled on Liv's old dressing gown, and followed suit. Arriving in the kitchen to the sound of the kettle, Lotta burst out laughing at the sight of Liv in front of her. Wrapped in a massive pink fluffy dressing gown, Liv had a flannel slapped to her forehead and ginormous, oversized sunglasses on her face. Lotta giggled. 'I take it you're not feeling great.'

Liv groaned. 'You're not wrong. Why did you let me do that? What the heck.'

'Me! I didn't have a lot of choice in the matter! You were knocking them back like they were going out of fashion. No one was going to stop you from where I was standing,' Lotta bantered.

'Why did I do that? Why? Why? Why? I feel like death warmed up.' Liv groaned, clutching the flannel to her forehead.

Lotta wished she knew why Liv had been on such a mission. She'd still not got to the bottom of what was wrong with Liv, despite a fair amount of digging the night before. 'No idea, but nothing was going to veer you away from a road of many glasses of wine.'

'Never again. Never,' Liv said, wincing as the flannel slipped off her head and landed on the worktop. She poured the tea and passed over a mug to Lotta. 'Toast?'

'Yes. Marmite. Lots of it, please.'

Five or so minutes later, they were in Liv's sitting room.

Lotta shovelled hot buttered toast with Marmite into her mouth as fast as she could, in the hope that it would do something for both her head and her queasy stomach. 'Goodness. I feel like crap. I'm getting too old for this. What were we thinking?'

Liv shook her head. 'It's not like we've done it for a very, very long time. At least there's that.'

'True,' Lotta said and then swore as she dropped a piece of toast, Marmite side down, on Liv's dressing gown. 'We won't be doing it again for a while, either. I'm so not up for doing that again.'

'Nope. I do feel a bit better, though. I needed to let off some steam, and it certainly did the trick after what I've been through.'

Lotta didn't waste a second in jumping down Liv's throat. 'Why would you feel better if there's nothing wrong with you? You told me repeatedly last night that everything is okay with you. What have you been through? What is going on?'

'I'm busted, aren't I?' Liv sighed.

'You so are.'

'Hmm. And there I was thinking I'd got away with it.'

'Are you finally going to tell me?' Lotta questioned. 'It's *so* obvious something is going on with you. It's been the same since you requested cottage pie. I've been patiently waiting. I know what you're like.'

Liv shifted in her seat. 'Look, it's nothing.'

'Sorry, not good enough.'

'James says he's changed his mind about trying for a baby,' Liv blurted out and promptly burst into tears. The sobs came thick and fast, along with snorts and the odd wail or two. Lotta was beside Liv on the sofa like a shot. She swore repeatedly over and over as she put her hand around Liv's shoulder, until the heaving sobs had softened to the odd sniffle here and there. 'When did he say this?'

'Ages ago. I thought I was fine at first. And then...' Liv

paused for a bit. 'And then I was so not fine. So not. My body feels like one great big clock. I'm running out of time. I may have run out of time already. It just really upset me. Like a lot.'

Lotta sighed. 'Oh, right, blimey.'

'I know.'

'What did he actually say?' Lotta could see the pain etched on her cousin's face, and it made her heart ache.

Liv sniffled, held a screwed-up tissue under her nose and looked at Lotta. 'He said he wants to wait for a bit. I just don't understand why he changed his mind. We had talked about having a baby for ages. Now he's suddenly not interested? I feel like I'm running out of time.'

Lotta took a deep breath and put her arm around Liv. 'Maybe he has his own reasons. It's not as if he's said he doesn't want a family, just that he wants to wait for a bit.'

Liv shook her head. 'I know, but that doesn't make me feel much better. I thought we had a plan. I don't even know where to start about how it's knocked me for six. I just feel so lost. I want it so bad now. Like, it's really time.'

Lotta squeezed her hand. 'Hmm. It must be tough.'

Liv smiled weakly. 'I just have all these conflicting emotions zooming around me.'

'Welcome to my world,' Lotta said, attempting to lighten the mood a touch.

Liv chuckled and hugged Lotta tightly. 'I'm so glad I've finally got that off my chest.'

Lotta hugged her back. 'You should have just told me in the first place. Anyway, I'm sure he'll be fine. He probably just needs a bit of time.'

'I hope so.'

'You'll figure it out, Liv. You two are so strong,' Lotta reassured her. 'You're like couple goals personified.'

'But what if we can't?' Liv looked up at her with tears still glistening in her eyes. 'Then what?'

Just as Lotta was about to offer more advice and was picking up her tea, her phone buzzed and she jumped at the ringtone. She fished it out of her pocket and saw that it was a message from Dave. Her heart sank as she read the message. She looked up at Liv, shock all over her face. 'I need to call Dave.'

17

Lotta gazed out the window of the airport lounge at Heathrow, watching the planes take off and land, her eyes fixed on the gloomy and misty runway in the far distance. The dark, overcast skies mirrored exactly how she was feeling – bleak, sad, hopeless and grey. Relentless rain hammered down outside, and the foggy mist seemed to cling to everything around. As the rain lashed down, Lotta felt mostly numb at the news from Dave. Her mum had been admitted to hospital, and things were not looking great. The doctors had said it would be a good idea for her to come and not to waste too much time. The news had thrown Lotta's emotions all over the place, and she didn't know how to process what was going on inside. She'd phoned Jack in America, spoken to Anne at work, booked a flight, and jumped on the fast train without too much thought for anything else.

The sound of the rain hitting the windows matched the monotonous heaviness of her heart, and she couldn't quite sit still or focus on anything much at all. She picked up her Kindle, scrolled through, and then dropped it in her lap again and just stared out at the rain, letting herself feel the sadness of everything that had ever happened with her mum. Just as her mind was racing between memories, her phone buzzed with a video call from Jack. She put her earphones in, pressed to answer it, and waited. Jack appeared solemn and concerned, his face wrinkled into a frown on the screen. 'Hey. How are you doing? How was it getting to the airport? Any problems?' Jack asked, his voice tinged with worry.

Lotta forced a smile. 'It's been okay. Nothing too bad happened on the train.'

'Good, at least you haven't had any travel dramas yet,' Jack noted. 'That would make an already hard time much worse.'

'Nope, touch wood, everything is on time. How's everything with you in Texas?'

'Fine, but busy. How's your mum? Any further updates?'

'I haven't had anything else, no. I don't think there's much to tell.' Lotta's face fell, and tears threatened to spill down her cheeks. 'She's not good, Jack. The doctors aren't sure what's wrong with her. For them to tell me to come, it must be bad. Dave said she looks terrible and has lost so much more weight. She was thin enough when I saw her last time.'

'I wish I could be there with you,' Jack said, his voice filled with concern. 'I'm so far away. It's not great timing. I should have stayed.'

Lotta nodded, her heart heavy with the weight of the situation. 'I know. It's just tough being so far away and not being able to do anything. It's like I'm stuck here in a travel zone, waiting for the worst to happen. Who knows what the situation will be by the time I get there.'

Jack shook his head. 'It must be awful. You said you felt as if something was going to happen. This is clearly it.'

'I know.' Lotta let out a deep sigh. 'I could just feel something was in the air. Things were going so well too.'

'At least you've still got me,' Jack said with a little wink. 'I'm not planning on going anywhere. We'll get this over with, and everything will be fine.'

'Yep, I just don't,' Lotta's voice cracked, 'I just don't think this is going to end well. For the doctors to tell me to come. They don't just say that willy-nilly.'

'I know.'

They continued to talk for a while longer; Jack chatted about Texas as the rain poured down the window, and Lotta felt a bit better. Once the call ended, Lotta just sat looking a bit forlorn and lost and stared out the window watching the planes move around outside. She went over what Jack had said and pondered how she'd known somehow that something bad was going to happen. It had been there in her peripheral vision for ages. Like a blurry, dark cloud marring the landscape. Now the cloud had fully arrived in her world, and she didn't like how it felt. And the most worrying thing of all? Lotta felt as if it hadn't quite finished with her or delivered all of its news yet.

Lotta disembarked the plane with a heavy heart, dreading going to the hospital. The airport bustled with people and the sound of luggage wheels and travellers echoed throughout the terminal. She joined the queue for customs, pulling her cabin case behind her and constantly checking her phone for updates. Finally, she reached the customs counter and handed over her passport. It was scrutinised for a quick few seconds before being stamped and handed back to her. She shuffled through past the desk, hoisted her bag onto her shoulder, pulled her suitcase behind her, and headed towards the exit.

As she walked out, she observed the hustle and bustle of the airport all around her. People rushing, children running around with excitement, and couples hugging each other tightly. Happy people with lovely, happy families. It hit her in the face how all her trips to Singapore had mostly been chock-full of angst. There had never been a nice, smiley, happy mum with a balloon standing at the gate, waiting for her to emerge from customs. There hadn't been a single visit without her mum turning on her. All Lotta's memories were marred by the drinking and the nastiness. It made Lotta's heart ache, and bad.

Hustling along towards the taxi area, when she stepped outside, a wall of humidity and thick tropical air swirled around her. Her forehead immediately felt damp as the heat simmered around her head as she lined up for a taxi. After finally getting to the front of the queue and putting her case into the boot, she gave the driver the address of the hospital, and before she knew it, they were pulling up outside.

Lotta peered out the window at the entrance to the hospital. A large, circular driveway bordered by tall palm trees and a line of taxis and cars dropping off patients and visitors looked back at her. In a few minutes, her taxi was at the top of the queue, and as she stepped out onto the kerb, she was immediately struck by the busyness of the place contrasting heavily with her empty feeling inside. The building loomed before her, tall and imposing, its sleek glass windows and sterile façade gleaming in the bright Singaporean sun. A mix of glass, steel, and vertical lines looked back at her as she stood still, peering up at its clean, minimalist look, wondering what was going to be waiting for her inside.

As she walked over polished marble floors with a massive glass entrance that stretched from floor to ceiling, she approached a desk staffed by a team of efficient-looking receptionists. With her stomach swirling, she gave them the details she'd received from Dave on her phone and made her way to the lifts. Almost as if she was floating along, not really in her body, lost in a world of her own, Lotta only half took in what was beyond the reception area; a large atrium filled with natural light, walls adorned with pieces of modern art, the floors sterile and bright. The entire place had an air of efficiency and modernity that wrapped her in something, but she wasn't sure what.

Getting out of the lift and going through a labyrinth of corridors and doors, Lotta walked towards the ward, her heart heavy with worry and anticipation. Making her way to the reception desk, a young woman in a neat uniform was typing on a computer.

'Excuse me,' Lotta said softly. 'I'm looking for my mum's room. Button is the surname.'

A few minutes later, following the woman's directions, Lotta proceeded along a further maze of brightly lit corridors until she came to an entrance and saw a familiar figure pacing up and down outside the reception. Dave, looking pale and drawn with deep circles under his eyes, looked up and raised his eyebrows as he watched Lotta approach. Lotta could see the pain etched on Dave's face. His whole demeanour made her catch her breath.

She walked up to him and gave him a small, awkward hug, feeling his body shaking with emotion. Then she stood in front of him for a moment, not sure what to say, and so neither of them said anything at all. Finally, he cleared his throat. 'I'm glad you're here,' he said, his voice hoarse with emotion. 'Your mum… she's not doing well. It's been up and down.'

Lotta felt a lump form in her throat, and she swallowed hard to stop herself from crying. 'What happened?' she asked, her voice barely above a whisper.

Dave shook his head. 'I don't know. She just took a turn for the worse. The doctors are…' He trailed off, and Lotta could see the fear and uncertainty in his bloodshot eyes and pale grey skin. 'Not good,' he said, his voice cracking. 'She's in a bad way. They're keeping her stable, but…' He trailed off, unable to finish his sentence.

Lotta was lost for words, emotion rendering her voiceless, so she just nodded, and Dave gestured towards the doors. 'We can't go in there at the moment. They told me I needed to stay out here.'

Lotta swallowed, feeling a surge of emotion well up inside her as Dave led her to a line of beige plastic chairs. She sat down next to him and stared blankly ahead as a receptionist tapped away at a keyboard. The only noise in the place was a far-off beeping, the tapping of the keyboard, and the odd nurse walking up and down. Lotta felt as if someone was beating a gargantuan echoey drum in the centre of her chest. She closed her eyes and took a deep breath, trying to steady herself as the same foreboding feeling she had had before raced around her veins. Good things were not around the corner.

18

The next day, Lotta felt as if everything about her and around her was a blur. The day before had ended up with many hours of waiting around and many hours of distress. She sat on the edge of her hotel bed, staring at the Singaporean skyline outside the window. She couldn't stop thinking about the sight of her mum in the hospital bed, hooked up to various machines and wires – so small and frail, just a tiny cog in a process enveloped by machines and light. The constant beeping and hissing in the background as Lotta had sat by her mum's bed had suffocated Lotta. The lights, numbers, and lines felt as if they were measuring her mum's life. A life which seemed as if it might be on the way out.

In the screen that was her brain, Lotta couldn't erase the image of her mum's pinched, gaunt face, weight loss, and thinning hair. She replayed walking into the room in her head and remembered how her mum's eyes had flickered open. How they had locked gazes for a moment. How Lotta had known in an instant that even at that moment, she wasn't welcome. There had been a glimmer of recognition in her mum's eyes, together with a serious lack of love. Lotta's throat had tightened, she had fought back tears, and even though overwhelmed by the situation, she'd tried to put on a brave face. Old habits died hard. Should she really have bothered? Maybe not.

Now, alone in the hotel room, Lotta couldn't hold her composure any longer and felt hot streams of tears running down her face. She felt so helpless, so lost, so alone, and so far away from home. She mulled it all over as she sat forlornly on the bed. Deep down, she knew two things – firstly, that her mum still felt the same way as she always had and secondly, that there was nothing Lotta could do to change it. The look in her mum's eyes had flicked a switch on the ridiculous notion Lotta had clung to all the way through the journey from Pretty Beach, that perhaps things would be different. How wrong and how *stupid* she had been. Even without being able to really speak, her mum had let it be known that nothing had changed in the slightest.

Lotta replayed the scene at the hospital over and over again in her head, reliving how her heart had sunk when she'd seen the disapproving look in her mum's eyes. She'd realised that she'd been harbouring thoughts of a longed-for connection or some kind of reconciliation, but it was clear that, even in her state, resentment was still so very much at the fore. The coldness in her mum's semi-coherent gaze had been like the final stab to Lotta's heart. She had hoped that her mum's condition would have somehow brought them closer together, but it seemed that nothing had changed. Lotta had felt alone, rejected, and unwelcome all in one.

Lotta sat there feeling numb, with a lump in her throat. She realised that underneath, she'd always hoped that things would one day be different. But seeing her mum in the hospital bed, hooked up to machines and looking so frail yet somehow still being able to command the room, brought back a flood of memories. Not a single happy one.

With her eyes fixed on the rooftop of a glistening skyscraper, she pondered what the hell was going on in her head. She'd always tried to win her mum's approval, but it had always been that no matter what she did, it was never enough. She remembered walking on eggshells all the time, never knowing what would trigger her mum's anger. Never knowing when a fit of venom would arrive out of nowhere. Seeing the nasty, vapid, abusive face of the alcohol doing its thing. Always waiting for the jarring look of disapproval, which always came.

Even in this scenario, the weight of her mum's disapproval sat heavily on her chest. It was as if she'd been transported back in time to her childhood, where her mum's drinking had made everything in Lotta's small, tight, closed world unpredictable and unstable. She remembered the countless nights worrying and waiting for her mum to come home, the bewilderment and hurt that came with each betrayal. Memories from her childhood flooded into her brain. She reeled and almost rocked as she remembered feeling *so* scared and *so* alone as a child, wondering why her mum couldn't and wouldn't just stop drinking. Now, sitting in the hotel room, a tangled mess of conflicting emotions swirled around Lotta's head – sadness for her mum and the life she had led, but deep, tightly held anger and resentment. Bitterness for a childhood lost.

She had, though, still hoped for something. For some sense of reconciliation or closure or at least some kind of connection. But instead, she had been met with the same coldness and disdain that had characterised their relationship to a tee. It was an acerbic reminder of all the pain and disappointment that had come with her mum's addiction. A short, sharp, stinging slap in a small, sad face.

Next, her thoughts raced with questions and regrets. Had she done enough to help her mum? Could she have done more? Was it too late to make amends? The uncertainty, sadness, and guilt weighed heavily on Lotta's shoulders. She felt drained and powerless, and just so very unsure of what to do.

Another twenty-four hours had passed, a lot of which Lotta had spent in a dark, ugly tunnel of emotion at the hospital, and now she was sitting alone in the coffee shop outside the hotel. Staring blankly at its decor, she nursed a coffee. She scanned the walls adorned with arty black-and-white photographs of Singapore from the past. A large clock hung above the counter, and the little timber chairs perched around her looked sturdy and well-worn. The aroma of freshly brewed coffee filled the air, blending perfectly with the scent of hot buttered toast. The chatter of locals and tourists alike filled the small space, numbing what was going on in Lotta's brain. She took a sip of her kopi and sighed, pausing for a moment amidst the chaos of her emotions. She was disconnected, even after spending long hours at the hospital beside her mum's bedside, watching the steady rise and fall of her chest, listening to the machines beep and whir. There had been no change.

Lotta felt exhausted and drained, physically and emotionally. She'd barely slept since arriving in Singapore, her mind constantly racing with worry and fear. She couldn't bear the thought of losing her mum, and the finality of what that would bring.

The coffee shop buzzed with activity and people going about their day, but Lotta felt alone in her thoughts. She wondered what was going to happen next and how long it was going to go on. All she really wanted to do was curl up in bed and cry. She took a deep breath, trying to push away the heavy weight that had settled in her chest, and took a sip of her coffee.

Half an hour later, she'd taken the train to the hospital and had spent the whole of the visiting time just sitting, watching, and waiting. The whole thing left her heart heavy and her head sad.

Eventually she'd come back to the hotel and, at a loss for what to do, was at the rooftop swimming pool, the warm Singaporean sun beating down on her skin. From behind her sunglasses, with heavy red-rimmed eyes, she gazed at the cityscape surrounding her. Tall skyscrapers stretched up into the sky, the humidity cloaked her, and honking from car horns below floated up, landing beside the sunbed. As she sat with her Kindle, the pool glistened in the sunlight and the warm, bright light was a stark contrast to the storm of emotions she had brewing inside. Not being able to concentrate properly on her book, she got up and moved to the pool edge, where she sat with her legs dangling in the water, the coolness of it nice against her skin. Despite the warmth of the sun, she shivered slightly as she thought about her mum's condition and what was coming next.

She couldn't stop a sense of helplessness wash over her as she sat there. She had done all she could do, but it still didn't seem to be enough. Her mind was consumed with thoughts of what might have been, if her mum hadn't spent her whole life drinking. She sighed and leaned back on her elbows, closing her eyes and let the sun soothe her. After a few minutes, her watch told her her phone was ringing; she got up, answered it, and then sat back by the pool, the phone held tightly to her ear, her feet still dangling in the cool water. She could hear the concern in Liv's voice over the miles.

'It's just so hard, Liv,' Lotta said, her voice low. 'There's been no change since I arrived. It's like we're just waiting for something to happen. Waiting for her to…'

'I'm so sorry,' Liv replied, her voice soft. 'I wish I could be there with you. I should have come.'

'Jack said the same; it would have been totally pointless, though,' Lotta said, her voice thick with emotion. 'I just feel so helpless. I wish there was something I could do.'

'There's never anything you've been able to do where she's

concerned. We both know that,' Liv said, trying to offer some comfort.

'True,' Lotta agreed.

There was a pause on the other end of the line before Liv spoke again. 'Have you talked to anyone about how you're feeling?'

Lotta sighed. 'Pah! Not really, like who? I mean, I talked to Jack, but it's hard for him to understand. He's never met her, and he certainly won't get what she is like. Who would?'

'No, I know. Sorry, a bit of a stupid question from me. But don't keep everything bottled up,' Liv said. 'I'm worried about you.'

Lotta felt a lump form in her throat. 'Thanks, appreciate it, but I'm fine, actually. Well, I mean, obviously, I'm not fine as such, and I'm sad, but somehow, I'm okay. I'm sort of a mess but not. It's really weird. Like maybe, somehow, now I'll have some closure.'

There was a pause for a moment from Liv's end. 'Yeah, I get that.'

'You're probably the only one who does.'

'Just take care of yourself, okay? And let me know if you need anything. I can still get on a plane if you want me to.'

'I will,' Lotta said, feeling a little better and letting out a funny little chuckle. 'You have to laugh. I'm actually sitting with my feet in the rooftop pool.'

'There is that as a silver lining. I've got the heating on here.'

'Yup, I thought the same. God life is weird.'

Liv agreed. 'It most definitely, certainly is.'

Lotta's phone rang in the middle of the night. She groggily answered it, seeing it was Dave. 'Hello?' she croaked, her throat dry.

'Hello.'

Lotta instantly knew Dave's news and she was suddenly wide awake. 'I'm calling from the hospital. I'm sorry.' There was a pause. 'She's passed away.'

Lotta felt a sharp pain in her chest as if her heart had stopped beating and her whole world had come to a halt. Tears welled up in her eyes and she struggled to breathe. 'What?' she asked, her voice trembling.

'She passed peacefully in her sleep,' Dave said. 'I'm so sorry, Lotta.'

Lotta felt as if the hotel walls were closing in on her as she made arrangements with Dave. She hung up the phone in a daze, unable to process what had just happened. She sat on the edge of the bed, her head in her hands, tears streaming down her face. It felt like hours had passed before she was finally able to move. She showered and got dressed in shock, unable to focus on anything except the fact that her mum was gone.

As she made her way to the hospital, her mind was a jumble of memories and emotions. When she arrived, Dave was there in the lobby, his face a horrible combination of exhaustion and grief, his eyes red and swollen. He hugged Lotta as she struggled to hold back her tears.

'I'm so sorry, Lotta,' he said, his voice barely above a whisper. 'I know how hard this has been for you.'

Lotta nodded, unable to speak. She followed Dave to her mum's room, where she lay in the hospital bed, peaceful and still. Lotta took her mum's hand in hers, feeling the coldness of her skin. Lotta didn't move or say anything. Everything in the room was so still, apart from the torrent of tears streaming down her face as she sat almost statue-like, lost in thoughts and memories.

Lotta couldn't believe her mum was gone, that she would never see her again. The grief was overwhelming, consuming her completely. Her mind was a horrible amalgamation of distressing memories, hideous blank numbness, and deep, deep, deep sorrow. Lotta didn't want any of it to be real. Didn't want to be her. Didn't want to have to deal with it. But as with everything to do with her mum she was left with little choice but to take it on the chin.

19

Lotta sat staring out of the plane window as it taxied, trying to comprehend the fact that she had flown halfway around the world to the final closing of the curtains. For a long time, she had semi-prepared herself for the news, but nothing had readied her for the tidal wave of feelings that had crushed her. It felt huge and devastating and sad, all at the same time. Like a massive tonne of bricks had settled on her chest that wouldn't be moving anytime soon.

The long journey itself from Singapore had been a whirlpool of emotion. The numbness and disbelief had jarred against the humdrum of the trip. All the regular travelling things hadn't sounded quite as normal in Lotta's state of mind – the announcements over the intercom, the smell of plane food, and the mindless watching of the entertainment system. The disorienting cabin lights and expanse of nothingness outside the windows had felt as she did inside. Even the pages of a new book she'd bought at the airport did nothing to alleviate what was going on in her head.

As she waited to get off the plane, phones buzzing all around her with notifications, it felt like time and life were still moving, but Lotta's world had ground to a horrid, grief-stricken, black hole halt. The world outside kept spinning, even though, just for a little bit, she so very badly wanted to get off. When a crew member smiled and said goodbye as she stepped out of the plane, Lotta barely registered the exchange as her mind drifted back to her mum's hospital room. All she could hear was the constant buzz of the machines beeping, the drabness of the walls, and the horrible antiseptic but stagnant hospital smell. Along with the room, flashes of memories danced in front of her eyes – her mum's alcoholism, the shouting, and the pain, all jumbled together with the sadness and regret of the past few days.

As she entered the immigration hall with all the familiar English signs, the emptiness hit her like a physical force, and she blinked furiously to stop the tears from rolling down her cheeks. She'd flown all that way to say goodbye to someone who had never truly been there for her, and now all she was left with was the illusion of what could have been.

Standing waiting in the winding line to show her passport, the grief suffocated her. She felt more alone than ever before. The journey home had been the final nail in the coffin of a relationship that had been broken for too long, and now was just sadness and regret. As her mind unravelled, there was also an oddly welcome feeling of relief. Daughter guilt took a front seat.

She peered down at her phone and frowned. She'd expected a text from Jack. With the time difference, she hadn't heard from him, and they'd agreed to WhatsApp in case one of them was asleep. She checked again, saw nothing, headed for a seat, and typed in the trip planner for the times of the trains. Her eyes felt heavy, her body tired, and her emotions were drained as she squinted down at her phone. Not able to concentrate even for a second, and with everything feeling too much, she just stared at the mass of people around her. Tears again welled up in her eyes as she felt the force of what had happened. It was time to face the reality of her mum's passing and everything that had been left behind.

She sat there for ages, not really being able to move, almost paralysed by thoughts of the past. Just as she was chastising herself, her phone buzzed. She picked up and tried not to sound too bad as she spoke to Liv.

'How was the journey?' Liv asked, her voice laced with concern.

'Long and exhausting,' Lotta replied, her voice shaky. 'I don't even know how to describe how I'm feeling. It's just... a lot.'

'I can imagine,' Liv said softly.

'Thanks for calling.'

'Of course. Don't be silly,' Liv said. 'How are you holding up?'

Lotta paused for a moment, struggling to put her emotions into words. 'Honestly, Liv, I feel numb. Like I've been rolled over by a truck. I've been sitting here almost paralysed by memories,' she said finally. 'I didn't have the best relationship, but she was still my mum, you know? And now she's gone, and I don't even know how to process it. To be quite honest, I feel like a mess.'

'You must be,' Liv said, her voice gentle. 'Just take your time and let yourself feel whatever you need to feel.'

'Thank you,' Lotta said, her voice breaking a little. 'I really appreciate it. Thank goodness I've got you.'

'Have you heard from Jack?' Liv asked.

Lotta frowned. 'No, I haven't. I went to bed, and the time zones were all on top of each other, but I haven't actually heard from him since, oh, I can't even work it out…' Lotta trailed off. 'I've lost all track of time. I'm not even really sure what day it is.'

'Right. Only–' Liv replied, stopping herself mid-sentence.

'What?'

'Look, it's nothing, but I was just watching the news. Whereabouts was he? Texas, wasn't it?'

'Yeah. Umm, I'm not sure where exactly, but yes, Texas. Why?'

'There's been another one of those shootings...'

Lotta felt herself go cold for a split second and then brushed it off. 'What, in Texas?'

'Yes, sorry, I shouldn't have said anything,' Liv gabbled.

'No, no, it's fine. Where was it?'

'I don't know. In a mall somewhere. Hold on.'

Lotta waited, not knowing what to think. Liv spoke again, 'Maynisse County. Does that mean anything to you?'

'No. Nothing at all, but I'm not actually sure where he is. I did expect at least a message from him when I disembarked.'

'Sorry. I'm sure it'll be fine. I shouldn't have worried you,' Liv backpedalled.

'All good. I'm going to head for the train. Speak to you later.'

'Yes, text me when you get to Pretty Beach.'

'Will do. Thanks for checking on me.'

Lotta sat back down again and immediately typed Texas shooting into her phone, repeatedly shaking her head as she read the first news article that had come up.

Police in Maynisse County, Texas, have announced that three people have been killed, three others are seriously injured, and two wounded in a shooting today in a shopping mall. Their condition is said to be unknown.

Maynisse County police spokesperson Sgt Corey Galardo stated that one person has been taken into custody in regard to the crime. No description of the person has been given. A weapon was recovered from the scene.

The US has seen a string of mass shootings in recent times. Many people have been killed in shootings, including at Michigan State University and in California where eleven people were killed in a dance hall in the Los Angeles-area city of Monterey Park, and seven were killed in a coastal town.

Lotta closed the article and didn't know what to do. She had no real clue where Jack was. They hadn't even discussed where he was going properly. She'd meant to ask him to forward her his travel plans, and then it had slipped her mind. Her mind raced back to when she'd had the call from Dave when Jack was in the States. Tapping out a message, she pressed send to Jack's phone. As she sat staring at her phone, she realised that on the bottom right of the text, it didn't say it had been delivered.

Her whole face wrinkled into a frown, and her heart skipped a beat as she scrolled up to double-check the previous messages she had sent to Jack. All the rest of them showed the word 'delivered', but the one she had sent just before didn't say anything. She stared at it for a moment, feeling a rising sense of panic. Had Jack not received her message? There was a horrible grizzly feeling in the bottom of her stomach telling her that he was not okay.

She tried to push away her worries, telling herself that it was probably just a temporary network problem or his phone was switched off or out of battery. Even though they'd discussed the time difference issue, she'd not heard from him for ages. Her mind raced with all kinds of worst-case scenarios, and she couldn't help but feel a sense of unease. She pointlessly tapped the message again, hoping that it would finally go through. But nothing changed, and she let out a huge sigh through her nose. She needed this like a hole in the head.

Taking a deep breath, she tried to calm herself down. She knew it was possible for messages to be delayed or not go through for various reasons. But the little voice that had been in the back of her mind for a while was now standing in front of her, jumping up and down and screaming. She simply couldn't shake off the feeling of unease racing around her body.

She glanced around the airport, watching people rushing to and fro with their luggage. The bustle and noise of her surroundings only added to her anxiety. Picking up her bag and grabbing the handle of her case, she felt a sudden urge to get out of there and make her way home. She needed to get to Pretty Beach, have a shower, make a cup of tea, and try to somehow process what had happened. She closed her eyes and took another deep breath, trying to focus on her breathing and push away her anxious thoughts about Jack. But it was easier said than done.

By the time Lotta had made her way across London and was sitting on the crowded train, her heart was not only racing about Jack, but she was also tired, irritable, and overheated. Her mind was consumed by the news bulletin she had seen earlier about the shooting in Texas, and she couldn't help but curse Liv for telling her about it. Everything was probably fine anyway, and it would be a whole lot of worry about nothing. She tried to push the thoughts out of her head, but they kept creeping back in. What if something had happened to Jack? If it had, she didn't know what she would do or how she would cope.

As the train rumbled along, Lotta kept picking up her Kindle, putting it down again, and switching to the book she'd bought at the airport, but all of it was to no avail. As she continued to get radio silence from her phone, her anxiety grew and her grief multiplied. She couldn't stop fidgeting, tapping her foot against the floor, checking her phone for messages, and making up plausible reasons as to why she now hadn't heard from Jack for a long time. On top of her grief, sadness, and the exhaustion from the long journey, she felt like she was going crazy and would, at any given moment, burst out of her skin with worry.

Her thoughts kept circling back to the news bulletin; the images and words burned into her mind as she leaned back in the train seat and closed her eyes. Her mind was a jumbled mess, her heart pounding in her chest. All she could think about was not having heard from Jack. She prayed that he was safe.

Lotta's worry intensified as she continued to send Jack more texts but still received no reply. The messages informed her that they had not been delivered. It wasn't like Jack to be unresponsive. She tried to reason with herself that he was likely in meetings or had his phone on silent, but her mind wouldn't stop racing. Deep down, she knew he wouldn't have his phone switched off, but she tried to convince herself that that was the case.

As the train rattled on, Lotta's thoughts swirled around, spinning out of control, and she imagined all sorts of scenarios – maybe he was caught up in the shooting, or perhaps he had been mugged. He could be lying somewhere left for dead and no one knew. Perhaps he'd had something happen to him in the hotel room. He'd slipped over in the shower and was concussed. On and on her thoughts raced as she sat stuck in the train seat as it barrelled towards the coast, not being able to do anything.

When Lotta's anxiety reached a boiling point, she decided to call Jack's sister, even though they had only met a few times. Saying a silent thank you that for some reason she'd added Natasha to her phone, she dialled the number and waited. She tutted and sighed as it went straight to voicemail. She left a message, her voice quivering with emotion as she asked if Natasha had heard from Jack.

Watching the countryside whiz by outside the window, she was physically exhausted from the journey, emotionally drained from the hospital, and overall just completely and utterly spent.

Leaning her head against the window, feeling the vibration of the train against her cheek, her eyes grew heavy, and she felt herself drifting and calming down a bit. By the time the train finally started to slow down and she saw the familiar signs for Pretty Beach, she was feeling, whilst not better, a little less agitated.

Pulling into the station, as Lotta gathered her things, she took a deep breath and tried to compose herself. As she waited to get off, she tried calling Jack again, but it went straight to voicemail. Her heart sank, and she felt like crying. She tried to push the nagging thoughts to the back of her mind and focus. She would get home, have a shower, and recalibrate. At least she was now home.

As she stepped out of the station and hustled in the direction of Pretty Beach to the Breakers, she could feel the weight of worry bearing down on her shoulders. She clutched her phone tightly and quickened her pace, her thoughts consumed by the events of the previous week. Approaching her front door, she fumbled in her bag for her keys, her hands shaking with a mixture of exhaustion and anxiety. Finally, she managed to unlock the door and pushed it open, her footsteps echoing through the empty hallway. Weary from the journey and heavy-hearted from Jack's radio silence, her eyes scanned the room, taking in the familiar surroundings. Everything was just as she had left it, but it all felt so different now. The silence was deafening, and the emptiness of the house seemed to swallow her up. She dropped her bags on the floor, feeling completely drained, let out a deep sigh, and closed her eyes.

Before Lotta really knew what she was doing, she'd stripped in the bathroom, pulled the lever on the shower, and was standing with hot water rushing down over her head, face, and body. Never had a shower been more welcome or felt so good. In its own strange way, standing in the bathroom and being home in Pretty Beach to the Breakers gave her a sense of comfort, even if it was fleeting.

As she stepped out of the shower and wrapped herself in a clean fluffy towel, Lotta felt the weight of exhaustion and grief settle in her bones as she sat on the loo seat again checking her phone. Still with nothing from Jack, she pulled on a pair of her oldest, softest trackies and sank onto her bed, a sense of relief settling now that she was in the safety of her own home.

Fifteen or so minutes later, she was sitting in the library room, a mug of tea in hand. Feeling numb as if she was watching herself from afar, her mind still reeling from the events of the past few days, she took a sip of the tea, hoping it might calm her nerves. She couldn't shake off the feeling of being lost and alone, as if the world had suddenly become too big, too bright, and way too harsh. Lotta wrapped her hands around the mug, feeling its warmth seeping into her bones. It was all too much to deal with at once – the grief of losing her mother, the worry about Jack, and the exhaustion from the long journey. She leaned back into the sofa, closing her eyes, and a few seconds later, she was interrupted by the shrill ringtone from her phone. Seeing Natasha's name flash across the top of her screen. Lotta quickly answered it, hoping it was news about Jack.

'Hello?' she said, trying to keep her voice steady.

'Hi, Lotta, it's Natasha,' said the voice on the other end.

By the sound of Natasha's voice, Lotta instantly knew that something was *very* wrong. 'Natasha,' Lotta replied, her heart pounding. 'Is everything okay with Jack?'

'No, I'm afraid not. I'm sorry to have to call you like this,' Natasha said quickly. 'He's in hospital. He was involved in the shooting in Texas that's been all over the news.'

Lotta's stomach dropped from the library in Pretty Beach to the Breakers to the centre of the earth. Her hand shook as she held the phone. 'What? Oh my god. No! Is he okay?'

'Yes. I've only just had a call from Mum. We don't fully know yet what happened or what is going on,' Natasha said. 'The police notified Mum because she's the emergency contact on his passport. She's trying to get more information now.'

Lotta's mind raced, trying to process what was happening. 'What can I do?'

'I don't know,' said Natasha. 'I just wanted to let you know what's going on. I simply don't know what to do. Mum is beside herself.'

'Okay, thank you,' said Lotta, her voice trembling.

'I'm waiting for her to phone me, then I'll call you straight back,' Natasha said.

Lotta hung up the phone, her mind reeling. She felt sick to her stomach with worry and fear. She didn't know what to do or where to turn. She felt so alone. All she could do was wait and hope for the best.

~

Lotta's heart thudded in her chest as her phone rang again. She hesitated for a moment, knowing that whatever news she was about to receive, it would be stressful. 'Hello?' Lotta answered, her voice shaking slightly.

'I've been on the phone with the hospital. He's stable, but he's very unwell.'

Lotta felt her breath catch in her throat. 'Is he going to be okay?'

Natasha's voice was gentle but strained. 'They think he's going to be okay, yes.'

Lotta felt tears welling up in her eyes. It was as if the library room was spinning out of control around her. She shook her head over and over again. 'I don't know what to do. I'm so far away.'

'I know. I feel the same,' Natasha said.

Lotta nodded, even though Natasha couldn't see her. 'How is your mum?'

'She's very worried, obviously. She can't go out there because of her leg, as you know.'

Lotta hadn't even thought about that. 'Right, yes, of course.'

'I'm in the same boat because of the children and not being allowed to fly...' Natasha trailed off.

'Yep.'

'What are you going to do?'

Lotta didn't take much time to make up her mind. 'I'm getting on a plane. I have to go.'

'Right, okay, well, at least that takes one thing off my mind. He needs someone out there with him, at least.'

'Yes.'

Lotta hung up the phone and sat staring off into space. She didn't even know if Natasha knew she'd just walked in the door from Singapore and had lost her mum. Her mind was reeling with a million different thoughts and worries. She felt helpless and alone, thousands of miles away from the person she loved most in the world. She'd just lost her mum. She was going to Texas. Wild bulls wouldn't have stopped her. There was no doubt about that.

20

The following morning, Lotta found herself at the airport, her suitcase hastily re-packed, and her heart heavy with worry. As she queued for passport control, she glanced at her phone, reading and rereading the messages from Natasha updating her on Jack's condition. Each word was like a punch in the gut. A reminder of how quickly life could change.

Lotta felt a lump form in her throat as the immigration agent looked at her with raised eyebrows. She had weird, horrible palpitations and suddenly was aware of her very sweaty palms. She'd been so focused on getting to Jack in Texas that she hadn't thought about anything else at all. The agent's questions about her travels to Singapore and the US made her even more anxious.

'Travelling for business or pleasure?'

Lotta shook her head. That was a joke in itself. It definitely wasn't pleasure, that she knew for a fact. She considered telling the man with the huge head the details of her last few weeks. 'Umm, neither, really.'

'Neither, really?' he repeated, without his face showing anything at all, emphasising 'really' with a question in his voice.

Lotta fought the urge to fling herself over the desk and pummel him with all her might. 'I was visiting my mother in Singapore,' Lotta explained, trying to keep her voice steady. 'And then I got a call that my partner was in the shooting in Texas, you know, the one that's been all over the news…' Lotta looked for a bit of recognition about the dreadful shooting everyone had heard about, but the wide face looking back at her was blank. 'So I'm on my way there.'

Lotta waited for more questions to come about the shooting. Maybe some empathy. There was nothing. The agent raised his chin just a touch, then looked down and scrutinised the documents for a few overly long, self-important minutes before nodding and stamping her passport and saying nothing. Lotta could quite happily have told him exactly what she'd thought of his stupid grumpy demeanour as if he was play-acting at being a hot-shot immigration person in charge of completely inconsequential things like, you know, keeping the country's borders safe. Instead, she smiled, grabbed her passport, and scooted through, letting out a sigh of relief. All she cared about was safely boarding the plane and getting to Jack. The mission she had chosen to accept meant she would get to Jack whatever it took.

As she was walking through Duty-Free, Lotta's phone buzzed in her hand. Looking down, she registered an unknown international number displayed on the screen. Once she'd scanned the message, she realised it was Brandy, the woman she'd met at a ball when she was fake-dating Jack. Brandy was the partner of Jack's business associate in Texas.

Brandy: *Hi, Lotta, it's Brandy. I'm with Jack at the hospital. How are you holding up? I've spoken to Jack's mum.*

As Lotta stopped in front of a ginormous display of perfume with two immaculately presented women dressed head-to-toe in red in front of it, her fingers trembled slightly as she typed her response.

Lotta: *I'm okay, just worried sick about Jack. How is he?*

Brandy: *Don't worry. He's in good hands. We have the best here.*

Lotta's heart raced with anxiety.

Lotta: *Thank you. I hope so.*

Brandy: *We're still unsure as to what happened exactly. We don't have all the details yet, but Jack was in the wrong place at the wrong time. We do know he jumped in front of a stroller.*

Getting shot in a shopping centre was more than that to Lotta. Wrong place, wrong time? Just a bit. Because that happens every day of the week.

Lotta: *How can this happen in a shopping centre???? A mall!*

Brandy: *I wish I had more answers. All we can do is be thankful he's okay. I'm praying to the Lord.*

Lotta's hands were fully shaking now as she typed. She wasn't even going to get into a conversation about guns and malls. She didn't want to think about anything other than Jack.

Lotta: *Thanks for your message. Please keep me updated on his condition.*

Brandy: *I will. Try not to worry too much. What's the flight number? I'll get a car for you. And what about accommodation?*

Lotta's eyes landed on the brightly coloured perfume bottles as she considered Brandy's question. She had decided she'd get a budget hotel once she'd arrived in Houston, and it had not even crossed her mind, really, on how she was going to get to the hospital. She typed her flight number in and then told Brandy she didn't have anything sorted.

Brandy: *A car will be waiting for you at the airport. He'll have a board with your name. I'll get our city apartment ready for you.*

Lotta: *Thank you.*

Brandy: *We're all praying for Jack.*

Lotta closed her eyes and took a deep breath, trying to calm herself down. She knew she needed to be strong. She knew she needed to do some serious adulting, but all she actually wanted to do was duck out of life and being an adult. It was coming at her too thick and fast. She wanted to just hop off the adulting merry-go-round for a bit.

Putting her phone back in her pocket, she felt grateful for Brandy's kindness and the fact that she didn't have to worry about getting to the hospital. As she mindlessly held out her hand for a spray of perfume from one of the dressed-in-red women, she tried to focus on the practicalities of the situation rather than her overwhelming emotions.

About an hour later, her Kindle and the four thousand airport lounge snacks had somewhat alleviated her racing worry about Jack and the uncertainty of the situation. But despite the food and an accompanying glass of wine, she was fuddled. It was as if her brain was having to cope with too many things at once, and so it had just gone on strike. She felt almost paralysed as her body grappled to deal with grief, regret, sadness, and anxiety all at the same time.

Once on the plane, Lotta tried to distract herself with reading but found it difficult to focus. She half-wished the airline hadn't been quite so gleeful in the publicity of its free in-flight Wi-Fi because it meant that she was constantly checking her phone for updates from Brandy, Natasha, or anyone at all. Unable to settle, she sat staring straight ahead at the little aeroplane on the map on the screen in front of her as the flight seemed to drag on forever, stretching for what felt like an eternity. As the plane appeared to go at a snail's pace, her anxiety and worry continued to mount. The hours ticked excruciatingly by, each minute feeling longer than the last.

Finally, the plane touched down in Houston, Texas, with a thud, and Lotta's heart felt as if it might burst from her chest as she rushed through the airport and made her way through immigration. Swept along by a tide of travellers past bright lights and gaudy adverts, she constantly checked her phone, hoping for an update from Brandy.

As she finally stepped into the arrival hall, her eyes scanned the long line of men in cheap suits, waiting with bored expressions, holding iPads and phones in front with names on them. As she bristled along past the barriers, she scanned the crowds for her name on a board and the driver that Brandy had arranged for her. A little inward sigh of relief came at the same time as a small smile, as she saw her name on a board and walked towards it.

After saying hello, they made their way to just outside the terminal where the car was waiting. The driver helped her with her bags, opened the door, and Lotta climbed in, feeling grateful for the air conditioning after the thick, humid air beating down outside.

Lotta sank back into the seat of the luxury car, the soft cream leather enveloping her in comfort almost like a cloud. Not that it made her feel any better. She could have been in a horse and cart for all she cared. Nothing would have made her feel any better. Her whole body seemed as if someone was pulling it taut at either end. At any given moment, anxiety, grief, and emotion would make her snap in two. She stared into the front at the car's sleek dashboard adorned with polished chrome and glossy digital screens, and felt the scented air conditioning whisper against her skin as it sent cool air through the car in contrast to the blinding sunshine outside.

The car pulled out of the airport and onto the busy streets of Houston, and they weaved through heavy traffic. Lotta gazed out the tinted windows, watching the city pass by in a blur. She couldn't quite focus on anything, couldn't quite compute where she was and what was happening. As if somehow the tall, imposing buildings towering over the car, their windows reflecting the bright afternoon sun, were peering down at someone else. She didn't really even know what time of day it was.

Despite the heavy traffic, the constant honking of car horns, and the chaos of the thoughts going on in her head, the inside of the car was calm. Lotta closed her eyes and leaned back against the soft leather seat, her heart racing as she thought about Jack. Not long, and at least she would be there.

After a journey that seemed as if it had taken longer than it had to cross the Atlantic, they finally pulled up at the hospital. Lotta was struck by the imposing nature of the towering structures with their mirrored windows stretching up into the deep, intense blue Houston sky. She took a deep breath and stepped out of the car; the driver helped her with her bags, and before she knew it, just like she had in Singapore, she was approaching the lobby of a huge modern hospital. The luxury of the car's interior faded away as she entered and approached the stark, sterile atmosphere that bustled in a quiet hum of activity. Medical personnel in scrubs rushed past, pushing gurneys and wheeling patients' chairs. Harsh fluorescent lights, stark white walls, and a thick red line on the floor led the way to the emergency department. An airless disinfectant smell surrounded Lotta as she felt a tighter and tighter knot forming in her stomach. Finally, she'd arrived.

~

It had taken hours for Lotta to get anywhere near Jack's room. She'd naively thought she would walk in, sit down, and somehow everything would suddenly be okay. Jack would be alive, she would be there, and things would work out fine. Too easy. It hadn't happened like that at all. Nothing like it. Firstly, there was the red tape around who, indeed, she actually was. Then there was the fact that the place was crawling with police. Add on top of that, she was not American. The whole thing had not been easy or pretty. Lotta had had to stop herself from both screaming and blubbing many times as she spoke to numerous people in numerous uniforms for what felt like hours on end, answering too many questions.

After the long flight and painstaking car journey in the gnarly traffic, she'd assumed her arrival at the hospital would mean she would see Jack. That hadn't happened, and she'd sat in the coffee shop on the ground floor of the hospital for hours. Tired, grief-stricken, and anxious, all was not good in her world. But Lotta was nothing if not determined. Despite the time difference, she'd managed to get hold of Natasha, who in turn had spoken to Jack's mum, who had called the hospital and confirmed Lotta's identity and relationship with Jack. That had been the start of a lengthy process, and as Lotta sat in the coffee shop nursing a lukewarm, and quite frankly revolting, cup of American tea, she couldn't help but feel overwhelmed. Exhaustion was seeping into her bones; the weight of her grief lurked just behind it, and the worry about Jack felt almost too much to bear.

When the call finally came that she was allowed to see Jack, Lotta all but sprinted to his room. After all the obstacles and red tape, she raced up in the lift and along the corridors in a blur, pulling her cabin bag behind her.

Finally, after more red tape, stuff with her passport, and being escorted to a separate wing, she stood outside the door to Jack's room looking through the window, a nurse in a blue uniform by her side. Lotta's heart didn't go remotely near the red competition leotard it normally liked to adorn anytime it was anywhere near Jack. Instead, her heart sort of juddered, as if it was about to topple off the balance beam. Its ugly training gear was rumpled and grey and stained by sweat. It was not going to perform a perfect ten at all. A mixture of relief, fear, and distress rushed through her from head to toe at the sight of Jack in the bed, and her legs felt weak beneath her as she stood staring, trying to compute what was going on.

Sensing her distress, the nurse tapped her gently on the arm and pushed the door open slowly. The squeak of its hinges cut through the quiet as Lotta took the nurse's lead and stepped into the private room. Monitors and machines beeped and hummed around Jack's bed. His right arm was heavily bandaged from his hand to his shoulder, and a huge dressing sat on the right side of his forehead. Lotta felt as if her knees were going to give way. He didn't look like Jack at all. Where was Just Jack? He'd left the building, leaving only his body behind. Big, strong, grumpy Jack, who had done things to her heart, was lying in the bed as if someone had squeezed the life out of his body. He looked pale and weak, and almost childlike in his form. Lotta wanted to turn and bolt and run and run and run.

She felt the nurse pull a chair up beside the bed and she sank down into it, simply not knowing what to do. Too scared to touch him and almost too scared to look at him either, she clasped her hands tightly in her lap and stared at the screen on the machine beside the bed. Beep. Beep. Beep. Tubes and wires snaked around him, connecting him to a myriad of scary-looking screens, blinking and flashing and whirring importantly to themselves.

She was vaguely aware of the nurse saying something, the door closing gently, the stark walls, the incessant beeping, and the gagging smell of too-warm antiseptic air. As she sat there, lost as to what to do, she felt her whole body trembling. It was as if someone had plugged her into a wall and turned her on, whereby everything in her body vibrated ever-so-slightly of its own accord. She was, in fact, wired with electricity, sitting on an uncomfortable plastic chair, not knowing what to do.

Finally, after a long time staring and her voice barely audible through her constricted throat, Lotta spoke. 'Jack.'

Nothing happened at all. Not a single thing changed in the room. She felt a tiny smidgen of a smile cross her lips as she remembered how Jack would often greet her when she called. 'Lotta as in hotter,' he would say. Now he was motionless. No funny frown, no grumpy smile, no eye roll, no deadpan response. Nothing but the nauseating stillness and the incessant beep, beep, beep. It felt as if the whole world had ended.

Lotta Button pushed her nails into her palms and started to cry.

21

Lotta had been at the hospital for so long that she wasn't sure what the time was or what day it was. She wasn't sure what anything was. All she knew was that she was very tired, emotionally done for, and ready to crack.

Finally, walking away from Jack's room, on her way out she slipped her phone out of her pocket and reread the text message from Brandy she'd received while sitting in the coffee shop in the lobby. As she walked along the long gloomy corridor following the exit signs, the text told her everything she wanted to hear; Brandy had sorted her an apartment to stay in, not far from the hospital, there was a number for her to text when she needed to be collected, and she should not worry about anything at all.

Stopping in the middle of the corridor, Lotta read the instructions for the car and driver again, copied the number, and not sure if she was doing the right thing, wrote out a message that she'd like to be collected. The little dots underneath the message flashed instantly, and Lotta waited, staring at her phone. As the reply arrived, it told her that a driver would be with her in approximately fifteen minutes and that she would receive a text when he was in the waiting area outside the main hospital entrance. Lotta nodded, putting her phone back in her pocket. She couldn't argue with that. The last thing she needed to worry about was how she was going to get to wherever it was that she was staying.

Fourteen minutes later, when she was standing by the huge glass doors at the entrance, her phone pinged with a text instructing her to walk outside. She followed the directions to find a man in a suit hovering by a huge car with blacked-out windows and gigantic shiny chrome hubs. The man smiled, and in one fell swoop, she felt as if he'd not only dealt with her bags but scooped her up and deposited her in the back of the car. She might be distressed, grief-stricken, and weary, but she really could get used to this. This was clearly how the other half lived.

After ten or so minutes of sitting in the back of the luxury car, absorbed in what had gone on in the day, Lotta was brought back to the present moment as the car slowed down in a waiting area. The driver then hopped out and opened the door. As she stepped out onto the pavement and looked at the driver, she looked up at a towering building in front of them and frowned. She didn't know what she was expecting, but a regular old apartment hotel, something with mirrored glass, was in her mind's eye. What looked back at her was so far from that it didn't even feel real. She sighed to herself. All she wanted to do was collapse somewhere, and now this. As if she hadn't had enough of a day already.

As the driver put her bags beside her, she smiled. Sounding very English, Lotta pointed upwards. 'Excuse me. I don't think this is correct. I, umm, I'm meant to be at an apartment hotel. Not meaning to be rude. Sorry.'

'Yes indeed, ma'am. We're at the Eppleton Building – top floor penthouse, ready and waiting for you.'

'I was, umm, expecting something a little more...' Lotta trailed off. 'Are you sure we're in the right place?' She quickly pulled out her phone and opened the text. 'Brandy said it was their city apartment.' Her face was full of confusion.

'I've been driving for the family since I was nothing more than a boy, and this is definitely the correct building, ma'am. This is the city apartment.' He chuckled. 'One of them, anyway. You are most certainly in the correct place.'

Lotta looked up at the towering structure. It wasn't quite a Travelodge. 'Right, yes, okay.'

Lotta stared at the grand 1920s building looming overhead. The imposing structure towered above her as if a living testament to the architecture from a bygone era. The light glinted off the delicate detailing of the façade, and as she stood entranced, she was struck by the sheer scale of the building. Its ornate arched windows and sweeping lines exuded an air of timeless elegance. She just stood there for a bit with her head tipped back, staring. The building's arches and ornate cornices seemed to transport her to another time and place, far removed from the hustle and bustle of modern Houston going on around her. Far removed from sickening worry and horrid grief.

A car horn honked furiously, and Lotta stood almost in a daze as a man in a suit appeared from the huge doors, swiped her bag, and led her in. The hum of the busy, hot city and its choking, blistering heat seemed to fade as she approached the entrance, replaced by the echo of her footsteps on the marble floor and the murmur of conversations from people going about their business once they got inside. She felt as if someone had dropped her into a calmer world as the scent of polished wood, brass, and age hit her nose.

Despite her racing mind and jangled nerves, Lotta couldn't help but shake her head over and over again at the exquisite building. It was as if she'd stepped from the modern glass world of the hospital to moving back in time to another more glamorous, much more elegant era. In a flash, it did the job of just slightly softening her frazzled edges and travel-weary bones.

After being treated amazingly by the concierge, she'd refused an offer of help with her bags and made her way up to the top floor in the lift. As the doors opened, in a daze of polished floors and expensive-looking greenery, she'd crossed a large square lobby with two doors, heading for the one on the right.

Lotta propped her case up by the door, keyed the number on the text Brandy had sent her into the pad, and put her hand on the door plate. The door didn't budge at all and needed a hefty heave from her shoulder for it to open. Propping the bottom of the door with her foot and picking up her case with her right hand, she stepped into the apartment and gasped. She didn't know what she'd been expecting, but gloriously tall ceilings, highly polished floors, and lacquered black doors were not it. As she put her case down on a glossy black-and-white chequerboard floor and pulled her jacket off, her chin was on the floor. Houston was doing old-school art deco very, very well indeed.

Half in wonder, half in exhaustion, and with a hefty dose of jet lag, grief, and worry thrown in for good measure, she wandered around the apartment. Brandy may have called the place an apartment, but as Lotta walked around in awe, it was bigger than most houses she knew. A neutral colour palette peppered with deep 1920s emerald greens looked at her every which way she turned. Matte gold accents on the vases, candlesticks and picture frames added to the rich, old-fashioned feel. Elegantly patterned wallpaper showcased a selection of vintage artwork and photography, and a plush, deep green velvet sofa, flanked by a pair of curvaceous club chairs, cajoled anyone into a sit-down and gaze out over the city. Anyone who wasn't sick out of their mind with worry, anyway.

Sunlight streamed in through tall, arched windows, landing

in a gleam on the glossy fireplace. Everywhere screamed classy, deco opulence, and despite everything that was going on, and despite her almost overwhelming upside-down tiredness, Lotta felt a tiny bit of the stress mounted on her shoulders lift and float away.

The kitchen didn't disappoint; streamlined, glossy, original cabinetry juxtaposed against white tiling, brass hardware, a vintage-style oven, and a retro fridge. Lotta pulled open the fridge door in a bit of a daze, looking for milk. As she peered in, she found just about everything she could have wished for. Brandy was most definitely on the ball.

In the bedroom, a stately four-poster bed fitted with luxurious linens made her sigh and want to hop in, pull over the covers with her book in hand, and never, ever leave. Emerald green satin dress cushions adorned the pillows, and a plush throw at the end of the bed topped it all off perfectly. Lotta could feel a sense of history and glamour surrounding her. The exquisite attention to detail, the seamless blend of old and new, the quiet, understated luxury whispered of a time gone by.

As she opened further doors and peered into bedrooms, the weight of everything on her mind pressed into the side of her temples as if accompanying her as she walked around, lost in a world of her own. What to do now? What to think? How to behave? How to cope?

Staring at more of the apartment's luxury, she couldn't quite get her head around what had happened. It was as if someone with a pair of pincers had picked her up from her house in Pretty Beach and dropped her on the top floor of an art deco building in an American city. On their way over the pincers had thought it might be a good idea to grab a load of grief for good measure. She didn't really know what the time was, what she was doing, how she felt, or what to do next. She checked the time on her phone, squinted her eyes, and tried to work out the time difference and what time it was in England. Not having the brainpower to work it out, she strolled back to the master bedroom, opened a door in the corner, and gasped. A deep sunken bath surrounded by elegant black-and-white tiles, gleaming taps and beautiful lush palms in glossy pots looked back at her. In another time, without the turmoil going on in her life, the sight of the bath would have made her jump for joy. In less stressed times, she would not have been able to wait to dive into the glorious deep, square emerald green bath with a glass of wine and a book. Now she wasn't sure what she wanted. The grief from what had occurred in Singapore weighed heavily on her heart, Jack was in hospital, and she was worried out of her mind.

In a split second, her whole life, her whole world, had been turned upside down. She squinted her eyes as she stood staring at the green sunken bath. Jack had been involved in a mall shooting. She repeated the words over and over again in her head, as if repeating them might somehow make them make more sense. *Jack in a mall shooting. Jack in a mall shooting. Jack in a mall shooting.*

It was all so strange and unfamiliar. Even the word mall didn't feel right in her brain, all of it so very far away from her little life in England. This was something that happened to other people in other countries, other lives. And now, here she was, part of it. A character in a story she wanted the writer to write her out of right away.

Feeling grotty, tired, and beside herself with worry, Lotta leant against the sink staring at the bath, her mind racing with thoughts. After a few minutes of contemplation, she mindlessly shuffled over to the bath, picked up a glass decanter from a line of potions on the tiles, and poured a deep amber-coloured liquid into the bottom of the tub, put in the plug, and lifted the tap. Water gushed into the sunken bath, and lights danced through the frosted glass window. Somehow, as the sound of the water tumbling into the bath filled her ears, the space soothed and comforted. For a long few minutes, she stood stock still and watched as the bubbles began to form, creating a soft, frothy haze in front of her.

Turning the tap down to a trickle, she padded back through the apartment to the kitchen. She closed her eyes in thanks when she found a pack of individually wrapped packets of English Breakfast Tea and made herself a cup of tea using a jug as a teapot. A few minutes later, she was back in the bathroom, dropping her clothes to the floor and slipping down into the bubbly bath. As Lotta lowered herself into the tub so that the water was just about up to her neck, she slowly felt a tiny bit of the tension in her muscles begin to melt away. She closed her eyes. Allowing her thoughts to compute, she tried to make sense of the whirlwind of emotions that had engulfed her in the past few days. For a brief moment, Lotta let her brain empty. Flashes of her mum drifted away, the feelings as she'd read Natasha's texts left her head. The memory of standing at the immigration counter in a daze and at the hospital waiting to get in and see Jack – all of it floated away on the top of the bubbly water as she took slow, grateful sips of her tea.

As she lay there, enveloped in the warmth of the water and the softness of the bubbles, the chaos of her life began to slowly dissipate as the apartment, the bath, and the tea felt as if they had wrapped her in some sort of protective cocoon. She revelled in a few moments of respite from the grief, the worry, and the uncertainty that had been her constant companions for days.

As she finished her tea and the water began to cool, Lotta felt so tired but, at the same time, so awake she wasn't quite sure what to do. The tea and the bath had been a good call, giving her the chance to recharge and regroup. But now she realised everything was out of whack.

Feeling a million times better than she had when she'd got

in, Lotta got up from the bath and wrapped herself in an emerald green towel and sat on a little chair by the window for ages, just staring out and wondering what was going to happen next.

After drying off and wrapped in the towel, she stood in the hallway with her case splayed open on the floor, looking for her pyjamas, lost in thoughts about Jack, when her phone began to vibrate on a sleek, polished side table. Glancing at the screen, she saw Liv's name flash up. Taking a deep breath, she swiped the screen and answered.

'Hey, Liv,' Lotta said, trying to keep her voice steady and not burst into tears.

'Hi, how are you getting on?' Liv asked, her familiar voice instantly bringing a small smile to Lotta's face.

Lotta hesitated for a moment, her fingers fidgeting with the edge of her towel as she considered her response. 'It's been… a lot. I'm fine, though.'

'No, you are not. Don't even go there. You cannot possibly be okay.'

Lotta let out a little chuckle. 'Nah, I'm not. The journey was long and exhausting. I have no idea where I am, and Jack is in hospital. So no, honestly, I've been better.'

'Oh, I can only imagine,' Liv replied sympathetically, the concern evident in her voice. 'You must be shattered. I can't believe this has happened.'

'I know.'

'How was the hospital?'

Lotta held the phone to her ear with her shoulder and pulled on her pyjamas. 'Yeah, it was fine once I finally got all the red tape out of the way.' Lotta sighed, pacing back and forth in the hallway as she recounted the difficulties she had faced trying to get to Jack's room. 'It was an absolute nightmare. There was so much red tape, and the place was swarming with police.'

'I suppose it would be.'

Lotta's expression darkened as she recalled the ordeal. 'Getting in was a right faff. They didn't know who I was, and then there were all these police around. And not being American didn't help either. I'm not going to lie, it's been really tough.'

'You poor thing. It does sound like an absolute nightmare. Thank goodness he's okay.'

'It was,' Lotta agreed. 'Eventually, I managed to see him. It's all a bit up in the air, but it seems as if he's going to be fine.'

There was a long pause as Liv digested the news. 'Well, at least you're there with him now.'

Lotta nodded. 'Yeah. I'm just glad I'm here.'

Lotta could almost see her cousin's worried expression as Liv spoke, 'It sounds awful. I'm so sorry you're going through this.'

Lotta walked into the kitchen, opened the fridge door and stood peering in, the bright light from inside hurting her eyes. 'I'm fine. I just wish I could make everything okay for Jack, you know?'

Liv's voice was full of understanding. 'Of course, you do.'

'On a lighter note. You should see this place! I thought I was going to be in some crappy apartment hotel somewhere. It's so not that.'

'Where are you, then?' Liv asked.

'Good question. Brandy told me she'd sort it. These people are like tycoons, I dunno, old-school oil money or something, I think. Jack told me way back when we went on that fake date at the palace. Yeah, so he wasn't kidding. I have a driver. Like, for reals. It's almost comical. You have to laugh or you'd cry. Well, actually I'm crying a lot.'

'It could only happen to you, Lott. What do you mean you have a driver?'

'One was at the airport to pick me up, and one came to the hospital. I have his number to take me wherever I want.'

'Wow.'

'I know. And this apartment is something else.'

'Like what?'

'Like bigger than my house.'

Liv swore. 'At least that's good.'

'I've totally just had a soak in a sunken bath,' Lotta chuckled. 'You have to see the funny side of it. My mum just died, Jack has been shot, and I'm in a penthouse mansion on the top of a Houston skyscraper in a sunken bath, completely on my own, surrounded by art deco fabulousness and emerald green.'

Liv giggled. 'It's surreal, isn't it?' Liv mused.

Lotta sighed, running her fingers through her damp hair. 'The whole thing is just all so bizarre.' Her voice suddenly cracked. 'I just don't know what to do.'

Liv's voice softened. 'You'll be fine. You're stronger than you think.'

'I'm not, though. I'm so not.'

'Yes, you are. You have no choice. Get on with it. Don't start feeling sorry for yourself.'

'I suppose I don't. I can always rely on you to tell me what's what.' Lotta managed a small smile, grateful for Liv's usual unwavering support and no-nonsense attitude.

'Yep, you can. That's what I'm here for,' Liv said with a small, kind chuckle.

'I'll keep you updated on everything.'

'Okay. Look, get some rest if you can. You're going to need it.'

'Yeah, I'm going to go to bed.'

'Don't sit up reading for hours.'

'As if I would do that,' Lotta said with a small smile.

'Pah!'

'Ha ha.'

'Keep me updated. Text me night or day. Don't worry about the time difference.'

'Thanks, Liv.'

'No worries. Speak to you later.'

Lotta sighed as she put down the phone and continued to stare into the fridge. As usual, Liv had done the trick to calm her down, and she felt slightly better. But, really, Lotta Button had never felt worse in her life.

22

The next day, Lotta didn't want to think about anything much at all. She wanted, rather, to let her brain have a bit of time off. No thinking about how she might be letting people down at work, no worrying about Jack's family, no grief, nothing. She simply wanted to turn her brain off. Would it be possible for her brain to have a switch, please? A giant one that she could just flick downwards, which would then mean that her brain or, indeed, her whole body would not have to do any adulting anymore.

It didn't seem as if that was possible as she finished up her four hundredth cup of wishy-washy American coffee and made her way along the long corridor towards Jack's ward. There was a severe lack of switches in her head. A nurse raised her eyebrows in greeting as Lotta passed, and a door in front of her automatically opened inwards. Once she got closer to the ward, through security, logged in at the desk, and finally went past the police, she took a deep breath and got ready to see Jack. She braced herself for how he would be there, not Just Jack at all but propped up by pillows on the bed surrounded by machines. At least this one was alive.

Just as she stepped in, the nurse, who had been there most of the time that Lotta had, turned around with a beaming smile on her face. The nurse's eyes widened, and she stepped to her right and backwards at the same time so that Lotta could see the bed. Lotta stopped right where she was in surprise and nearly dropped her bag on the floor. She couldn't quite believe what she was seeing. Jack's eyes were open! Not only were his eyes open, but his skin seemed to have changed colour. It was as if someone had painted him with a brush of warmth. The cold, distant, grey look had disappeared.

Lotta flicked her head quickly from left to right and squeezed her eyes shut for a second, thinking that she was seeing things. She knew she wasn't when she heard Jack's voice. Not quite his voice as such, more like a whisper coming from the direction of the bed. 'Lotta, as in hotter.' He sounded hoarse and weak and just so very different. Lotta didn't quite know what to do. She wanted to scream and shout and bounce up and down and dive onto the bed. Instead, she stood stock still in shock, paralysed in the doorway, unable to move.

For a good, long moment, she didn't do anything but stare at him. She felt herself blink a few times and then saw the nurse smile again. Taking a few steps towards the bed, Lotta clasped her hands tightly together in front of her. 'Just Jack. You're awake.' Her voice choked with emotion as she reached the bed.

A small smile seemed to take Jack a lot of effort. The nurse walked around the end of the bed. 'He's going to be very tired.'

Lotta sat down slowly on the chair beside Jack and grasped his hand. She couldn't quite believe it when he squeezed it back. All she could do was think about how much she loved him, how scared she'd been, how grateful she was that he wasn't dead. 'I love you, Jack.' She gulped back an avalanche of tears. 'I love you, I love you, I love you,' she whispered over and over again, as if the more times she repeated it, it would somehow make up for what had happened.

Her hand clasped his more tightly. When he didn't reply but did look at her, she sat there happier and more grateful for something than she'd ever been in her life. Just Jack was awake, and it looked as if he was going to get better. They'd told her he would get better, of course, but she hadn't really believed it. Not deep down. Deep down, she'd thought that Just Jack was going to die. She'd thought that she'd leave the hospital and fly back to England alone, just as she had with her mum.

As Lotta clung onto Jack's hand, she took in the hospital room around her. The same walls painted a sterile shade of pale green that she'd stood staring at for hours on end, willing healthy vibes into Jack's veins. Now the walls seemed just that little bit softer, warmer, calmer almost.

Her eyes drifted to the bank of machines that stood sentinel at the head of Jack's bed. Their rhythmic beeping and whirring she'd initially hated, now provided an oddly comforting soundtrack. Despite the clinical feel of the impersonal room, Lotta felt as if everything was smiling, as the sense of relief, now that Jack was awake, flooded her from head to toe. A heavy weight had been lifted from her chest – from her head, from her bones, and from her heart. She could now breathe just that tiny bit more freely. As she stared back at Jack, her heart swelled with gratitude. Though his eyes looked tired and weak, Just Jack was actually back in the room.

As she sat there with the relief working its magic, Lotta's fingers entwined with Jack's as she remembered the day they'd first met. She'd been wearing a ridiculously ginormous green fascinator and had escaped from the nausea-inducing successful people around her at a table full of wedding guests. She remembered the ball she'd gone to when she'd thought he was in love with someone else, and the picnic when they'd sat in the hills of Pretty Beach. She'd admitted that she'd thought because of a pink jacket that there was another woman on the scene. All of it part of the Lotta and Jack story, as she sat, willing him to get better.

She leaned in closer to Jack and smiled. In the small, sterile hospital room, Lotta knew more than anything else that she wanted to be with Jack forever. As they sat there together, Lotta could see the exhaustion etched on Jack's face, his eyelids growing heavier by the minute. His whole body started to sag, and he was slowly drooping as the effort of being awake took its toll. She whispered, 'I'll be here when you wake up.'

With a barely perceptible nod, Jack allowed his eyes to fully close, his breathing gradually evening out as sleep claimed him. Lotta watched him for ages, ensuring he was asleep, before carefully extracting her hand from his and reaching for her phone.

She could barely contain herself, and excitement bubbled up inside her as she tapped out a message to Liv back in England.

Lotta: *Liv! Jack's awake. He's talking! He's still very weak. I can't tell you how relieved I am. I'll keep you updated, but it seems like he really is going to be okay. I didn't believe the doctors...*

She hit send and waited, feeling a little less alone as the familiar 'whoosh' of the sent message filled the room. Almost immediately, her phone buzzed with a reply.

Liv: *Amazing news! I'm so happy. Thank goodness. Love you loads! xxx*

Tears of gratitude pricked at the corners of Lotta's eyes as she read Liv's message. Texting Liv made it feel real that Jack was actually going to get better. With a sigh, she tucked her phone back into her pocket and turned her attention back to Jack. As she sat by his side, she imagined him getting better and the both of them flying home. It couldn't come soon enough.

About half an hour later, as quietly as she could, she tiptoed up from her seat. Her whole body was fizzing with an overwhelming mix of relief and happiness. Stepping out of the room, she closed the door gently behind her and stood just outside the door next to the handwashing station. The hospital corridor was dimly lit, the atmosphere hushed, and the smells of the day wafted around her. Lotta stood by the wall, her fingers scrolling through her contacts to find Natasha's number. She took a deep breath, preparing herself for the conversation. She tried to inject some stability in her voice, rather than screaming at Natasha that Jack had been awake.

Pressing call, she held the phone to her ear, trying to keep her voice calm and slow as she spoke into the receiver. 'Natasha, it's Lotta. He's awake, and he's been talking.'

Lotta could hear the happiness and relief in Natasha's voice. 'Oh my! That's such good news. Thank you so much for calling. How is he? How are you holding up?'

Lotta smiled, her own relief mirrored in Natasha's words. 'He didn't say much at all. The nurse said that he will still be very weak, but the doctors are optimistic about his recovery. I'm just so grateful he's awake. I didn't really believe it before, you know?'

'I know. Me too! It's been a rollercoaster, especially not being able to get there, but knowing he's on the mend is a huge relief. Huge. Massive!'

The conversation continued, and in the confines of the quiet corridor, Lotta's heart felt lighter than it had in days. It looked like Just Jack was back.

23

A few weeks or so later, Lotta had become somewhat attached to the apartment in the art deco building, and she had quite the routine going. She could also get used to living the kind of lifestyle where everything was serviced. There were no chores involved in the penthouse apartment at the top of Eppleton Building. Beautifully prepared food appeared in the fridge and a little fairy magically laundered Lotta's clothes. Another fairy also changed the bed, put out clean towels, and put expensive, beautifully scented lotions and potions by the emerald green sunken bath. Not that she wanted to stay. She couldn't wait to get home, but there could have been a lot worse ways to spend her time in Houston as Jack continued to heal.

She mused it all as she got ready to meet Brandy and then go to the hospital. She'd spent the early morning working on an event for Christmas involving a group of top airline directors, and had arranged to meet Brandy for a coffee not far from the hospital.

Grabbing her jacket from the dresser in the hallway, she checked her Kindle was in her bag and took the lift down to the lobby. She headed for the metro, not faffed to bother with texting the driver. Putting the address Brandy had given her into her phone, she followed along with the directions. About fifteen minutes later, she was standing on the pavement, squinting and shaking her head in surprise at where Brandy had chosen for them to meet. She had sat with Brandy a few times in the hospital coffee shop and thought she knew what Brandy was about. She'd expected a Starbucks or similar, not what was presenting itself to her.

She shook her head as she took in a bookshop in front of her. The exterior of the quaint, two-storey building boasted white wooden panels. A whimsical, hand-painted sign with the bookshop's name hung above the entrance swaying gently in the breeze. A weathered wooden bench sat beside the door, inviting passersby to pause and take a moment. To both the left and right of the door, large glass windows adorned with charming book-themed decals shone, and an abundance of leafy green plants in hanging baskets thrived in the sunshine.

A bell tinkled overhead as Lotta stepped inside, and she found herself completely and utterly surrounded by shelves full of books. Books, in fact, were everywhere; in stacks on the floor, piled up on tables, and jumbled on top of chairs. Even for a seasoned bookshop-goer, it was unfathomable, and Lotta stood still for a second, mesmerised. The scent she loved hit her squarely between the eyes; books and sofas and pages and reading wafted through the air, instantly transporting her to a world she knew and loved. A place that took her away from everything going on in her strange new fragmented world.

Mostly gobsmacked, she meandered down the narrow aisles as the well-worn wooden floorboards creaked beneath her feet. A kaleidoscope of colours greeted her as she scanned row upon row of book spines. The haphazard arrangement of the shelves seemed to stretch both up to the ceiling and away through tiny corridors at the back. Lotta didn't know where to look or walk first.

Dust motes danced in the air as she stood staring at a little gathering of round tables topped with books and lamps. In a corner, two plush deep pink armchairs beckoned, nestled amidst a nook lined with floor-to-ceiling shelves. All of it made her heart sing, the perfect spot for getting lost in a book, a sanctuary from the world outside. Lotta felt as if she had entered another hushed sacred world, part of a secret society of readers all strolling around doing their thing. For a brief moment, as she wandered around aimlessly, she felt the weight of her worries slip away as her eyes moved from book to book.

Never had Lotta been more pleased that she'd arrived somewhere early. She'd already earmarked the little gap in her morning for a spot of Kindle diving before meeting Brandy, now she could rock it to the hilt. She wandered further through the old building until she came to the coffee shop at the back. A long counter ran from left to right, books were wedged here, there, and everywhere, and tiny little tables were packed with people sitting with books.

Nestled among towering bookshelves, the coffee machine seemed to blend seamlessly into its literary surroundings. Lotta inhaled the rich aroma of freshly ground coffee mingled with the bookshop smell she knew and loved. As she stood in the small queue for a coffee, she gazed around. Mismatched tables and chairs were scattered throughout; people sat with cups of steaming drinks, and a large triple-width black paned window framed a greenery-filled courtyard beyond. The soft clink of china and the gentle hum of the coffee machine provided a soundtrack that slowly began to decompress the tightly wound layers of worry on the inside of Lotta's head.

The walls groaned under the weight of books, while the sun dappled down onto the timber floor. A plush sofa and cluster of armchairs arranged around a low coffee table was the epitome of bookshop delight. As Lotta took in the atmosphere, she felt a tiny bit removed from her actual life.

An hour later, Lotta had taken full pleasure in her surroundings. Just as she'd closed the cover on her Kindle, she saw Brandy on the far side of the room, her attention drawn to the entrance by the sound of a boisterous laugh. Brandy, with her voluminous blonde hair that defied gravity, swept into the room, her larger-than-life presence filling the space. As Brandy approached the table, Lotta couldn't stop staring at her hair, a masterpiece of hairspray and expert blow-drying. It framed Brandy's plump smiley tanned face, adorned with bold makeup and bright red lips. Dressed in a tight-fitting floral dress that hugged her curves and designer handbag, Brandy's entire demeanour exuded a sense of over-the-top extravagance. She seemed to almost ooze luxury as she squeezed in and out of the tables.

With a big grin, Brandy approached Lotta's table, her eyes twinkling. 'Well, hi there,' she drawled, extending a manicured hand to touch Lotta's arm and kissing her on the cheek.

'Hello. How are you?' Lotta said as she inhaled Brandy's strong, expensive perfume.

'Oh, I just love that British accent. Would you just listen to that? It's just so charming!' Brandy pulled up a chair and sat down. 'You said you love books, so I thought y'all might like it here.'

'Like it? I love it. I'm in my happy place. I want to sleep here,' Lotta joked.

'Good. Wow, you sound better. How is Jack this morning? I'm so pleased he's on the mend. We all are. Thank the Lord.'

Lotta nodded towards her phone. 'He messaged me earlier, and he's feeling good. He's like his old self. The human body really is amazing.'

'Ahh, good! You guys will be going home soon.'

Lotta sighed. 'I can't wait to get home, if I'm honest.'

'Yes, I bet.'

Lotta reached across and touched Brandy's arm. 'I wanted to say thank you for everything you've done.'

'Don't be silly!'

'I mean it,' Lotta added seriously.

'It's nothing! I haven't done anything at all.'

Lotta was actually aware of that. It wasn't lost on her that Brandy was surrounded by staff. She was still grateful, though. 'I would have been in a right old pickle without you.'

'A pickle?'

'Yeah, you know, in a state.'

'Well, it was the least I could do.'

'Thank you.' Lotta joked again, 'I must say, I could stay just so that I could get in that bath every day.'

Brandy laughed. 'I don't think anyone has used it for years.'

Lotta chuckled. 'I've been in it constantly.'

'So I've heard.' Brandy side-eyed.

As they began to chat, mostly about Jack, Lotta couldn't help but compare their stark differences. Brandy's exuberant personality and appearance seemed a world away from Lotta's more understated English-ness. The contrast between Brandy's Texas drawl and her own clipped British tones was striking, but despite that, as she had done in the hospital, Lotta found herself drawn in by Brandy's warmth.

As Brandy chatted, Lotta was suddenly filled with the image of Brandy at the ball, where she'd been spilling out of her red dress and had suddenly not looked very well at all. She'd then projectile vomited into a hastily grabbed champagne bucket. Lotta chuckled inside and turned herself back to the conversation as she heard Brandy ask a question.

'So, what will you do about flights?' Brandy asked.

Lotta raised her eyebrows. 'I don't know. I haven't really even thought much about it.'

Brandy flapped her hands. 'We'll sort it out. Don't you worry about that.'

Lotta frowned. 'No, it's fine. I'm not letting you do that too!'

Brandy was very quick with her response. A little too quick. 'I insist. We insist. One less thing for y'all to worry about.'

Lotta was well aware that Brandy was very rich, not concerned one little bit about money and being kind, but it felt too much. 'No, no. I couldn't.'

Brandy almost jumped down her throat, and Lotta was taken aback. She was insistent. 'I'll sort out the flights.'

Lotta didn't like to say anything else. The woman was fairly riled up about it. 'Okay,' she conceded.

Brandy squinted her eyes and leant across the table. 'Jack said he likes to fly British Airways.'

Lotta screwed her face up. She couldn't give two hoots about what airline they went with. What a strange question. As far as she was concerned, she just wanted to get home. She'd swim if she had to. 'Sorry, what? You've already spoken to him about it? When? We don't even know what the doctors are going to say yet.'

Brandy coughed and spluttered. It was like she was backpedalling, but Lotta didn't know about what. 'Y'all don't want to have to worry about anything.'

Lotta just lifted her chin. There was no way she was going to say anything to Brandy. The woman had been brilliant – so kind, so generous, and so nice. But it was weird the way she was talking about the airline, as if she had some sort of ulterior motive. Lotta took a sip of her coffee as Brandy bit into a gigantic white chocolate muffin and put it to the back of her mind. If a Texan billionaire wanted to book her flights back to England, she wasn't really going to argue about it too much. Go for your life.

24

An hour or so later, Lotta walked into the hospital. She made her way through the now familiar corridors, went through the palaver of checking in at the desk, and then proceeded to the private wing. As she got to the door, she stopped in shock at the sight of Jack. The turnaround was astonishing. He was looking *almost* back to his old self. She said a silent prayer and closed her eyes slowly for a second. It all could have ended so differently. She was well aware of that.

Jack looked towards the door as it creaked as Lotta opened it. He smiled. A big smile as the old Jack did. 'Lotta as in hotter.'

'Hi,' Lotta said, smiling.

Jack tilted his head. 'How are we?'

'Good,' she replied, clasping her hands together.

'Great,' Jack said, beaming.

'Have the doctors been?' Lotta asked, raising an eyebrow.

'Yeah. They said I'm great,' Jack responded, nodding.

'Wow,' Lotta exclaimed, her eyes widening.

'So we can get home soon,' Jack stated, leaning back on the bed.

Lotta frowned and looked over toward the table by the bed, where Jack's laptop was open. 'Have you been working?'

'I have,' Jack said and rubbed the back of his hair. 'There's only so much Netflix a person can watch.'

'Gosh, you must be better.'

'It's amazing how I turned the corner and almost overnight started to feel back to my old self,' Jack remarked, his eyes sparkling. 'Whatever they pumped into me worked.'

Lotta touched him on the arm. 'Yeah, we don't want to run before we can walk, though.'

'No,' Jack agreed, shaking his head.

'You must be sick of it in here,' Lotta said, glancing around the room.

'Yup, pretty much,' Jack replied with a small shrug of his shoulders. 'I'm not complaining.'

'No.'

'I *am* bored, though. I'm bored senseless.'

'Hmm, yeah. What else has been happening?'

'Nothing! That's about the sum of it.'

'Brandy said she came in last night when I didn't.'

'Yep, she did,' Jack agreed, nodding.

'How was that?'

'Fine,' Jack said, glancing away quickly.

'She said you were so much better. Because she hadn't seen you for a few days, she really noticed the difference.'

'Yep,' Jack responded, taking a deep breath.

Lotta pulled the chair closer to the bed. 'She was going on and on about flights. In the end, I just had to agree. She said you insisted that you always fly British Airways. I don't know what she was getting herself in a two and eight about.'

Jack's body language changed instantly. 'Was she?'

'Yeah. Why is she so bothered?' Lotta asked, her brow furrowing. 'Did you say something?'

Jack dismissed it with a wave of his hand. He seemed to

squirm a little bit. 'No idea. I think she feels like all of this is her fault somehow. It must be something to do with that.'

'Right. So, you're going to let her book our flights, are you?' Lotta questioned, her eyes narrowing. 'Why would you do that?'

Jack shrugged. 'Dunno.'

'You seem weird,' Lotta said, tilting her head in question.

'I *am* weird,' Jack replied, smirking. 'You already know that.'

'Jack! What are you up to?' Lotta exclaimed, folding her arms.

'I'm not being weird,' Jack insisted.

'You so are,' Lotta countered, shaking her head.

'I just thought if she wants to book it, let her,' Jack explained, looking thoughtful.

'But whatshername at your office books all your flights. I thought we would just do that,' Lotta said, raising an eyebrow.

'Nah,' Jack replied dismissively.

'Right, okay. You *are* being weird,' Lotta insisted, leaning back in her chair and narrowing her eyes.

Jack sighed. 'I'm not.'

Lotta felt as if something was going on, but she didn't know what. She decided to leave it. 'It's going to be a long journey.'

'Yes, but I can't wait to get out of here. We'll be back before we know it,' Jack reassured her, giving her a smile.

'It felt like a very long time when I flew here.'

'It's ten hours. I've done it enough times,' Jack said, stretching his arms out.

'I suppose that isn't that long really, when you think about it.'

'Nope, just a working day. Or six or so films,' he quipped, chuckling.

'Ha. I wasn't watching films when I was on that flight here.'

'I'm sorry this has all happened,' Jack said apologetically, his smile fading.

'Don't be ridiculous! How can you be sorry?' Lotta asked, waving her hand dismissively.

'I don't know.'

'As if you purposely got shot in a mall,' she said, rolling her eyes.

'Are we calling it a mall now?' Jack bantered, raising his eyebrows.

'Too funny. I actually am. I heard myself saying that when I went into the one near the apartment on the way home from here yesterday,' Lotta admitted, laughing.

'We definitely need to get home, then,' Jack concluded, grinning. 'We can't go around calling shopping centres malls and asking for ketchup with our fries.'

Lotta looked at him, hardly believing that he was laughing and joking, hardly believing that Just Jack was fully back. She had never ever been more relieved in her life.

25

There was one thing Lotta would miss about Houston – the emerald green sunken bath. It really was an art deco beauty, the whole bathroom was. As Lotta lay in it up to her neck in bubbles, she realised that she'd spent many hours in it deliberating. A lot of the time she'd been grieving her mum, but somehow the low down bath had helped. There was something about the whole room that had a really good vibe, which had been much welcome when she'd been a blubbering mess when she'd first come home from the hospital. It had helped her when, in between Jack worries, she'd sobbed about her mum. It was as if the room had seen her through tough times.

A rectangular sunken bath surrounded by original art deco tiles with its very own little built-in seat had swiftly moved onto her house goals, indeed her life goals. Reaching out and leaning forward to top up the bath with hot water, she sighed as she contemplated Dave's latest message. She'd come to the conclusion that she wasn't going to take the trip to Singapore for the funeral. Her decision hadn't come lightly, but it had come about when she'd been sitting back in the bookshop on her way home from seeing Jack. She'd been merrily minding her own business after buying a few books and was treating herself to a sit-down after the mind-blowing visit where Jack seemed so much better. As she'd sat sipping on a cup of tea, paired with a very large slice of chocolate cake, she'd overheard a couple of ladies sitting next to her. They were talking about how sometimes you just had to do what *you* wanted to do in life. Lotta's ears had pricked up, and she'd earwigged like crazy at their conversation. They'd seemed so wise, worldly, and knowing – an influence that had been sorely missing in her journey.

She'd slyly turned around and had a good old gawp at them too. They'd reminded her of an older, wiser version of Brandy. They also reminded her that she'd missed a motherly figure in her life. And it was then, as she was sitting with her cake listening, that she'd thought about all the times her mum had let her down. All the occasions her mum had failed to turn up. All the times Lotta had sat in assemblies at school, her mum, not one of the parents on the side. Her mum, not being interested in anything. Her mum, comatose on the kitchen floor. Her mum's snide, snarky comments. Her mum, not coming out of her room. The rows of own-brand cornflakes in the cupboards. Empty vodka bottles down the back of the sofa.

And as the women's conversation pinged back and forth behind her, a great big penny had dropped in Lotta's mind. The penny had 'closure' written across the middle of it, and as it had plopped down into the middle of her brain, it shut a door. To be quite frank, it slammed the door hard and locked it shut. Locked it to the hurt, the heartache, the guilt, and the what-ifs. In a bookshop in Houston, two Texan ladies with hair bigger than Lotta's head had finally set her free.

Lotta nodded her head over and over again as the penny brought with it the clarity that had been missing for way too long. This time, Lotta would be the one who wasn't there for her mother, because, finally, Lotta Button was too busy doing something else. Something more important. Lotta Button was taking care of someone much, much, much more important. Lotta was taking care of herself.

As Lotta lay in the bath mulling it over, she didn't waver a single, solitary bit from her decision. The penny dropping had given her the closure she'd needed. Yes, she was respectful. Yes, the woman had given birth to her, but that was where it ended. Lotta had paid her respects a million times over the years. She didn't need to be leaving Jack and traipsing to a funeral where the person involved hadn't even liked her. She didn't need to stand at a service where her very existence had pained the person immensely.

She picked up her phone from the side of the bath, didn't care about the fact that the room might echo down the phone, and pressed the number for Dave.

'Hi,' Dave answered, sounding tired.

'Hi, Dave. How are you getting on?' Lotta asked.

'Yeah, not too bad, actually.'

'Good. Look, Dave. I'm sorry, but I've decided that I'm not coming to the funeral.'

'Okay.'

'I hope you understand.'

'Of course. I know it was tricky between you and your mum.'

Lotta nodded. He had *no* idea. No idea at all. None. Dave had no clue what it had been like growing up in a house with her mum. He had no idea what it was like to be ten years old and wondering what was going to happen that night. He didn't have an inkling of what it felt like to wish that the neighbours would somehow realise what was going on. He had no idea to be sitting in class pretending everything was okay. He had no inkling whatsoever of the feeling as a child to hope that someone, somewhere, would help. She swallowed all the thoughts and clung to the penny for dear life. It was cold and hard and *lovely* between her fingers. 'Thanks.'

'I was speaking to the funeral director. She said we can

stream it. Apparently, people do it all the time. It's extra, but I thought you might be interested in that.'

Lotta wasn't sure what to think, but she agreed. It wouldn't do any harm. 'Okay, thanks. I'll pay for it.'

'No, no, you don't need to worry about anything like that.'

'Thanks, Dave.'

As Lotta ended the call and put her phone on the side, she leant her head back on the tiles and looked up at the ceiling rose in all its deco glory. The end of the call had signified so much in her life. The end of an era that had marred and scarred her for too long. Lotta felt strangely calm, oddly cleansed, and happily released. With the drop of the penny, she'd turned a corner in her life, and it felt so good she almost didn't know what to do with herself. She did know that the reprieve was sweet.

26

Jack had not been at all happy about being in a wheelchair. In fact, he'd pooh-poohed it and insisted that he'd be able to walk when they'd been dropped off at the airport entrance. It hadn't lasted long. By the time Lotta had got him to the desk, she was not having any of it, and she'd more or less pushed him in.

After being whisked through immigration because of his injury, both of them had chuckled when a buggy came along to collect them and take them to the lounge. The same thing had happened to take them to the gate. As they'd sat on the back of the buggy and whizzed past weary travellers, both of them had joked about the benefits of what had happened in the mall. When they got to the boarding gate, Jack became jittery. Assuming he was nervous after the trauma, at first, Lotta kept quiet. But as it got worse as they were making their way to the aircraft door, she started to get concerned.

Once on the plane, Lotta frowned at Jack. 'Are you okay?'

Jack didn't look okay at all. He looked flustered. His voice was strange too. Like a sort of growl. 'Yep, fine.'

Lotta didn't know what to do. She'd never seen him behave in a stressed manner. 'Sure?'

'Yes. Why do you ask?' Jack snapped.

'You seem jittery. Do you need me to do anything for you?' Lotta offered. Inside she was terrified he'd taken a turn for the worse, and they'd started the journey home way before they should have done.

'Like what?' Jack replied.

'I don't know, but you've been odd since we got to the gate. I'm worried.'

'I'm fine. Just sit down,' Jack insisted.

Lotta shook her head. Jack was being really peculiar, and he'd kept looking at his phone when they'd arrived at the gate. She sat down in the seat next to him as the crew member asked her if she wanted a glass of champagne. She accepted and leant over towards Jack. 'I could get used to living life as Brandy does. Imagine her *actual* day-to-day existence.'

Jack let out a strange laugh, and Lotta sat back in her seat with a frown. He must be nervous about flying with this arm. As another crew member dished out hot towels, she sat back and held hers up to her face. She wondered if the pain was kicking in or if he needed to take more painkillers – the hospital had packed them off with all sorts, maybe it was time to give something a go. Stealing a quick glance at him, she decided that he was just nervous and thought that she'd keep quiet. There was no doubt about it, though, he was definitely agitated.

Once they'd taken off, Lotta wasn't sure what to think other than that Jack was not her kind of traveller. He'd called the crew member with the button multiple times, and he'd been jumpy, fiddling with everything around his seat, adjusting the tray table, fussing with the overhead light, putting the slippers on and then taking them off. Lotta had tried to ignore it, putting it down to the fact that he was recovering from trauma and realising that they might have a rocky road ahead of them yet.

About an hour into the journey, and when she was stuck in a good book, Jack leaned over. 'Did you order your meal?'

She frowned. He'd seen her do it. 'I did, yes.'

'What did you ask for?'

'The chicken.'

'Do you want to go to the bathroom?'

Lotta screwed up her face. 'Err, no. Why?'

'I thought you might need to.'

'No, I don't.'

'Right, okay.'

Lotta frowned and looked back down at her Kindle. Ten minutes later, Jack tapped her on the hand. 'Want to go to the back and have a look out the window?'

She shook her head. 'No, not really. I'm quite happy here with my book.'

Jack was sort of garbling. 'I think it would be good for me to get up. Get the circulation going.'

Lotta wrinkled her nose and nodded to herself that he must be behaving strangely because of the strength of the painkillers. 'Do you? You could barely step out of the car. I'm not sure if that's a good idea.'

Jack tapped her hand. 'No, no, come on.' He jerked his head towards the back of the cabin.

Lotta was irritated. To be frank, she was tired of it all. A nurse she was never going to be. Her seat was set up nicely, she was well into her book, and she was very much enjoying Brandy's lifestyle of first-class on a plane. She didn't want to move all her stuff, get up and go and stand at the back. After everything she'd been through, she did not have any inclination to go and look out of the window. 'I'm good, thanks.'

'Come on,' Jack said through gritted teeth.

Lotta sighed but plastered a small smile on her face, put her Kindle in the slot in front of her, pushed her tray table back, and got up. Jack stood up and started to walk towards the back of the plane. She shook her head and rolled her eyes to herself. 'What are you doing?' she asked.

'I always like to get up and have a bit of a walk when I'm flying.'

'Right you are. What, even when you've just been involved in a very traumatic event and have a serious injury where you're meant to be resting? When the doctors have told you not to do anything?'

Jack almost snarled. 'I'm fine.'

Lotta promptly shut her mouth and followed his gaze out the window on the door. He kept looking around and through the cabin to the seats at the front. 'Sorry, are you okay? Do you want to go back?'

He flicked his hand towards the window. 'No! I'm fine. Happy here looking at the clouds.'

Lotta squinted and moved closer to the window.

About five minutes later, Jack nudged Lotta on the arm. 'You go back.'

'What?'

'Go back.'

'What, to my seat?'

'Yeah, I want to stay here for a bit on my own.'

'Okay then.' Lotta frowned. 'Now you want me to leave you here?'

'Yep. Go on.' Jack's voice was weird and sort of panicky. Lotta was not liking the way he was behaving at all.

She kept looking back towards Jack as she walked to her seat. She then noticed that the crew member who had served her the champagne was also looking at her strangely. She shook her head as she got to her seat. She'd been asked if she wanted the dinner on demand, and she'd said yes. Now her tray table was covered in a tablecloth, and there was a covered plate on her table. Strange - would they not have waited until she was back in her seat? She sighed, squeezed herself behind the table, and sat down. For a minute, she just sat there, realising that Jack didn't have anything on his side. She looked to her right where another passenger was sitting to see if he had any food. He quickly glanced away, and she realised that he'd been staring at her since she'd sat down. Part of her wondered if someone was filming her for a strange, joke-y YouTube video. She picked up her Kindle and thought she'd wait for Jack. Thinking better of it, she sighed, put the Kindle back, and pulled off the lid on top of the plate. Some sort of package.

She side-eyed left and right. She couldn't believe it; she was part of some sort of strange internet viral joke, and Jack was clearly a part of it. She wasn't really happy. Not sure what to do, she turned the package over and frowned even further and started to fumble with the string. Once opened, there was a small blue envelope with a pink sticker closure and inside a card with a handwritten note.

'Stand up and turn around.'

She wince-frowned, sighed, wondering what the heck was going on, pushed the tray out of the way and turned around. Looking towards the back of the cabin, Lotta gasped and frowned, screwing her eyes together. Four cabin crew members with deadpan faces stood directly ahead of her. Each of them held up a sign.

Will. You. Marry. Me?

Lotta flicked her head back and forth and leant on the seat. Then she turned around to see if the signs were meant for someone else. There was no one there. She put her left hand to her mouth and fumbled to step into the aisle, knocking her tray table, spilling the plate all over the floor and down the aisle. Tears streamed down her face as she looked down at it. She then looked up to where she'd been standing with Jack, looking out the window. He was now beside her in the aisle.

Her voice was barely above a whisper as her tears turned to full-on crying. 'For real?'

Jack's face didn't crack. 'Oh yes. For real.'

Lotta put both her hands in front of her face and shook her head repeatedly. She couldn't do anything but cry as Jack leaned on the chair and held out a box. 'I love you, Lotta, as in hotter. I love your silly books, I love how hard you work, I love how you never gave up, and I love how you love me back just as much as I love you. I don't know what I'd do without you.'

Lotta looked around the cabin, tears streaming down her face. The confined space and bright overhead lights made the moment feel surreal. As she sobbed and shook her head, her heart swelled with emotion as the cabin seemed to fade away, leaving just her and Jack standing in the aisle. She couldn't believe it. 'For real?'

'Yes, for real,' Jack repeated with a chuckle.

'I never thought...,' Lotta said with a judder and then paused. 'I never thought anyone would want to.' She stopped mid-sentence.

'I always want to be with you, Lotta. Getting shot does that for a bloke,' Jack deadpanned. He held out an open box where a ring glittered under the cabin lights.

'I didn't expect this,' Lotta just about blurted out between sobs. 'I'm too old to get...'

She glanced behind her at the crew with the signs. The passengers all looked at her expectantly. Lotta continued to sob. 'I just... I can't... I can't stop crying,' she said, waving and flapping her hands in front of her face.

'Well, what's the answer?'

'Yes, yes, yes, of course! I love you, Just Jack.'

Jack smiled. 'I love you too.'

27

After the fast train back to Pretty Beach, Jack had tried to hide his exhaustion, but Lotta could read him like one of her books. As she'd witnessed him seem to sag, she was worried they'd acted too hastily about getting home. As she sat sneaking looks at the diamond on her finger, Jack had become more and more tired. Once in Pretty Beach to the Breakers, she'd packed him off to the shower and made a cup of tea, and it hadn't been long before they'd fallen into bed and dropped off to sleep almost immediately as their heads hit the pillow.

The next morning, Jack was dead to the world. After surreptitiously checking that he was both breathing and looking a healthy colour, Lotta slipped out of bed. As quiet as a mouse, she padded down the stairs and took a pot of tea into the library room. As she pushed open the door, every part of her body let out a huge sigh of relief. Jack was alive, and they were home. And she was getting married. Mind-blowing. As she opened the curtains and then the doors to the garden, the fresh Pretty Beach air welcomed her as never before. Lotta was so pleased to be home. Part of her vowed never to leave.

She looked around the room as the comfort of her books

wrapped her up in feeling safe. She'd never felt more grateful. After many cups of wonderful English tea, one after the other, relishing in dipping into her TBR pile, eating half a packet of Rich Teas and spending time just staring at her bookshelves, Lotta kept playing the proposal reel in her mind. The jumble of emotions it had brought up hit her again, but out of all the things she felt, mostly, she was surprised. She'd never really thought she'd get married. Of course, she had here and there when she was young. Like everyone else, she'd fallen for the white dress and happy-ever-after fallacy. But despite years of attending a long round of family weddings, she'd eventually worked out for herself that it wasn't ever going to be her walking up the aisle in a frothy cloud. Plus, by the time she'd gone through the relationship mill, she wasn't sure she wanted it anyway. But here she was, having said yes to a man she'd met by chance in a hotel. It was all rather bizarre.

Checking the time, she realised it was late enough to call Liv. She couldn't wait to tell her her news. She pressed the button and waited for Liv to answer, barely able to keep a smile from her face.

'Hi. Home safe and sound?' Liv asked, an air of concern to her tone.

'We are, yep.'

'How was the rest of your journey after being personally transported around the airport on the back of a buggy?' Liv joked. 'It's a bit of an extreme way to get on one of those things.'

Lotta chuckled. 'Yeah, it was, umm, fab.'

Liv didn't pick up on Lotta's cue or the tone in her voice. 'How did Jack cope with the flight? I was worried about that.'

'He was fine. More than fine, actually.'

'Ahh, that's good. Hopefully he's fully on the mend and back to his old self soon.'

Lotta got up from the sofa, strolled over to the French doors and stood looking out over the garden towards the sea in the far distance. 'Liv, are you sitting down?'

'What? What's happened? Oh, no...'

'So, Jack proposed,' Lotta said bluntly.

'What? Whaaaaat?' Liv shrieked. 'When?'

'I still can't quite believe it, but he proposed in the air,' Lotta said, realising that her hands were slightly shaking as she told Liv her news.

'What? Like on the plane? That's so romantic!' Liv gushed.

Lotta let out a shaky laugh, and as she continued to tell Liv the story of Jack's proposal, she beamed. 'The cabin crew held up the signs that said "Will. You. Marry. Me?" I couldn't believe it. I thought it was some sort of joke at first,' Lotta said, shaking her head. 'He left this blue envelope with a heart on my table. Sorry, I mean the crew did that, but yeah, I thought it was one of those weird meme things.'

'Oh my goodness! That's so sweet. I can just picture it,' Liv said with a dreamy tone to her voice.

'It was amazing. I was in shock. I kept making him confirm it was real.'

'I'm so happy for you. You deserve all the love in the world,' Liv said. 'After everything that's happened.'

Lotta felt grateful that Liv got it. Liv was one of the few people who knew how Lotta had gone through the mill in love. 'Thank you. Apart from that, I'm just so grateful Jack's alive,' Lotta said, her voice full of emotion.

'Yes, and you two are perfect for each other,' Liv said. 'This is so exciting! The best news ever. I am so happy for you!'

'I know. I just feel so lucky,' Lotta replied.

'You really are,' Liv said. 'How exciting!'

'The thing is. I never thought anyone would want to marry me, Liv. After what happened with you know who... I felt worthless and useless. Looking back, he stripped me of my self-worth. I never ever thought anyone would commit to me.'

'Don't be silly! I can't believe you would even *think* that, let alone say it. You're amazing. Don't you ever forget it. Of course, someone wants to marry you,' Liv said.

'I guess you're right because Jack *actually* does,' Lotta said.

'Tell me all the details,' Liv said, her voice full of excitement. 'Did Jack video it?'

Lotta took a deep breath and began to recount the full story, describing the signs the flight attendants held up and the moment when he got out the ring. As she spoke, even though Liv couldn't see her, she gestured with her hands, her eyes shining with emotion.

When Lotta finished her story, Liv let out a high-pitched squeal. 'That's so amazing! Woohoo!'

'I know, right? I still can't believe it. The thing I feel the most is shock.'

'You deserve all the happiness in the world, Lotta. You really do,' Liv said sincerely.

Lotta felt a lump form in her throat at her cousin's words. There had been a lot of times in her life when she'd felt as if she didn't deserve anything, let alone happiness. She took a deep breath and let out a shaky laugh. 'I love you, Liv. Thanks for being there for me, for, well, you know, the last few years, forever,' Lotta said, her voice full of emotion.

'Love you too. And I can't wait to see you two and celebrate,' Liv said excitedly.'Just wait until Timmy hears. He'll have a fit! We won't be able to bring him down from dancing on the ceiling about this.'

Lotta felt joyous, content, and, most of all, loved as she stood looking out at the sea. She'd never been happier in her life.

28

Lotta walked through Pretty Beach in the direction of the ferry on her way to work. She'd left Jack with his right arm propped up on a pile of pillows on the sofa in the library room. He had his laptop at his side, the soup she'd made was ready and waiting in the fridge, and cinnamon buns were by the kettle for afternoon tea. Not that he was incapable of looking after himself, just that she wanted to make sure that he didn't do too much. He'd thought that he was going to go to work. She'd put paid to that.

As she got to the sea, the colours behind the wharf made Lotta catch her breath. The sun had painted hues of light pink and pale orange in the sky as she waited for the ferry. Salty air, still cool from the night, filled her lungs as she joined the queue. Some of the faces around her were now familiar faces, all preparing for their daily commute. A woman in a medical uniform smiled, she recognised the man who owned the curry house with who she presumed was his wife, and the ferry hand raised his eyebrows in recognition. It felt so nice to be home. So far away from Texas.

As she stepped onto the ferry, Lotta loved the unsteady

rocking of the boat beneath her feet and the sea breeze in her hair. Taking her favourite spot on the upper deck, as the ferry came to life and they set off towards the coast, she left her Kindle in her bag and let her eyes wander over the sea towards the horizon. Lotta always appreciated the early morning ferry rides to work, sitting on the top deck in all weathers had become a time for her when even the pages of a book took second place. A place where the world seemed to pause for a moment. She'd now seen the sea in all sorts of weather, but today, the water was calm and inviting. It glistened as rays of sunlight danced on its surface, seagulls soared overhead, and a faint smell of diesel wafted in the air.

She leaned against the railing in front of her, watching as the Pretty Beach shoreline slowly receded away to a blur. The quaint pastel houses and lighthouse in the far distance got smaller and smaller as the ferry chugged along on its way. She watched below as it cut through the water, leaving a trail of frothy white in its wake, and took long, slow lungfuls of the crisp air, cleansing her of Singapore and grief and Houston and stress.

As the ferry glided up the coast, an array of scents filled the air; the briny aroma of the sea intermingled with the freshness of the ocean breeze, coastal flowers, and a subtle aroma of fish and seaweed – a tapestry of seaside smells. Lotta smiled to herself. Not only was she so glad to be home and on the ferry, but she realised that living in Pretty Beach made her feel alive.

About half an hour later, she was sitting on a bench not far from the entrance to the arcade, untying her trainers and putting on her heels. She felt so happy to be back at work, happy to be back to her routine, and happy to be safe. She wouldn't be going anywhere anytime soon. Striding purposefully into the building, she took it all in with a gleeful look on her face. Before she knew it, she was in the inner lobby and then opening the door to the office. In a split second, Marie was up and out of her seat. 'Hi! Oh my goodness, I'm so pleased to see you!' Marie hugged her hard.

Lotta was a bit taken aback by the hug, but she beamed. 'Hi.'

'You must be exhausted!'

'I'm fine,' Lotta reassured.

'Thankfully, Jack is okay. We've all been so worried and concerned,' Marie said, still holding Lotta's arms.

As Marie let her go, Lotta touched the back of her hair, and as she did so, Marie frowned and pointed. 'What? What is that?' she said, pointing to Lotta's left hand. 'Oh my flipping heck!'

Lotta felt herself blushing. 'Umm, it's what it looks like.' She smiled sheepishly.

Marie swore. 'Oh! What? Ahh!' She clapped her hands in excitement. 'What? When?'

'It all happened on the plane,' Lotta explained.

'Sorry? What do you mean?' Marie asked, her eyes wide with curiosity.

Lotta took her bag off her shoulder and followed Marie through to the sofa and the kitchen area. 'Jack asked me to marry him on the plane,' she said, a dreamy look in her eyes.

'I'm gobsmacked,' Marie said.

'I know, I was too,' Lotta replied, sitting down.

'What, and he presented you with that rock?' Marie asked, pointing to the ring.

'Yeah, not quite. The crew were in on it,' Lotta said, chuckling.

Marie's eyes were wide. 'Hold on.' She held her hand up in a stop sign. 'We need a coffee and a full debrief on this.'

Five minutes later, they were sitting on the sofa, both with a coffee. 'He made this big fuss about getting to the back of the plane to look at the door and the clouds. To be honest, it was irritating the heck out of me. Then I went back to my seat,' Lotta recounted, gesturing with her hands.

'Oh, this is so romantic.' Marie sighed. 'I'm so there in my head.'

'I know, haha,' Lotta agreed, grinning.

'Did you have any idea?' Marie asked, leaning forward.

Lotta screwed her face up. 'None! Not at all. I never thought anyone would want to marry me.'

Marie frowned. 'Sorry? What does that mean?'

'Oh, I don't know. Anyway, so yeah, there was a blue envelope with a heart telling me to turn around. Then the crew each held up a sign, and it was the question, the proposal.' Lotta scrolled through her phone to the pictures of the aircrew with the signs and showed Marie.

Marie looked down at Lotta's phone. 'You have *got* to be kidding me. This is amazing,' she said, shaking her head in disbelief.

'I know. I didn't know what to do,' Lotta confessed.

'I would have paid to be there,' Marie said wistfully.

'I just cried and cried and cried. There's a video too. He got one of the other passengers to take it with his phone.'

'So he planned the whole thing.'

'Yep, I had no idea.'

'What, like none at all?'

'No. Of course not! Brandy, the woman with the apartment that I told you about, was funny about flights. And now, as I look back, it all makes sense. She was in on it,' Lotta said. 'I pieced together a few things with hindsight, but no, at the time, I didn't have a clue.'

Marie looked at the ring. 'It's gorgeous. How did he plan it all? What, from like the hospital bed?'

'Yeah, apparently, Brandy was in on the ring. She got the cleaner to look at a ring of mine in the room. Jack said that they were going to guess that bit, but then one day, I'd left my rings by the sink in the bathroom, and so that was just lucky,' Lotta explained.

'Wow, what a story, Lotta! I am so jealous!' Marie exclaimed.

'I know, I can't believe it. It wasn't on the cards at all,' Lotta confessed.

'How very exciting. Have you set a date?' Marie asked.

'No, not really, but I think it's going to be soon. No one more than us knows that you don't know what's around the corner. I mean, who would have thought what happened in Houston would happen to Jack, right?' Lotta said.

'I know, it makes you think, that's for sure,' Marie agreed. 'Is it going to be a huge wedding?'

Lotta paused for a second. 'I don't know, is the honest answer. I never really thought I was going to get married.'

'Big white dress, something in the country, ahh, loads of flowers.'

'Yeah, I'm not sure, actually. Maybe we'll just sneak off, just the two of us.'

'You don't fancy all the pomp?'

'I don't know, it just seems a bit...' Lotta paused to consider. 'Wasteful, pointless, something like that.'

'Yes, well, weddings certainly are a lot of money.' Marie nodded in agreement.

'I know. It's not the money, though that is a consideration.'

Marie's face wrinkled into a frown. 'What is it then?'

More that I just want something simple and meaningful. Lotta shook her head. 'I need to muse it for a bit, I suppose. It's all a bit of a shock. A huge shock, more like.'

'It's so exciting.'

'I know,' Lotta said as she picked up her coffee cup and took a sip. Lotta Button was getting married. Hoo-blooming-ray.

Lotta stepped out of the arcade and decided to get a coffee out in the fresh air. As she stood in the queue near the bandstand, she looked over towards the sea and smiled. A thick line of clouds edged the horizon, and the sun dipped in and out, landing on the water in sparkles. As she waited, she flicked through one of her digital TBR piles, deciding on what book to start next.

'Afternoon! How are you?' the woman behind the counter said with a warm smile. 'I hear you've had a run of it. Usual?'

'Yes, please.' Lotta nodded, rolled her eyes, and smiled. 'I should say so.'

'Marie said your partner was involved in that terrible shooting in the US. I'm so sorry to hear that,' the woman said, her expression turning sympathetic.

'Thanks,' Lotta replied, appreciating the concern.

'How is he?' the woman asked, leaning in slightly.

'He's actually fine now,' Lotta answered, her voice carrying a hint of relief.

'Wow, that's good news then. I've been asking Marie for updates,' the woman said, her eyes lighting up.

'He was very lucky,' Lotta confirmed.

'He jumped in front of a pram, is that right?' the woman inquired, raising her eyebrows in surprise.

Lotta nodded. 'He did.'

'Can't argue with that,' the woman noted, nodding her head. 'I'd keep him if I were you.'

'I know. I intend to,' Lotta said, her lips curving into a grateful smile.

'Anyone who does something like that out of instinct tells you something.' The woman nodded as she handed over a coffee.

Lotta agreed. 'Thanks.'

'See you later,' the woman said cheerfully, waving as Lotta

left.

Lotta nodded and said cheerio. As she walked over towards the bandstand, the air felt amazing; clear, fresh, pure, and *English.* Oh so nice and simply English. Never had she been more pleased to be home and living on the coast. Never had she been more grateful for her life.

As she got herself comfy in the bandstand and propped her coffee beside her, she turned her Kindle on. As the sun glinted through the panes of glass and warmed her through, she was lost for a while. About fifteen minutes later, her coffee was finished, and as she tapped to turn the page, the diamond on her left hand caught the light. It made her catch her breath. She still couldn't believe what had happened on the flight. She couldn't believe Jack had proposed.

After the drama of it all, and as the cloak of excitement and happiness had lifted slightly, Lotta had suddenly asked herself if she did actually want to get married. What did it even mean to her? She'd never really thought about it much. It had been a sort of unspoken thing that it just wasn't the way her life was going to go. She'd been to loads of family weddings and events and Liv had had a big, fabulous wedding, but Lotta had been on the sidelines in all of it. Silly little Lotta Button, who, more often than not, attended things on her own. Silly Lotta Button at the table, squeezed in between the successful people. Silly Lotta Button no more. Silly Lotta was getting married.

Staring out to sea, her mind scooted back to the country manor hotel and the bar where she'd met Jack. She thought about the fascinator, the secondhand dress, the shoes that killed her, and how she'd been at a very low point in her life. She thought about the huge wedding, the massive amounts of money, the guests dressed up to the nines, all of it. The indulgence. As she watched the waves down on the shore in front of her turn over and over, she cocked her head to the side and considered. Did she really want all of that? Did she want people in a huge room who didn't really mean that much to her at all? The more she thought about it, the more she wasn't sure. She wanted something simple; her, Just Jack, whoever he wanted from his family, Timmy, and Liv. Really, they were the only people who knew the real Lotta. The only people she wanted in her world. Did she need a big, huge wedding? Or did she want something small? Her little life was tight and few, and she liked it like that. Just as it was. Her wedding would be the same.

The more she thought about it, the more she knew what she wanted. A tiny affair, a simple celebration of her and Jack. A bonding of the two of them that meant everything to her. And as she sat gazing at the sea, she thought about where. A church? A registry office? A fancy old building country manor house, like the one where they'd met?

And suddenly, it came to her. There was only one place Lotta Button wanted to get married. It was so obvious and so perfect that a tear pricked at the corner of her eye. Lotta was going to get married in a library, totally and utterly surrounded by books.

Lotta checked her watch and hurried as she closed her computer down. She was meeting Liv for a drink; she was pressed for time because she had been caught up at work. Grabbing her coat and bag, making sure she had everything she needed, she headed out the door in a rush.

Cool evening air hit her as she pulled her blazer tighter and marched down the street, her heels clicking rhythmically on the pavement. The pub was not far, nestled in a long row of quaint old shops and cafés. As she approached the entrance, she spotted Liv through the window, sitting at a corner table with a drink in her hand. Lotta smiled at the sight of her cousin. Liv was her rock and always had been.

As she pushed open the door, a buzz of lively conversation flooded her ears as she made her way through the pub. It was cosy, dimly lit, and filled with a mix of locals and tourists alike. She weaved her way through the crowd, exchanging nods and smiles with a few people, before finally reaching Liv's table.

'Hey,' Lotta greeted Liv with a beam. 'It's so good to see you!'

Liv looked up from her drink, her face lighting up. 'Hello.' She jumped up from her seat to give Lotta a hug. 'We have so much to catch up on! I'm still getting over the proposal. I must have watched that video a million times,' Liv gushed.

After putting her bag down and going to the bar, they settled into their seats and sipped their drinks. Lotta was determined that the conversation wasn't going to be all about her. Before she let Liv go on too much about the proposal, she asked about James. 'So, what's happened with that?'

'Nothing,' Liv said glumly, swirling her drink absent-mindedly. 'I don't know what to do, really. I suppose I've just accepted it now.'

'There's not a lot more you can do,' Lotta replied, offering a sympathetic smile.

'I know.' Liv sighed.

'He'll come around,' Lotta tried to reassure her.

'The thing is, I don't want that,' Liv said, looking up from her drink with a sad look in her eyes.

'What do you mean?' Lotta asked, furrowing her brow.

'I mean that I don't want him to come around. I want him to want it. I think it would be awful to start off like that,' Liv explained, her voice firm. 'You need to want to try for a baby, surely?'

'True, yeah, sorry, I shouldn't have said that,' Lotta said, realising her mistake.

'It's fine,' Liv reassured her with a weak smile.

'You're right. He needs to want it just as much,' Lotta agreed, nodding.

'I'll just wait,' Liv said, taking a sip of her drink.

'I guess it's really your only option,' Lotta concluded, reaching over to give Liv's hand a supportive squeeze.

'Yep,' Liv replied with a resigned nod. 'Anyway, that is so not why we're here. We are here for a Liv and Lotta celebration.' Liv chuckled and held up her glass in a toast.

Lotta groaned. 'I'm not getting hungover like the last time we met. That was terrible. I said never again, and I meant it.'

Liv chuckled. 'Ha, no. So, have you had thoughts on the big day?'

Lotta hesitated, playing with her napkin. 'I have.'

'What then?' Liv asked, curious.

'Don't laugh,' Lotta warned.

'Oh no, what does that mean?' Liv raised her eyebrows in anticipation.

Lotta took a deep breath. 'A library.'

Liv screwed up her face. 'What? In the library room at your house. Won't that be a bit stressy? It's too small, surely?'

'I want to get married in an *actual* library,' Lotta explained.

'Is that even a thing?' Liv questioned, tilting her head.

'I don't know, but I'm going to find out,' Lotta replied, determined.

'What did Jack say?'

Lotta smiled. 'He said he doesn't care, but I haven't actually broached the library thing yet.'

'Right.' Liv nodded.

Lotta continued, 'He also said that he'll sort it, whatever I want.'

'Wow, that's good,' Liv said, impressed. 'I wonder what he can do to make that happen.'

'I don't know, but I'm going to find out,' Lotta joked.

Liv giggled. 'Lotta Button gets married in a library. Timmy's going to die.'

29

Once Lotta had realised she wanted to get married surrounded by books in a library, it had taken her all of about two seconds to know exactly which one. She'd spent a lot of her time in the amazing London libraries when she'd lived in Chelsea and had been on pilgrimages to libraries all over the country. But her favourite library in Oxford was top of her list to marry Jack.

She hadn't even mentioned it to Jack, but after long sessions studying the library's website, she'd decided a day trip to Oxford was on the cards. Sitting on the fast train, she swiped down the library's social media account over and over again and read through.

Nestled in the very heart of Oxford, the library stands testament to the city's rich history and undeniable charm. These ancient walls have seen countless stories unfold, and now, they offer the most stunning setting for your special day.

The grand library, with its many beautifully appointed rooms, is licensed for civil weddings and partnerships, each one radiating a sense of romance and elegance. Whether you envision an intimate ceremony or a lavish celebration with all your loved ones, the library will provide the perfect backdrop to make your wedding dreams a reality.

So come and let your love story unfold in this timeless venue, where history and romance intertwine to create memories that will last a lifetime.

Lotta had decided to take herself off for the day to check out the library, just to be sure it was where she wanted to be. Once she'd changed trains and arrived in Oxford, she stood in a queue to get a coffee and began to stroll through the old streets. As it always did, the beauty of Oxford hit her all at once. The grandeur of the architecture, the cobbled streets, and the atmosphere made her heart skip a beat. She took a deep breath and set off towards the library with a spring in her step.

As she strolled through the streets, she marvelled at the buildings surrounding her, each one whispering a story with their intricate details and ornate façades. As she sipped her coffee with her book bag swung over her shoulder, church bells filled the air, a flurry of bicycles whizzed past, and Lotta drank it all in. She revelled in the old buildings, the students zipping around with backpacks slung over their shoulders, locals leisurely pedalling along the quiet back streets, and people on phones sounding busy.

Despite the hustle and bustle, there was something soothing about the streets. As she was lost in a world of her own, Lotta ambled in and out, captivated by the beauty of it all. The closer she got to the library, the more certain she was that Oxford was the place of wedding dreams.

As she approached the library, she was struck by its sheer grandeur. The towering stone walls and the imposing archways took her breath away. She stepped inside, and a hush of time and books descended. She embraced the sheer volume of knowledge and time as the smell of old books and polished wood filled her nostrils. Entering the main room, she was overwhelmed – the high ceilings, the stained glass windows, the intricate carvings, and the shelves full of books.

As she spun around with her head up and her heart pounding in her chest, she knew it was exactly where she wanted to get married to Jack. It somehow felt as if it was meant to be. Peering up at the ceiling, a member of staff with a huge stack of books in her arms smiled and approached her.

'Everything okay? Do you need any help at all?' the staff member asked.

Lotta went to say that she didn't need any help, but then she changed her mind. 'Thanks. I was, I am, rather, thinking about getting married here.' The words alone seemed strange as they came out of her mouth. Lotta Button was getting married. Come again, please.

'Ahh, right. It's certainly a nice place for a wedding.' The woman chuckled. 'You're in luck, actually. Lucinda, who is in charge of our weddings, is out the front here today, as it so happens.'

'Oh, no, I didn't make an appointment,' Lotta said, shaking her head.

'She won't mind showing you around and having a chat if you like,' the woman said with raised eyebrows.

Lotta considered for a second. It certainly wouldn't do any harm. She had already made her decision. The library was her first and probably only choice. 'That would be fantastic. Thank you.'

'Hang on. I'll just put these down, and I'll go and get her,' the woman said, nodding towards the books she was carrying.

The woman returned shortly with a tall, poised woman in her late thirties with long, curly hair. 'This is Lucinda. She is in charge of weddings here.'

'Hello, it's lovely to meet you.' Lucinda extended her hand with a warm smile. 'I'm Lucinda.'

'Hi, Lotta,' Lotta replied, shaking her hand.

'What a lovely name. So, you're interested in having your wedding here?' Lucinda asked.

Lotta nodded. 'Yes, I am. I was just admiring the ceiling, actually. It's quite beautiful.'

'Ah, the ceiling is one of the most stunning features. Along with the books, of course!' Lucinda said with a proud smile. 'And we're licensed in three of our rooms, so we can tailor things for just about anything you want, really.'

'That's wonderful,' Lotta said, feeling a bit nervous.

'When were you thinking? Next year? The year after?'

Lotta bit her lip. Of course, the library would probably be booked out for years. There was no way she was waiting long. After what had happened with Jack and how she'd seen life on the edge, she didn't want to hang around. 'I don't know, actually.'

'We're fairly booked up. We do have some available dates, but it really depends on the size of your party and which room you'd like to use. Our 200 guest room is always booked into the foreseeable future, that's I think two years out at the moment, maybe three, but the other smaller rooms have some spare dates.'

Lotta was put off. The last thing she wanted was to be on a conveyor belt of weddings. It all left a bit of a sour taste in her mouth. 'We were thinking of a very small wedding…'

'We have beautiful choices for that,' Lucinda said with a nod. 'If you'd like, I can show you around and give you more details about each room.'

'That would be wonderful, thank you,' Lotta said, feeling grateful for the help but not sure if she wanted to be in a wedding machine.

Lucinda led Lotta through the library until they came to a

small room with shelves upon shelves of books surrounding them. 'This is our Inner Library,' Lucinda said, smiling proudly. 'It's one of our smaller rooms, perfect for intimate weddings.'

Lotta shook her head over and over again as she was immediately struck by precisely what she had been looking for. The wooden floors creaked as they walked over them, the walls were lined with tall bookshelves filled with leather-bound books, and beautiful old-fashioned pendant lights hung from above. 'It's beautiful,' Lotta said, her voice barely above a whisper as she ran her hand along the spines of the books, taking in their musty scent.

'It's a popular choice,' Lucinda said with a smile. 'It can seat up to fifty guests comfortably.'

Lotta nodded, picturing her small wedding in the intimate space. 'That sounds perfect.'

'We can decorate the room to your liking,' Lucinda continued. 'We have a team of florists and decorators who can transform the space into your dream wedding.'

Lotta felt a flutter in her chest at the thought of her wedding coming to life in the room. 'That would be wonderful.'

'And the catering can be tailored to your tastes,' Lucinda said. 'We have a list of recommended caterers, but if you have a specific cuisine in mind, we can work with you.'

Lotta smiled. 'It all sounds perfect.'

'Of course,' Lucinda said, placing a reassuring hand on Lotta's arm. 'We want your wedding day to be as perfect as possible.'

'What about the ceremony? Where does that take place?'

'You have a few options,' Lucinda said. 'Some couples choose to have the ceremony in the Inner Library itself, while others opt for the grander areas. It all depends on your personal preference.'

Lotta thought for a moment, picturing herself walking down

the aisle in each of the spaces. 'I think I'd like to have the ceremony here,' she said finally. 'It feels more intimate.'

'I completely understand,' Lucinda said with a nod. 'It's a beautiful space for a ceremony.'

Lotta smiled and nodded. She'd found her perfect venue. Now all she needed to do was sort out a date.

30

Lotta burst through the front door of Pretty Beach to the Breakers, her cheeks flushed with excitement. 'Hello!'

Jack was sitting in the breakfast room, his laptop in front of him. He frowned as he looked up. 'You look pleased with yourself. What are you up to?'

Lotta kissed him. 'I have the best news ever.'

'Really?'

'I've found it. The perfect wedding venue.'

Jack smiled at her enthusiasm. 'What? Where is this perfect venue then?'

'One of the libraries in Oxford!' Lotta exclaimed, dropping her handbag on the table. 'I went on a secret mission.'

'I thought you were acting weirdly.'

'I wanted to see whether or not I'd love it. I did.'

'Okay. Sorted then.'

Lotta's smile faded slightly. 'Only thing is, it's super expensive. Even for the package we'd want.'

Jack wrapped his arms around her waist. 'Lott, not being funny, but have you not quite clocked that I can afford stuff? We don't have to worry about the cost. I already told you that.'

Lotta gazed up at him uncertainly. 'But that's not the point. Weddings are expensive enough, and this is next level. We're talking eye-wateringly expensive.'

'So what? It's small and intimate and what you want,' Jack insisted. 'Just our closest friends and family. All that matters is we're getting married in a place that means so much to you.'

'I guess so.'

'You get to have your dream wedding, whatever it takes.'

Lotta put her arms around his neck, overwhelmed. How did she get so lucky? But still, a twinge of guilt remained. 'Are you sure? I have enough debt on my plate…' She left her sentence dangling in the air.

'Not a problem. I will sort it.'

Lotta gazed up into Jack's eyes, feeling as though she might burst with joy. 'Are you really sure? I don't want you to feel like you have to spend a fortune because I want it in a library.'

'I just survived a mall shooting, Lotta. The only thing that matters is that we're getting married. The venue, the flowers, the dress – you do all those details. You're all I need for it to be the perfect day.'

Lotta blinked back tears of happiness. How did she find this man, who seemed to know exactly what to say to assuage her worries and make her feel like the luckiest woman in the world?

'Besides,' Jack added with a chuckle. 'Let me spoil you.'

Lotta sighed. He was right – she'd spent so much of her life before she'd met Jack worrying, that it was habitual. She needed to stop fretting and enjoy it.

'The library it is, then!'

Jack laughed. 'Done.'

'We're really doing this, aren't we?' she asked softly.

'Are you getting soppy on me, Lotta Button?' Jack asked as he took her hands in his, giving them a squeeze.

'I think I might be.'

'You're stuck with me now.'

'Shame. I think I am.'

'Stuck with me and marrying me. Glutton for punishment. Is it because you feel sorry for me because I got shot?' Jack deadpanned.

Lotta giggled. 'Totally.'

'That's why I asked you. I knew I'd guilt you into saying yes.'

'I still have to turn up.' Lotta joked. Inside though, none of it was a joke. To her, it was the best thing that had ever happened in her life. The wedding, the library, their marriage – it felt as if her real life was just getting started. She couldn't quite believe it. She was marrying Jack in a beautiful historical library, surrounded by books—what could be more perfect for a life-long bookworm? Who even was she? What was this gilded life? Her excitement returned in a rush of warmth that spread up and down her body. Lotta Button was getting wed. In a library, no less. But more than that, more than all the stuff, the venue or the dress, Lotta was happy because she was loved. And it felt completely and utterly amazing.

31

Lotta sat at the table in the quaint tea room, watching the steam rise from her cup of tea. Since she'd been back from America and the experience of vile cups of watery tea, every time she'd had a cup, she'd embraced it like never before. She sat staring into space as she waited for Timmy and Giles to arrive. Lotta had been friends with Timmy for years, and they'd seen each other through thick and thin. When Lotta had told Timmy her news, he'd been over the moon. When Timmy swept into the room, Lotta could see his excitement written all over his face.

'Hello, darling!' he gushed, practically jigging in excitement.

Lotta beamed as she stood up to give Timmy a hug. 'Hi. It's so good to see you,' she said as they hugged tightly.

Timmy pulled away and looked at Lotta expectantly as he and Giles sat down. 'So, spill the beans! How's the wedding planning going? A wedding in a library! Only *you* could want that, Lott. Love, love, love it!'

Lotta grinned, feeling a bit giddy at the thought of it all. 'It's going well. All we need is a date.'

'Ooh, do tell!' Giles said, leaning forward in his seat. 'I love a wedding, especially one with a love story like yours. It's so romantic!'

Lotta giggled and poured tea from the teapot into the cups, passed them over and leaned back in her chair, relishing every single thing about the moment. 'Small and special is what I'm thinking.'

Timmy's eyes widened in surprise. 'Oh, really. I wanted a huge bash. No. How small are we talking?'

Lotta shook her head. 'Sorry to disappoint you. Basically just us, plus James and Liv, Jack's family, and a couple of close friends. I've thought about it loads. It's what I want,' Lotta said with a dreamy sigh. 'A small ceremony surrounded by books. It doesn't get any better than that, as far as I'm concerned.'

Giles smiled and clapped his hands. 'What's not to love?'

Lotta nodded. 'Yeah, we're keeping it simple. Some flowers and candles, but nothing too over-the-top. We want the library and the books to be the main focus.'

Timmy looked thoughtful. 'What about your dress? Have you found the perfect one yet?'

Lotta's smile faltered slightly. 'Not yet. I've tried on a few, but I just haven't found the one. It's been a bit frustrating, to be honest.'

Timmy reached across the table and took Lotta's hand. 'Don't worry, darling. You'll find something. And if you need any help, just let me know. I love wedding dress shopping!'

Lotta laughed, feeling grateful for Timmy's enthusiasm. 'Thanks. I might take you up on that offer. On the other hand, I don't have your sort of budget.'

'Have you seen anything you like at all?' Timmy asked, his eyes sparkling with interest.

'Not yet,' Lotta replied with a smile. 'I'm thinking of something simple. I just haven't seen anything that's even close.'

'Hmm.'

Giles chimed in. 'Yeah, I guess if everything else is simple, the dress will need to be the same.'

Timmy beamed. 'Sod that for a laugh. I'm telling you here and now. I am ordering a bespoke suit. It has to be done.'

Lotta chuckled. 'You'll be better dressed than me.'

'You know me. Never knowingly underdressed,' Timmy replied, grinning from ear to ear.

Lotta took a sip of her tea and chuckled, knowing full well that Timmy would be dressed up to the nines. 'That is so true.'

'What about the reception? Will that be in the same place?' Giles asked, his eyes twinkling with curiosity.

Lotta bit her lip, suddenly feeling unsure. 'I think so. We've mostly been focusing on the date and the ceremony.'

'I think, in for a penny, in for a pound,' Timmy said.

'What, like, have the whole thing in the library?' Lotta questioned. 'You think so?'

'Yeah, I mean, it's not like you're going to get the chance again.'

'True,' Giles agreed. 'You'll be in your element, completely surrounded by books. So why not make the most of it?'

'Yeah.'

'Well, that's it then. All too easy,' Timmy said. 'Let the foofing begin.'

32

Lotta had looked at so many wedding dresses she was sick of the sight of them. She grimaced at the huge ones, shuddered at the skinny slip dress style, and gagged at anything with a sparkle. At a loss of knowing what she liked, she'd even flipped through her favourite books to reread scenes with weddings and dresses. None of it had inspired her. Not even a sniff of inspiration. She'd also camped out in the library room, rugged up on the sofa and watched a few classic movies. Nothing. Nada. Not a single thing had taken her fancy.

Liv had made an appointment with a wedding dress shop, but Lotta wasn't looking forward to it in the slightest. It was strange indeed. She'd spent so many years as a wedding guest, oohing and ahhing at dresses she'd seen float past her down the aisle in a cloud of frothy, tulle white, that she would have thought she'd be clued up on the dress of her dreams. In fact, it was the opposite. All of it was a jumble of sparkle and silk that wasn't quite floating her boat.

She had so many different looks and styles in her head that she almost wanted someone to take the decision away from her entirely. She would have been quite happy with just a couple of options, and being dictated to that she had to take one of them, and that would be that.

With her feet curled up under her, she looked around at the library room, her eyes scanning the rows upon rows of books, and mulled over the dress problem. As she pondered, her mind wandered to Jack. It was so much easier for him. He was wearing a suit and a nice tie and he couldn't have been less bothered if he'd tried. The same went for Timmy and Giles. Although no one could say that Timmy's outfit was simple, or that he wasn't bothered. He'd totally gone to Savile Row and had a bespoke suit made just for him. But it had all been quite easy. There had not been any real brain power involved.

Lotta sighed. First World problems and all that but even Liv was sorted. Staring into space, she shook her head at the whole thing. She still couldn't quite get her head around the fact that the wedding was happening at all.

Her mind went backwards and forwards over the two of them and landed on the day when she'd first met Jack. She laughed to herself as visions of them floated through her head. She remembered when he'd helped her with the red carpet when she'd first moved into Pretty Beach to the Breakers. She thought about their lovely picnic in the hills of Pretty Beach, and she pondered when she'd first clapped eyes on him when she'd been sitting in the bar with the huge green fascinator on her head. She chuckled to herself as she thought about the fascinator and how its size had nearly overpowered not just her, but the whole room. She'd bought it in a charity shop for a fiver, along with a matching dress.

Suddenly she'd jumped off the sofa so quickly that she almost stumbled as she got to the library door. Practically running up the stairs, her thoughts were consumed by the green fascinator and the dress she'd worn the day she'd met Jack. Bursting into her bedroom, she flew around the sleigh bed and opened her wardrobe doors. Digging through her wardrobe, she flicked to the end until she found the green dress and pulled the hanger from the rail. Then, rummaging in the bottom of the wardrobe, she found the fascinator tucked away in a box and flipped off the lid.

Repeatedly nodding to herself, she held the dress up against her body as memories of the day she'd met Jack flooded her mind. She remembered ordering a large glass of wine at the bar as a sense of doom at the trajectory of her life had circled her. She remembered him sliding onto a stool, asking for a whisky, and not sounding too happy. She remembered her fascinator bumping him. She remembered how handsome he was.

Staring into the mirror with the green dress held up against herself, she smiled as she thought about their first conversation. The way he had told her that he pretended to be mean at functions, how he had made her chuckle inside. His sort of grumpy, nonchalance. The sparkly red leotard. Standing in front of the mirror with the hanger behind her neck and the dress draped over her body, she nodded. This was the dress that had started it all. It was simple, classic, beautiful and most importantly, made her feel good. There was one problem, though. It was green. She wanted something exactly like it, but in white.

With a smile on her face, she put the dress down and grabbed the fascinator, slotting the hair band into her head, and then whipped off her jeans and put the dress on properly. Spinning around in front of the mirror, the heavy satin bias-cut fabric with the slit in the front, moved as if on its own. The sleeves were gorgeous. She nodded; it was perfect. She felt good, and the memories of the day she had worn it felt happily poignant.

As she looked at herself in the mirror, she knew she wanted this dress for her wedding. It was simple, beautiful, and pushed all her buttons. In white, it would seal the deal. It would be perfect. With the fascinator wobbling, she squinted and tried to imagine something similar in white. She envisaged a veil, a gigantic bunch of flowers in front of her, and her hair in loose curls. Most of all, she imagined the scene with her in the simple dress surrounded by an avalanche of books.

Daydreaming, as if her life depended on it, she revelled in the fact that she, Lotta Button, was doing this thing. Lotta Button was getting married. She pictured herself walking towards Jack as she stood in front of the mirror. She pictured his face. She thought about her heart.

Gathering the hem of the dress, she craned her neck to the inside seam to attempt to read the label. She had no idea where the dress was from, having bought it in a charity shop. A few seconds later, she was typing the brand into her phone. Five minutes after that, she was one *very* happy bookworm. The brand of the green dress had a wedding arm. The wedding arm had a floor-length version of the dress in white. The dress did not fall under the umbrella of charity shop prices. She didn't care. Lotta was sold. She'd sell an arm if she had to.

Picking up her phone and still with the fascinator on, she video-called Liv. She felt giddy that she'd found a solution and garbled as soon as Liv's face came onto the screen. 'Guess what?'

Liv frowned and wrinkled up her nose. 'Why are you wearing that? Are you going to the races?'

Lotta was speaking very quickly, almost tripping over her words. 'I want to wear my green dress for my wedding and this,' Lotta said, pointing to the fascinator.

Liv's eyes widened. 'Are you serious? Wow, You're going to get married in green. Right. Err, not really my cup of tea but…' Liv turned her head this way and that, contemplating. 'Okay. We can work with that, I suppose. Hmm. Each to their own.'

'No! I'm getting it in white. They do a wedding version.'

'Oh wow! I love that dress on you. The shape of it is fabulous.'

Lotta beamed with excitement, 'You think?'

Liv leaned in closer to the phone, her eyes shining with excitement. 'I love it. Tell me more about the wedding version!'

Lotta started scrolling through the pictures on the website, copied the link, sent it to Liv, and waited as Liv looked down at her phone. 'Look at this one! It's got this beautiful train, and the fabric is gorgeous.'

'They're all stunning,' Liv said. 'And what about the fascinator? Blimey, I'd forgotten how big that thing was.'

Lotta laughed. 'Remember I was wearing it when I first met Jack at the bar? I'm going to get something similar, but with silk flowers or petals, I dunno.'

'Yeah, yeah. Perfect,' Liv said with a sigh.

'Hair up and some vintage-style jewellery. What do you think?'

'Yes, yes, yes,' Liv said, nodding her head enthusiastically. 'That would be perfect. You're going to look absolutely stunning. So simple and so classy. Love it.'

Lotta felt fabulously pleased with herself. Not only couldn't she believe that she was actually getting married, but it would be in a dress she loved. 'So, we're going to London to buy a wedding dress,' she singsonged.

'I cannot wait. I've literally been waiting for this moment for like fifteen years,' Liv said, her eyes twinkling with affection. 'I'm so happy for you, Lott. I really, *really* am.'

Lotta was full of it too. She loved that Liv was happy for her. But right at that moment, no one, not a single person in the world, could be happier than her.

33

Lotta must have been the only bride in history totally head over heels in love with getting married, in love with the groom, and in love with life but also totally more interested in going to a bookshop than going to a wedding dress shop. She smiled as she made her way from the underground station through a street market to one of her favourite bookshops. The sounds of the London street filled her ears. A stall owner called out to passersby about fresh cherries from Kent, the smell of a crepe stand filled the air, and the colours from a flower stall made her smile.

Lotta had been to the bookshop many, many times when she'd lived in London and turned the familiar left at the end of the market, along the pavement until it narrowed a bit, past a little Italian deli, a post office, a curry house and then there it was – squat and tucked right in the corner. A tatty old black Pashley bike was parked out the front – not a pretend bike or a bike just for show with flowers in its basket. The bike was transport and how the owner got to work. Lotta loved that. Curved paned windows greeted the street, a toppling display of books was stacked up inside the window, and window boxes full of trailing ivy and dancing pink petunias sat in baskets to the front. A double-width doormat requested that patrons please wipe their feet.

Lotta pushed the old door and sighed inside as the bell above tinkled in her ear. As she stepped onto the worn timber floorboards, the old bookshop smell hit her squarely between the eyes. It had been similar in Houston but nowhere near as good. She inhaled deeply. Pretty Beach air was good, but to Lotta, this was better. Much, *much* better. A tiny assistant with an oriental patterned pale blue jacket, huge dark brown eyes, and the most perfect skin Lotta had ever seen, raised her eyebrows in greeting as she zipped past with an enormous pile of books in her arms.

Everywhere Lotta looked, books greeted her. New books, old books and everything else in between. Piles of paperbacks littered the floorboards, coffee table books sat on the steps of old ladders, vintage piano music was stacked up on upside-down fruit crates, photography books graced old chairs, and towers of the classics were crowded on and under tables. Lotta spied the owner behind the desk in the corner, reading glasses on his head, phone to his ear, pen in hand and a book held out in front of him. A vintage reading lamp glowed, classical music played, and brown paper bags were stacked up in piles on a sales table pushed up against the desk.

A strange feeling swept over Lotta as she retraced the steps of her past and made her way to her favourite section at the back of the shop. She suddenly realised that despite how much she loved it, the shop made her feel sad. Sad for the Lotta she had left behind when she'd moved to Pretty Beach. That Lotta, not that she'd known it then, had been a person who had been zapped by life. Squashed by the needs and wants of a man-child who'd had little to no interest in her and what she required from the world. Lotta shook herself over and over and over again in an attempt to flick the memories from her brain as she stared up at shelves full of books. The difference between the person she'd been then and the person she now was so huge, it took her breath away. With the oh-so-wonderful benefit of hindsight, that gorgeous thing that no amount of money can buy, she realised that she was looking back at the face of someone who was depressed. Someone who had been so very low. Someone who had been buried underneath someone else's life. It had not been nice.

Lotta closed her eyes together tightly as feelings flooded through every single cell of her body. Now, in the cosiest corner of the shop where a faded old gold wingback chair sat beside a fireplace and a small pretty lamp glowed, she slowly lowered herself down into the chair and leant her head against the back. Rummaging in her book bag, she took out her phone, flipped the camera and then stared at herself on the screen. This person was different from Lotta from before. This Lotta looked together, her eyes shined, and her face had colour. This person looked happy. And as she sat, staring in disbelief, it dawned on her who and what this person was. For the first time in her life, this person, Lotta Button, was loved.

She gulped and blinked and gulped and blinked as she stared at her phone screen and realised, as she sat in the corner of the bookshop wedged in between all manner of books in all shapes and sizes, that Jack had given her the one thing she'd never had in her life. He simply loved her. Her mother had never had the capacity to love anyone, and certainly not Lotta. Dan, her ex-partner, had most definitely not loved her, and really except for Liv and Timmy, there had never been anyone that important in her life. But now the person staring back at her in the camera was a loved person. Someone whose whole aura was soft and glowing. It was so deliciously good, it was quite spellbinding. Lotta sat that way for ages, hugging the knowledge tight.

An hour and a half later, Lotta had spent the most delightful time not only surrounded by books but delving into them left, right and centre. She had six new books squeezed into both her book bag and a carrier bag, and she was on the way back out to meet Liv.

Liv was standing on the corner of the pavement, just along from the bookshop by a lovely old London pub. Lotta walked up and hugged her in greeting, 'Hi.'

'Hey, how was it in there?' Liv asked, pointing to the bookshop. 'As good as you remember?'

Lotta smiled in response, 'Better. My gosh, that place makes other shops look like amateurs. I don't know how but it's like you go into another zone in there.'

'No, *you* do.' Liv laughed. 'Other people just walk around normally and buy a few books.'

'Maybe.'

'Other people do not have book fantasies like you.'

'Oh yes, they do.' Lotta giggled.

'Nope.'

'They do, Liv! Why do you think people want to get married in a library? Why do you think bookshops are so popular? It's not just me.'

'I'm not saying that. I'm saying that other people do not go into a higher state and do that funny sniffing thing when they walk in the door as you do. Sorry, Lott, I've never seen anyone do that.'

Lotta wrinkled up her nose. 'What?'

'You did it, didn't you? I know you did.'

'What?'

'When you walked in, you inhaled deeply and said to yourself that you loved the bookshop smell.'

Lotta chuckled. She'd done exactly that, but not only that, she'd added that that particular shop had the best smell. 'I might have done.'

'Nuts.'

'That's why you love me.'

Liv slotted her arm into Lotta's. 'Correct.'

Lotta looked at the time on her phone. 'We'd better get going.'

'I've been waiting for this day for a very long time.' Liv sighed. 'I'm so looking forward to it.'

Lotta wasn't quite as enthusiastic. She would happily have asked Liv to pick the dress up for her so that she could spend longer in the bookshop. No matter. 'Hmm, me too,' she lied.

Liv stopped. 'Lott! You're doing that casual voice. You totally would have preferred to stay with the books, wouldn't you?'

'No, no,' Lotta breezed.

'I know that voice,' Liv admonished. 'You're a nightmare.'

'Well, I mean it isn't as if I don't know what the dress is like. It's the green one but longer and in white.'

'That's not the point. This is a *momentous* occasion. Up there with one of the big five things in life. Hang on.' Liv rummaged in her bag, whipped out her phone, and held it up in front of them. 'Selfie. I'm going to document this even if you're not that bothered about it.'

Lotta beamed into the camera. 'I love you, Liv. Thank you for being here for me.'

Liv put the phone down and smiled. 'Of course.' She then frowned. 'You okay?'

'Yeah, yeah, I'm fine. It's just something that happened in the bookshop.'

'What?'

'Nothing major. It was just that as I walked around, I realised how sad I used to be when I lived up here. Like my soul was sad, you know?'

A cloud crossed Liv's face. 'Despicable Dan does that to a girl.'

Lotta frowned. 'I was depressed, wasn't I?'

'I guess you were.'

'I'm sorry you had to deal with that.'

'Don't be ridiculous! You're not apologising for that.'

'No, I mean it. I looked at myself in that bookshop. I actually *look* like a different person, not just feel like one.'

'You do. You're not wrong about that. I love you, whoever you are, though. Warts and all. Weird bookshop fetishes and all. And I cannot wait for you to marry Jack.'

Lotta glowed. 'Same, Liv. Same.'

34

Lotta strolled through the garden with her cleaning bucket hooked over her left arm and the vacuum in the other. When she'd got back home from Houston and regrouped both herself and her new business, she'd reopened the reading retreat again and had been more than surprised when, almost straight away, bookings had come in. It was as if making it unavailable for a bit had driven up demand. As she hustled through the garden looking at the old building, she sighed. After weeks without even the chance of visitors because of her trip to both Singapore and then Houston, the little place felt somehow bereft. But with a new booking for a couple of best friends wanting to spend the whole weekend reading the latest release from their favourite author, Lotta was determined to make everything perfect and to get her side business going again.

Unlocking the door, she smiled as she looked around. Tiny specks of dust particles swirled in the sunshine streaming in through the windows, and with fresh eyes, she saw the place in a whole new light. It was gorgeous. Gorgeous and needing to be cleaned.

Putting her bucket down and rolling up her sleeves, she took off all the cushions from the sofa, plugged in the vacuum, and started to work the nozzle back and forth over the seat cushions. The sofa had only been sat on a few times – she was going to do it anyway. As she worked her way around the room, she thought about how the little place had helped her move forward with her life. She'd thrown herself into it with the hope that it would help pay off her credit card debt or what was actually her ex's debt. She didn't really care whose it was now, all she knew was that she wanted well rid. And now, she could see that in the long term, the reading retreat would help her achieve that goal.

Humming along to the radio as she worked, Lotta scrubbed and polished until there wasn't a speck of dirt anywhere. She plumped the cushions on the sofa, lining them up just so, and arranged little piles of carefully curated books here, there and everywhere. Fresh flowers went on the coffee table, a stack of crisp towels was neatly folded in the bathroom, and lavender diffusers filled the rooms with scent. A basket of L'Occitane wrapped soaps went beside the bath, a fresh-scented candle was ready to be lit, and a pile of washcloths sat next to the sink. Once clean linens were on the bed, and the kitchen was shining. Lotta filled the fridge; locally-made cheeses sat on a wooden board, milk filled a vintage glass milk bottle, a pack of bacon was ready to be opened, and eggs in a white china egg carton took pride of place. No stone was left unturned.

Lotta nodded to herself. The reading retreat had been a lot of work to get off the ground. It was also not a mean feat to get it ready for visitors, but as she did a final check, she realised that right before her eyes, she'd created the place she'd always dreamed about staying in but had never been able to find. Her little touches were the icing on the cake, creating a sanctuary where guests could, should they so wish, hibernate and read to their hearts' content. A bookworm's heaven.

Lotta stood in the pebbled courtyard of the reading retreat, and on hearing a car outside the gate, she went outside. She waved as a little blue Citroen puttered up towards the house and parked on the verge. Assuming that the car was her guest, Hailey, Lotta smiled. Hailey emerged from the car, brushing her fringe out of her eyes, and grinned at Lotta. 'Hi, I'm Hailey. Sorry, I'm late. The traffic was chocka getting into Pretty Beach. Is it always like that?'

'No worries at all. I'm Lotta. Sorry about the traffic – no, not always. There's a boat carnival this weekend. I should have mentioned it in my email.'

'Well, I'm here now. My friend is coming via the train,' Hailey said, letting out a huge sigh. 'I am so pleased I'm here. Downtime has officially arrived.'

'Busy life?' Lotta asked.

'Ahh, you know what it's like. I work in the media. Always some drama or another.' Hailey rolled her eyes and then looked down towards the retreat. 'Honestly, this place looks like heaven. Just what the doctor ordered. It was a friend of a friend who recommended it. Emily.'

Lotta felt a little surge of pride. Her first guest Emily had been the same in her response to the place, but Lotta was still nervous about how it would go down. If Emily had recommended it, Lotta must have done something right. 'Ahh, yes, Emily. She had a nice relaxing time, I think. This place will sort you out. The air here is fabulous.'

Hailey looked over towards the sea and then turned towards the vintage umbrella in the corner of the courtyard. 'From what I can see so far, I'm not leaving. Ever. You'll have to force me out.'

Lotta laughed as she led Hailey over towards the door. 'Okay, do you want me to give you a guided tour? Or let you be?'

Hailey slipped her shoes off by the mat. 'I think I'll be fine, actually.'

'Great. You said you were here for a book release, is that right?'

'Yes. The latest in a trilogy. It's dropping at midnight. We're staying up for it,' Hailey said with shining eyes. 'Don't worry about us, though, we'll be as quiet as mice.'

'Sounds glorious. What else have you got planned?'

'Zilch. That's why we liked the look of this place. We plan to sleep, eat, read, and go for walks. That's about it. My life has been so busy recently, I've forgotten what it's like to stop.'

'I hear you,' Lotta replied. 'Well, you're in the right place.'

Hailey sighed. 'Yes, it looks that way. I can't bear to be away from work sometimes, but once I get away, it's lovely. Now all I need to do is unwind.'

'Sounds like you deserve it. You'll definitely get nice walks and recharge time here,' Lotta stated firmly as she turned and pointed up towards the cliffs. 'The best walk is up to the lighthouse. It's breathtaking, honestly. The views are spectacular all the way along the coast.'

'Brilliant. We might do that this afternoon then once my friend Louise arrives.'

Lotta stood on the doorstep of the retreat and pointed into the house. 'There's a document on the iPad with some of my favourite walks around Pretty Beach. The cliffs are stunning, but if you fancy something a bit flatter, head to Princess Pier. It's very pretty in the evening, too, with all the lights.'

Hailey frowned. 'Princess Pier? Ooh, that sounds nice! What's there?'

'It's an old pleasure pier which has recently been completely renovated. It makes for a delightful evening stroll. You can get fish and chips or ice cream, sit on a bench and just watch the waves and all the lights on the water.'

'Sounds perfect,' Hailey said. 'I think we'll head that way tomorrow.'

Lotta pointed down the road that led into Pretty Beach. 'Just go down along there and once you stroll through to the other side, you can walk all the way along the promenade to the pier. Oh, and on the way back, stop by the funicular railway. It's a cliffside lift that opened in the 1880s. Still runs today. Honestly, it's amazing.'

'A funicular railway, how divine!' Hailey exclaimed. 'Sounds like this place is full of hidden gems.'

Lotta smiled, very pleased inside that the attractions of Pretty Beach were at her disposal. 'Too many to discover in one weekend. You'll have to come back again!'

Hailey laughed. 'At this rate, you won't be able to get rid of me! Right, sounds like we're going to have a lovely weekend – the book release, a stroll to the pier, some al fresco fish and chips, a ride on the funicular and maybe an ice cream if we're lucky.'

'Enjoy the book.' Lotta chuckled. 'Let me know if you need anything. I'm always here to help.'

'I will, but I doubt you'll hear a peep from us.' Hailey grinned. 'The recharging starts now.'

Lotta waved as she turned and headed back to the house and smiled broadly to herself. The retreat had another visitor, and Pretty Beach was weaving its magic on her guests. Just as it had done her.

35

It had been a fairly uneventful journey to the florist in Oxford to talk about wedding flowers, and Lotta had spent most of it with her nose in a book. Once she and Jack had arrived in Oxford itself after navigating gridlocked traffic, they'd been for a coffee and were walking along a narrow back street, making their way to a florist Lotta had originally come across by way of Pinterest. From the pictures she'd spent way too long studying, and the reviews, the florist promised to be amazing. She'd booked an appointment, had a chat with one of the florists on the phone, and was looking forward to having them as part of the wedding.

After getting lost in the puzzle of backstreets, they finally arrived at the tiny shop, and Lotta gazed across the road in delight. She clutched Jack's arm. 'Wow, it's better in real life than it looked on Instagram. It's so sweet! Like something from a book. Just what I wanted. Yes, yes, yes.'

She stopped for a second at the little shop tucked away on the other side of the winding cobblestone street. Outside, an antique table struggled under the weight of galvanised buckets bursting with peonies in the palest blush, and an old-fashioned sign swung above the door. The whole exterior of the tiny shop was painted a soft ballet-slipper pink, and matte gold embellishments wound around the windows and door. A pale pink Dutch canopy swooped over the length of the building, peppered with pink paper lanterns that danced in the breeze coming up the street.

Jack smiled as Lotta jigged up and down in excitement. 'It's right up your street, Lott. I can see why it comes so highly recommended. Let's just hope it's as good on the inside as it is out here.'

Lotta squeezed Jack's hand. 'Oh, I think it will be. I have a good feeling about this place.'

They crossed the street in anticipation, and as Lotta pushed the door, she gasped – the inside of the shop was even better than what had greeted them on the pavement outside. Pale oyster pink-washed walls were lined with shelves displaying vases, ribbons and hundreds of jugs. Masses of bunches of upside-down dried flowers were gathered on the ceiling, and a round wooden table in the centre held blooms of every colour, scenting the air with a heady fragrance.

A woman emerged from a door at the back of the shop, wearing a fluttery floral dress and an apron. 'You must be Lotta and Jack,' she beamed, hurrying forward to shake their hands vigorously. 'Thrilled to have you. I'm Cath, head florist here at Poppies. You're in luck, you got landed with me.' She laughed at her own joke. 'I'll keep you out of trouble.'

'Hi,' Lotta said, gazing around in wonder. 'The shop is gorgeous. Thanks for having us.' She heard herself gushing.

Cath laughed. 'Thank you! It's an experience, not a flower shop. That's what I like to tell people.'

'Yes, I saw that on your Insta page. It's what had me sold.' Lotta chuckled and looked around. 'It's certainly living up to the pictures.'

'I mean, you're getting married and choosing your flowers. It needs to be gorgeous. That's what I always say,' Cath noted with a glint in her eye. 'Weddings need to be special all the way through in my book.'

'Totally,' Lotta said as she leaned into a pink rose and inhaled deeply. 'Wow.'

Cath beckoned. 'Rightio, come on through.'

Lotta and Jack followed Cath through the shop to a small area to the left behind a counter. Lotta looked around with her chin on the floor. This was not your average florist's run-of-the-mill bridal appointment. It was as if they were in the pages of one of Lotta's books.

Cath proceeded to make a pot of tea, a two-tier homemade carrot cake arrived on the table, and tiny vintage glasses of water topped with edible flowers were dished out. Cath busied around chatting and asking questions, and then a large iPad on a stand came to life, showcasing a presentation of different types of bouquets. After a few minutes and by way of elimination, Lotta was quickly and expertly led to exactly the bouquet she liked. She'd walked in with not really a clue about what she wanted. By the time the tea had been drunk and cake eaten, her dream bouquet was done and dusted. Even Jack was impressed.

Once Cath had quickly ascertained that Lotta wanted a jumble of pale pink roses in an oversized, soft hand-tied posy, Lotta moved on to the next thing. She pulled the green fascinator from a bag and presented it to Cath with a flourish. 'This is the hair thing I was emailing about.'

Cath chuckled, studying the fascinator with a bemused expression. 'I think I've seen it all now. Phew, that's huge.'

'I want to somehow incorporate this.' Lotta gestured at the fascinator eagerly.

Cath frowned, brows furrowing. 'Green to go with the dress and pink flowers?'

'No, no, sorry, I meant the look of this.' Lotta pointed at the arrangement of feathers and netting on top of the hairband.

'Right.' Cath turned the fascinator over in her hands, assessing its potential. 'You're wanting the same flowers in your hair as the bouquet, I presume? It might be too heavy.'

'I don't really know.' Lotta shrugged.

'Hmm.' Cath tapped her lip, deep in thought.

'It's just that this fascinator was there when we met. It's part of our story, as it were. I was sitting at a bar and it bumped into Jack. I wanted to somehow incorporate it.' Lotta smiled at the memory of her sitting at the bar with her Kindle.

'Shouldn't be too much of a problem,' Cath noted with a decisive nod. 'I did something similar, gosh what must be ten years ago now. A jumble of flowers and petals. How will your hair be?'

Lotta hadn't thought a huge amount about her hair. 'Soft updo or curls.'

'Too easy.' Cath smiled, clearly formulating ideas.

'I was just wondering if I can just, you know, leave it with you.' Lotta shrugged, smiling.

'Said no bride ever.' Cath laughed, waving a hand.

'Not me. I'll leave it totally in your capable hands.'

Cath gathered the fascinator, turning it over once more with a practised eye. 'You won't be disappointed.'

Lotta sighed in relief. The visit to the florist meant that everything for the wedding was more or less sorted. Once they had decided on the venue, it had all been quite straightforward.

Cath sliced another piece of carrot cake and passed it over to Jack. 'A pink flower crown. I wish they were all like you and wanted to leave it to me.' Cath chuckled.

As Lotta looked back through the little shop, she was sure that Cath would do a fabulous job. It was as if the whole place had somehow weaved its own kind of magic as they'd sat totally surrounded by blooms, drinking cups of tea and eating cake.

Lotta felt a sigh of inner relief as another thing in the library wedding of dreams was ticked off. It was all going swimmingly well, but most of all, she couldn't wait to marry Jack.

36

A few weeks or so after the florist appointment, everything with the wedding was sorted. The fact that the occasion was a very small and modest affair, meant they'd not had to beat to the drum of availability, and everything had slotted together nicely without any problems.

Lotta's life and world had slipped back into a lovely regularity, one she cherished after the chaos of Jack's accident and her mum. She'd had two stays at the reading retreat, both of which had resulted in repeat bookings and recommendations. The winner of her retreat weekend competition was booked in to stay and the retreat was slowly starting to gain momentum. Her book review work was coming in thick and fast, and she'd spent most, if not all, of her spare time ticking wedding boxes or dealing with her ever-growing TBR pile.

She was at work after a very full day where she'd been shadowing Marie and her events, and if anything could have gone wrong, it had done. It had been one of those strange manic times where the day had flung itself from one disaster to the next. As she stood in the kitchen making a cup of tea, Lotta's mind was a whir, going over the day's events. The balls of her feet were on fire, and it felt as if someone had tightened a band around her forehead.

It was way past lunch and afternoon tea, and Lotta was so ravenous she could have eaten the teapot itself. She grabbed her sandwich from the fridge, put it and the cup of tea down on the table, sat down and eased her heels from her shoes. She loved her job, but they certainly got their money's worth when the days were full of problems. At least it stopped her mind from thinking about anything else.

As she stopped herself from hoovering up the sandwich too fast, she stared at the coffee table, and her mind moved from her day to what was going on in her life. She frowned to herself as she thought about Jack and his manner that morning. He'd been quiet and distant as he'd dropped her off at work, and she hadn't liked it at all. The more she thought about it, the more she had to admit that he'd not been right for a few weeks. She couldn't put her finger on why. He'd been quite short with her a few times, snappy even, and she put it down to his ongoing convalescence.

Squinting, she tried to pinpoint when she'd first noticed Jack acting strangely. Once she actually stopped and thought about it properly, she realised that the signs had been there for a while, she'd just chosen not to see them. As she pondered Jack, she suddenly put her sandwich down as a thought came to her. Perhaps he was having cold feet about the wedding. It was really the only thing she could put his distance and moodiness down to. There had been a few things that had happened, and the more she thought about it, the more she realised with clarity that they were big old red flags waving at her.

She nodded to herself as she went over a few times she'd sensed Jack wasn't quite right. The first thing she'd spotted was he hadn't really wanted to talk too much about where they were going on their honeymoon. In actual fact, he'd been quite unexcited about it. When she'd shown him a video showcasing a hotel in Venice, he'd sighed and turned back to the football. Then he'd been really busy at work. Not that that was unusual, just that he'd stayed away just a few more times than normal. He'd also had some very early starts and corresponding early nights. More than that, though, overall, he'd simply seemed withdrawn. Lotta had even casually mentioned it to Jack's sister, but she'd said she hadn't noticed anything at all.

Lotta turned it over and over in her head and went cold. Of course. Maybe the whole plane proposal was a knee-jerk reaction to what had happened to him in Houston. Now that he was home, he was regretting the proposal, and this was his way of dealing with it.

She looked down at the solitaire diamond on her hand, fiddled with it so that it was centred on her finger, and held her hand out in front of her. She frowned as she surveyed the ring and thought about the plane proposal. It had been a lot of effort to go to for someone not one hundred per cent certain.

Lotta sighed heavily and took a sip of her tea, feeling the warmth spread through her chest. The more she thought about it, the more she was concerned that Jack was having second thoughts about their wedding. It was unsettling, to say the least. She'd been so caught up in the excitement and the pure self-indulgent romance of it all and swept off her feet by the proposal, that she hadn't stopped to consider that for the past few weeks, he had been not himself. She'd not read the writing on the wall.

As she finished her sandwich, Lotta pondered his behaviour and mulled it over a bit more. On second thoughts, was she obsessing? She didn't want to jump to conclusions and create an issue where there might not be one. Jack had been through a lot, and he was very busy at work. Maybe it was just that.

She tidied up her plate and mug and took a deep breath,

gathering her thoughts. She reminded herself of the effort that must have gone into the proposal. Surely he wouldn't have done that if he wasn't genuinely committed to their future together. She nodded her head, trying to convince herself. He was clearly just a bit nervous. Not one for fuss, he was probably over all the preparation. Plus, he'd flung himself back into work since coming back from Houston. Also, he was tired. Yep, that was it.

With that thought in mind, Lotta decided that she was likely overthinking the situation. She would keep an eye on things but not jump to conclusions or make assumptions. Trying to convince herself but not feeling that reassured, she went back to her desk, turned on her computer, and tried to focus on work. Just as she was finishing off writing up the post-event notes, Marie bustled in. She stopped short when she caught sight of Lotta's expression, her brow creased with the events of the day. 'What a day! Everything okay with you? Goodness, I'm shattered!'

Lotta glanced up and offered a weak smile. 'Yeah, I'm okay. I'm just getting stuff written up now. I can tell you one thing, I'm glad I was shadowing on that. Phew.'

Marie chuckled and rolled her eyes. 'I need a long soak in a deep bath or a bottle of wine. Maybe both. Could anything else have gone wrong today?'

'It sure was coming at us thick and fast. That bloke who complained about the height of the table. I mean, really?' Lotta shook her head in disbelief. 'Some people have way too much time on their hands.'

'Yup, I wanted to deck him.' Marie clenched her fist in frustration. 'I don't want another day like that for a long time.'

Lotta sighed, rubbing her temples. 'Nightmare.'

Marie frowned. 'Are you sure you're okay? You seem a bit off-colour.'

'Just got a few things on my mind.' Lotta fiddled with a pen on her desk.

Marie leaned in closer, her eyes filled with genuine concern. 'Sorry, have I done something to upset you?'

Lotta hesitated, her fingers tapping nervously on her desk. 'Ahh, no, it's nothing, really. Nothing to do with work.'

'I'm all ears.' Marie smiled.

'Well, it's just... I don't know.' Before she knew what she was doing, Lotta had blurted it out. 'I think Jack's been acting a bit off lately.' Lotta bit her lip, looking down.

Marie frowned, placing a comforting hand on Lotta's arm. 'Off? How?'

Lotta sighed, brushing a stray strand of hair behind her ear. 'I don't know if he's distant or something. I'm worried he might be having second thoughts about the wedding.'

'Distant?'

'Yeah, as I was sitting here eating my sandwich, I realised that it's been the last few weeks.'

'Have you talked to him about it?'

'No,' Lotta admitted, shaking her head. 'I don't want to jump to conclusions, you know? Maybe I'm just overthinking it.'

Marie nodded thoughtfully. 'It's probably just a few pre-wedding nerves.'

'I suppose so.'

'Maybe it's worth talking to him.'

Lotta bit her lip, considering Marie's words. 'I don't know. The time doesn't quite feel right. You know?'

'Hmm, tricky one. He has been through a lot.'

'I know. I just thought maybe we've jumped into all of this too quickly.'

'Are *you* the one having second thoughts?' Marie frowned.

'Goodness, no! At least, I don't think so. But it has been very quick, and he's been through a huge trauma.'

'You both have.'

'Hmm. Yeah. Anyway…' Lotta trailed off.

'You'll work it out. I'm sure he's fine.'

Lotta smiled gratefully at Marie. She felt a little lighter now after sharing her concerns, but there was something in the back of her mind chipping away at her. A little voice that was telling her that something with Jack wasn't right. She wasn't sure if he was fine at all.

37

The following weekend Lotta strolled along the coastal path next to Liv on the way to Pretty Beach lighthouse. The sea breeze carried the tang of salt in the air, and puffy white clouds scudded across a deep blue sky. The waves crashing onto the beach below accompanied their walk, gulls danced overhead, salty sea breeze whipped through their hair, and sunshine glinted off the lighthouse in the distance.

Lotta shoved her hands in the pockets of her jeans and sighed. Liv glanced over, concern creasing her brow. 'You're very quiet today.'

'I'm fine,' Lotta said breezily, forcing her face into a big smile.

Liv shook her head and tutted. 'You're doing the casual voice. I knew something was wrong.'

'I'm not. Honestly.'

'Don't even try to deny it,' Liv said, exasperated. 'You seem so out of sorts the last few times we've chatted. What's wrong?'

Lotta bit her lip and hesitated for a moment before responding. 'I don't know. I can't seem to shake these weird feelings lately.'

'What sort of weird feelings?'

Lotta stumbled over her words, not sure what to say. 'I don't know.'

'Wedding jitters?' Liv picked a leaf and twirled it around in her fingers.

'Maybe.' Lotta scuffed the toe of her shoe against a rock, sending it skittering over the edge of the cliff. 'Anyway, everything's fine.'

'It's so not. Don't even try to pretend. You know I pick up on things with you, especially when you're doing the acting casual and breezy thing. Just admit it.'

Tears suddenly stung at the corners of Lotta's eyes as she nodded. 'I'm just so worried about everything.'

'Like what? Everything's sorted with the wedding. All we have to do is wait for the big day.'

Lotta decided to tell Liv. Since she'd mentioned Jack's distance to Marie at work, she'd decided to try and bury it, but it hadn't really worked. 'Jack's been acting strangely, and I'm not sure what to do. I'm worried. I'm really worried. He seems distant, like he's pulling away. I can't put my finger on why.'

Liv stopped, turning to face Lotta with a frown. 'Has he said something?'

Lotta shook her head. 'That's the problem. He hasn't said *anything*. It's like he doesn't want to discuss the wedding. What if he's having second thoughts?' Her voice broke. 'He must be. It's the only thing I can put it down to.'

'Oh, dear,' Liv said as they sat down on a nearby bench overlooking the lighthouse.

Lotta sighed, glad that she'd told Liv, releasing the doubts she'd bottled up.

Liv made a wincing sound and shook her head. 'I'm sure it's just pre-wedding apprehension.'

'Come on though, Liv. Is that really a thing? It's not. Not if you're our age and you're sure.'

'I think so. Remember James?'

Lotta shook her head and frowned. 'No, actually, I don't.'

'He was the opposite. He went all strange and nervy. He was running around like a headless chicken. Remember, he was driving everyone nuts with the planning and organisation. Surely you remember the email about the backup weather contingency plan that not only included a rain plan but an extreme heat version. Like we were going to get that in the English countryside. You must remember he bought all that sunscreen from Boots.'

Lotta screwed up her nose. 'Oh, yeah, he did too! Ha ha. He couldn't sit still either.'

'Maybe this is Jack's way. It's a huge thing to be getting married.'

Lotta shrugged. 'Maybe.'

'You have had a lot on your plate, too. It's been a whirlwind,' Liv acknowledged.

'I know.' Lotta sighed. 'I've questioned myself that maybe we've been too hasty.'

Liv raised an eyebrow. 'It has been very quick.'

'It has.' Lotta looked at the ground, her hands in her pockets. 'I threw myself into it because, well, because of what happened to him. You don't know what's around the corner. He could have died.'

'No, true,' Liv agreed, looking out towards the horizon.

'Ahh!'

Liv glanced at her, concerned. 'Have you thought about postponing the wedding, just for a few months?'

Lotta gazed at the lighthouse, deep in thought. 'You think that would help?'

Liv squeezed her arm. 'I don't know. Just a suggestion. It would give you a chance to breathe and talk properly. Make sure you're both on the same page before the big day.'

Lotta turned to Liv with a watery smile. 'Maybe I've just got too caught up in all the planning and lost sight of what really matters. The thing is, I thought we *were* on the same page. Surely that's the whole point.'

'Maybe just take a step back from the wedding planning for a bit. Give yourself some time to think about what's really important to you and what you want.'

Lotta raised her eyebrows, considering Liv's advice. 'You might be right, Liv. I've been so wrapped up in everything that I haven't given myself a chance to breathe. Then there was the streaming of the funeral. That was massive for me. There's been one thing after another. He's probably feeling the same way.'

Liv smiled encouragingly, gently squeezing Lotta's shoulder. 'Once you've cleared your head, you might feel better.'

'I know what I want,' Lotta asserted, splaying her hands out in front of her. 'I want more than anything to marry Jack. It's not like I'm the one having second thoughts.'

'No, no, but you have had a lot going on.' Liv gestured with her hands. 'I mean, your mum. Have you even processed that?'

Lotta furrowed her brow. 'What?'

'Not being funny, but it's like you've completely brushed it under the carpet,' Liv pointed out, her tone gentle.

'Have I?' Lotta looked away, biting her lip.

'You've not even said a word about it,' Liv continued. 'Have you even dealt with the grief?'

'I guess I haven't,' Lotta admitted, her voice barely above a whisper. She knew precisely what she'd done; run away, not thought about it, and focused on other things.

'Plus, you've had what happened to Jack and then boom, you're back here and full on into planning a quick wedding.' Liv shook her head. 'It's all too much in a way.'

'You're right.' Lotta sighed, realising the truth in Liv's words.

'Maybe it's just all been too fast,' Liv suggested softly.

'Hmm.' Lotta nodded in agreement, her gaze fixed on the distant waves. She took a deep breath, inhaling the fresh sea air, and gazed up at the lighthouse. Maybe Liv was right.

38

It was a while since Lotta had voiced her concerns about Jack to Liv. Rather than things getting better with him, though, the opposite had happened. There had been a couple of occasions where both Jack's manner and his actions had convinced Lotta that something was not only wrong with him but *very* wrong with him.

Lotta had decided to go for a walk to try and clear her head. So she'd popped an audiobook in her ears and was winding her way through Pretty Beach. The sun warmed her face as she strolled along the main streets, lifting her spirits as she soaked up her surroundings. She smiled at the row of pastel-coloured shops lining the laneway painted in shades of soft pink, baby blue, and pale yellow. She gazed at the overflowing hanging baskets spilling with petunias and geraniums, adding pops of colour to the street, and looked up at the bunting fluttering overhead in the sea breeze. As she strolled underneath its criss-crossed layers, it seemingly celebrated the best of the weather perfectly. It did not in any shape or form reflect her mood.

Outside the bakery, a queue of customers snaked from the open door, where people strolled out with coffee in hand and bread tucked under their arms as they enjoyed the pleasant weather. The mingled aromas of fresh bread, sunshine, cinnamon, and roasted coffee beans filled the air as Lotta ambled along with her book playing in her ears. Every few steps, she passed oversized white pots filled with healthy palms, and outside the local café Maisy's, every table was taken with people sitting in the sunshine.

As Lotta strolled along, she could see a sliver of turquoise at the end of the street, the waves sparkling under the sun. Though she tried to focus, she couldn't quite concentrate on the story filling her ears. Instead of losing herself in the rom-com playing, worries about Jack filled her mind. Her agitated state was almost in direct contrast to the seemingly chilled and carefree people enjoying the sights, and cheerful surroundings of the unhurried pace of Pretty Beach life unfolding around her.

As Lotta wandered past the post office and chemist, she noticed what were now becoming familiar faces – Suntanned Pete was standing chatting to a woman in a sari, and Clemmie, who had helped with the working bee on Lotta's garden, waved from the other side of the road. Lotta might have had turbulent thoughts going around her head, but as she waved back to Clemmie, her heart swelled at being recognised. As she walked along, she finally gave up and turned off her audiobook, pulled out her earphones, and let the little town by the sea do its thing. About fifteen minutes later, she was calmer and a little less tightly wound, even though she was still thinking about Jack.

As she arrived at the ferry wharf, she spotted a familiar face in the distance. Xian, owner of the local bakery, was sitting on a bench near the ferry terminal with a huge checked laundry bag, nearly as big as she was, sitting on her lap.

Approaching the bench, Lotta smiled. 'Hi, Xian. How are you? It's a beautiful day, isn't it? The laneway was heaving with people.'

Xian returned Lotta's smile, her eyes crinkling with warmth.

'Indeed, it is a stunner of a day. Long time no see.' Xian patted the bench. 'Come, sit down with me and enjoy the view.'

Lotta gratefully accepted and plonked herself down next to Xian. 'What are you doing here, sitting on your own?' Lotta asked.

'I'm on my way to play bridge,' Xian replied, pulling a silver flask out of the laundry bag, pressing it to her lips and swigging it quickly. 'Holly just dropped me off early so I could sit and watch the water for a bit. It's good to sit here and observe the goings on of the world. It does wonders for one's state of mind.'

Lotta's gaze followed Xian's to the ebb and flow of the water as a ferry bobbed out of the harbour. Seagulls swooped and dived overhead, their calls mingling with the rumble of the ferry's engine. 'Not a bad spot,' Lotta noted.

For a moment, they sat in comfortable silence, people watching and observing another ferry come in from the opposite direction. Lotta could feel the weight of her thoughts pressing down on her. Xian seemed to read her mind as she peered at Lotta, her brow crinkling. 'You look worried. Anything this old chicken can help with? Is something bothering you? A problem shared and all that.'

Lotta hesitated, but before she knew what she was doing, she found herself telling Xian all about Jack. As she confided her doubts, Xian listened attentively, nodding every now and then. When Lotta finished, Xian patted her hand gently. 'You've had a lot going on by the sounds of it.'

Lotta ran her fingers through her hair, anxiety creasing her forehead. 'I know. It's been quite the ride the last few months.'

Xian nodded, her eyes full of understanding. 'That terrible business in Houston. That's a lot to deal with for anyone. It will take a long time to get over that if you ask me. You mark my words.'

Lotta sighed, looking down at her hands. 'I know. My cousin Liv said the same thing.'

Xian leaned back on the bench, crossing her ankles and resting her hands on top of the laundry bag. 'It could be Jack dealing with the trauma of it all. Making him a bit distant.'

Lotta frowned, her fingers fiddling with the hem of her shirt. 'He says he's fine.'

Xian chuckled softly. 'I bet he does. That's probably his way of not wanting to admit it. Strange how we all say we're fine when a lot of the time we're actually not.'

Lotta looked out at the water, her gaze distant. 'I've thought about maybe postponing the wedding if it's that that's bothering him. When he proposed, I just went a bit gung-ho about it. Maybe I should have waited and given us both a bit of time to get used to the idea.'

Xian shrugged, her eyes following a seagull as it soared above them. 'Ahh, no time like the present sometimes.'

Lotta bit her lip and gazed at the churning wake from a departing ferry. 'I'm just so afraid that if we postpone the wedding, something else might happen.' Her voice trembled slightly. 'It was awful in Houston.'

Xian smiled softly, her eyes full of wisdom, and she took a quick swig of the flask. 'What will be will be, as they say. You can't make things go right or wrong, for that matter. That's what I've learnt in all my years.'

As people bustled around them, boarding and disembarking, a ferry horn sounded. Lotta sighed. 'I suppose so. I just don't know what to do.'

'Have you said anything to him about it? Have you mentioned that you've noticed he's distant?'

'I just haven't been able to find the words. Every single time I've gone to say something, I've bottled it. I know, yes, pathetic is the word.'

'You just have to either get on with it or ask him outright. No point dwelling on it forever. My advice would be to talk to him,' Xian said gently. 'Speak honestly, even if it's hard. The wedding can always wait.'

'You think?' Lotta asked, squeezing the thumb and forefinger of her right hand into the corners of her eyes.

'I don't think, trust me, from experience, I *know*. You'll just obsess and go around and around in circles, not knowing what's really going on. It probably has nothing to do with the wedding. If you mention it, at least you'll know one way or the other.'

'Thank you, Xian,' Lotta murmured, feeling a weight lifted off her shoulders. 'Yes, I do need to just come out with it and ask him precisely what is going on.'

Xian patted her hand. 'Let me tell you. I don't think Jack would have proposed like that if he hadn't meant it.'

Lotta nodded in agreement. But deep down, she wasn't really sure if Xian was correct.

39

The next day, the morning sun streamed through the tall windows of the library room, casting a warm glow on Lotta's desk and books. Lotta sat on the velvet sofa with her legs crossed and her phone propped up on an old wine box on the coffee table, preparing to begin a live on her Insta account. She took a deep breath as she looked around the room, watching the sunlight play on the spines of the books and tried to focus.

As she logged in, she quickly went over her notes on her latest book review and made sure the book was to hand. Her mind was far from the book, though, and all she could think about was Jack's strange distant behaviour and Xian and Liv's advice. She needed to stop dicking around, talk to Jack, and get it out in the open. She knew it and so did the little voice in the back of her head.

As she glanced around the room, taking in the familiar surroundings; the armchairs, the soft rug underfoot, and the beautiful blue velvet curtains, none of it really worked its usual magic to soothe her frazzled worry wort mind. She checked her appearance on her phone screen; angst was evident all over her face. Chilled and relaxed, she was not. The conversation with

Xian the day before was weighing heavily on her mind. As she sat, waiting for the time to tick over, she nodded to herself and decided that it was time to act. She was going to take the bull by the horns and go straight to Jack's after the live and ask him outright what was going on. When she'd first been going out with him, she'd obsessed about a pink jacket on the back of his office door – that had turned out to be nothing, but she'd let herself get tied up in all sorts of knots about it. As she stood staring at her phone, she attempted to reassure herself that this would probably be the same.

With a final adjustment of her hair and a reassuring smile, Lotta made a decision as she clicked the button to begin the live stream. She would get the review done and dusted, drive over to Jack's, and find out exactly what was going on. She was planning on going to his house later anyway, she'd just bring it forward. He'd said he was working from home all day, so she knew he would be in.

Once the book review was over, Lotta stood in the hallway of Pretty Beach to the Breakers, her bag open on the floor as she mentally ticked off what she was going to say to Jack. She'd decided that whatever happened, she was going to get what she was feeling out in the open. She was over the obsessing and constant churning in her head that deep down he regretted asking her to marry him. She'd been on the end of a man dictating her life and look how that had ended up. There was no way she was going to let it happen again.

After zipping her bag closed, she flicked through her phone to make sure she had an audiobook to accompany her on her drive and, after a moment's consideration, settled on a rom-com set in Spain. She hoped the tale of tans, sunshine, and sangria might be a welcome distraction and keep her from talking herself out of confronting Jack. She clicked to make sure the book was safely stored on her phone, unplugged her charger, put her sunglasses on her head, and grabbed her book bag and jacket. After giving the house a final once-over, ensuring everything was locked and satisfied that she had everything she needed, Lotta scooped up her keys and headed out the door, locking it securely behind her. As she climbed into her car and started the engine, she connected her phone to the car's sound system, scrolled through her audiobook library, and pressed play. The narrator's voice filled the car as she reversed off the drive. As she pulled away from her house, she was determined that by the end of the day, things would be clearer. One way or the other, she would know what was what with Jack. She might no longer be engaged, but she would also no longer be sitting on a shelf under the dark and dreary wing of Doubting Thomas.

By the time Lotta was barely out of Pretty Beach, she'd given up on the audiobook as her mind raced. The coastal road stretched out before her, winding around the cliffs as another lovely day, which did not reflect her clouded mind, shone brightly overhead. Lotta pressed the button on the steering wheel to turn off the audiobook, realising she couldn't focus on the story as thoughts of Jack swirled around in her head.

As she drove, a salty sea breeze blew in through the open car window bringing with it seagull squawks, the scent of seaweed, and a faint whiff of brine. Lotta kept her eyes glued to the coastal road, every now and then glimpsing to the right as the sea glittered, and to her left, a patchwork of fields and hills passed the window. As she got further and further away from Pretty Beach and closer and closer to Jack's place, the more her stomach churned. Every now and then, she passed through a small village, the narrow streets lined with whitewashed cottages and bustling cafés. The idyllic coastal country scenes contrasted sharply with the turmoil she felt inside.

Driving along with nothing much but silence, Lotta found herself reflecting on her relationship with Jack. She chuckled as she remembered when she'd vomited from food poisoning and he'd held a bin bag in front of her. She smiled at the first night he'd spent in the tiny bed just off the breakfast room in Pretty Beach to the Breakers. Memories flooded through her mind, and she felt sick at the thought of the phone call that had told her about the shooting in Houston. The more she thought about Jack and their relationship, the more she was almost sure she was obsessing. Clouded by uncertainty and fear, she'd let her mind imagine all sorts when the truth was that Jack was probably, as Liv had said, suffering from a few pre-nuptial nerves.

Another side of her was beside herself at the thought of Jack changing his mind, and everything she'd thought they were slipping through her fingers. A horrible nasty little voice chanted that Lotta Button was not getting married in the morning.

She took a deep breath, trying to steady her racing thoughts. She knew she had to get on with it, face the issue, and figure out what was going on. The thought of the difficult conversation made her heart heavy, but as she pressed down on the accelerator, she knew that by the end of the day, she would know where she and Jack stood.

~

After pulling up outside Jack's house, Lotta sat in the car for ages, just staring at the front door. His car was on the drive, and she was psyching herself up to go in and come right out with what was on her mind. Once on the doorstep, she put her key in the lock, slipped off her shoes, and called out. The house was deathly silent, and she could see through into both the sitting room and study that Jack wasn't in either of them. Padding across to the kitchen, she opened the door and walked in. As usual, it was immaculate with not a thing out of place. She walked over to the kettle, put her hand near it, and felt for heat. Stone cold.

After walking around the whole house, checking out the

garden, and peering into the garage and the car, Lotta whipped out her phone and messaged Jack.

Lotta: *Hey. What are you up to? xxx*

Jack: *Working.*

Lotta shook her head. Jack had told her the day before that he had intended to work from home. Maybe he'd gone into the office.

Lotta: *Where? In the office???*

Jack: *No. Why?*

Lotta: *Just wondering.*

Jack: *What time are you coming over later? Do you fancy a takeaway?*

Lotta: *Not sure. Where are you now?*

Jack: *At home.*

Boom. Lotta felt the ground tilt underneath her feet. She'd known something was wrong with Jack. Now she had the evidence to back up her suspicions and racing mind. Unless he was in the shed at the bottom of the garden, he was very much not at home. Lotta stared at her phone, heart pounding. Jack had lied to her as quickly and as casually as that. This was obviously the beginning of the end. She sank down onto the couch, queasy with the realisation that all her concerns, and what she'd tried to convince herself was just obsessing, were correct all along. Her phone pinged again.

Jack: *What are you up to?*

With shaking fingers, Lotta typed: *We need to talk.*

Lotta watched as the dots flashed. The pause before Jack's reply seemed endless, and her head swam.

Jack: *About what?*

Lotta squinted and suddenly she felt very, very angry. So angry it was as if pure red steam was pouring out of her nose, ears and anything else you care to imagine. Fury zipped around her body. She was not going to have this. It simply wasn't fair.

Another man was not going to do this to her. No way, José. Her thumbs flew over the phone keyboard.

Lotta: *About why you feel the need to LIE to me. I know you're not home.*

Lotta glared at her screen and waited in anticipation for another lie. An excuse, maybe. But none came. Instead, there was nothing. There were no flashing dots and no response. Her phone was as dead as a doornail. She gazed out the window to the garden as a bird on the lawn went about as normal, pecking at the grass, while her world tilted on its axis, and she began to shudder uncontrollably. She just sat at the kitchen island, staring out into the garden, looking back at the kettle, deciding on whether or not a cup of tea would help and simply not knowing how to behave or what to do. She'd been right all along. Jack had asked her to marry him as a knee-jerk reaction to getting shot, and now he was having second thoughts.

After fifteen minutes of staring at the kettle, her phone suddenly rang with Jack's number. She snatched it up and listened. He didn't even say hello. 'I'm sorry, I can explain…'

'Can you?' Lotta cut him off. Anger warred with angst as all her worries came crashing down around her ears. 'I've known something was wrong for ages, Jack. Now I find you outright lying to me. Do you want to call off the wedding? Just call it.'

Jack's voice sounded as she'd never heard it before. 'No! Of course not.' He seemed distressed. 'I just... I don't know. I should have told you the truth right from the beginning.'

Lotta wiped her eyes, wishing he was there so she could see his face. She really didn't have a clue what to think. 'The truth about what, Jack? Right now, I feel like I don't know you at all. If you don't want to go ahead with the wedding, at least have the decency to tell me. I mean, is this really how you treat someone? Just no. It's not right.'

Silence. Then, 'I've been going to see a counsellor.' Jack's voice was raw, filled with pain. 'I didn't want to ruin everything with the wedding planning. You were so excited and into it. It would have put a dampener on everything. Then there was Mum, she was so looking forward to everything. Yeah, so I just kept quiet.'

Lotta shook her head, not quite able to compute what he was saying, and she couldn't work out what was going on with his voice. 'What?'

'To deal with…' Jack paused for a second. 'With what happened in Houston. I didn't want you to know how much I've struggled. I thought I could handle it alone. I was fine at first. I was just pleased to get through it, but then I started to get flash-backs…' Jack's voice trailed off.

Lotta pressed her hand to her mouth, holding in a sob. Everything made sense now – his distance, the funny mood swings. It was all a misguided attempt to shield her when all she'd been concerned about was her own selfish needs and wants about a wedding in a library. Brat sprang to mind. 'Oh my god! I'm so sorry. I've been talking about nothing but the wedding! Why didn't you tell me?'

It was as if Jack was pouring anguish down the phone. 'I wasn't really sure what it was. I mean, I don't *do* not coping. The doctor said a few counselling sessions would sort it. So I thought, why bother to make an issue of it? I thought I'd just go along, deal with it and put a lid on it once I'd seen someone.'

'The doctor? What do you mean, doctor?'

'Yeah, I went to the GP when I had that nightmare. Remember? Not long after we first got back.'

Lotta closed her eyes. 'You said you were fine! I told you you weren't. I feel awful. Terrible. I knew you weren't right all along.' Lotta's heart ached. She'd been too busy flitting her head through libraries and weddings, peonies and floral fascinators. 'I can't believe how selfish and self-centred I've been. You were recuperating from a terrible thing and all I could talk about was books and dresses. Bloody hell, Jack!'

A shaky sigh, then, 'You haven't been selfish. I tried to hide it. I didn't want to ruin things.'

Lotta wiped tears away from the corners of her eyes with her cuff. 'Don't be ridiculous. Jack, you got shot! In a mall! You threw yourself in front of a pram. That's pretty huge from where I'm standing.'

'I thought it was nothing because I'd recovered physically, and then when I got back to work, it hit me like a tonne of bricks. Like it was all I could think about.'

'Have you told anyone else?'

'God no! Just the GP and now the counsellor.'

'What? So you've been keeping this to yourself the whole time?'

'It's not something you bring up over a cup of tea. How many people do you know who've been shot in a mall?' Jack deadpanned. 'Oh, hi, nice to meet you, I'm Jack. By the way, I was in an American mall shooting recently. Fancy a cup of tea?'

Lotta paused for a second, a smile crossing her lips and shaking her head. Same old Just Jack. 'Where are you?'

'I've just come out of the counselling session.'

'Want me to come and pick you up?'

'No, I'll be fine. I'll see you later. Where are *you* then?'

'I'm already at your place. That's how I knew you weren't here.'

'Oh, right, yes, of course. Okay then. Actually, yes, I'd love it if you could come and get me. It's just down the road. I'll text you the address.'

Lotta ended the call, heading for her car keys with a gigantic surge of relief flushing through her veins. She had never felt better and worse, both at the same time. Just Jack hadn't changed his mind. Just Jack needed her big time.

As Lotta drove towards the counselling office, a mixture of emotions swirled inside her.

She felt a deep sense of relief that she finally knew what was going on with Jack. She was also relieved that it wasn't about the wedding or her. At the same time, she felt wretched. A deep sense of guilt circled her. She'd been so wrapped up in the wedding plans and what mattered to her, she'd not seen the writing on the wall. She also felt nothing short of stupid. Had she really thought they would step off the plane, roll on back to normal life, and continue as before? Had she not thought about anyone else but herself? She knew that as the case. She knew she hadn't thought about Jack at all.

As she approached the building, she gulped as Jack saw the car and waved. Now she knew what he'd been up to, it all made sense. Pulling the car over and pressing the button to unlock the central locking, she took a deep breath. Her eyes scanned Jack's face as he got in and her breath caught in her throat as she could see he was *so* not himself. Her heart clenched – he'd just got on with the aftermath of being caught up in something terrible, and she'd not really taken much notice at all. Sure, she'd asked him how he was feeling and if he was okay, but overall she'd not done enough. Nowhere near enough. Not even close.

As Jack smiled and put his seatbelt on, Lotta reached over and took his hand, giving it a squeeze.

'Lotta as in hotter. How are we?' Jack asked, raising his eyebrows.

Lotta didn't know what to say. Jack, as he always did, was attempting to lighten the moment, but she wanted to be serious. She forced a smile as Jack adjusted himself to the passenger seat. 'So, how was it?'

Jack let out a small chuckle. 'Well, you know, just your average day discussing being shot.'

Lotta winced. 'It's so awful.'

Jack laughed, the sound a bit more genuine this time. 'I suppose it is when you think about it like that, yeah.'

'I'm really sorry about the nightmare. I'm sorry I didn't press it more. I'm just sorry, full stop, really.'

'It's fine. I was purposely hiding it from you,' Jack said.

'I'm proud of you, you know. Facing it couldn't have been easy.'

Jack looked down at their entwined fingers and sighed. 'I just wish I hadn't kept it from you for so long. I kept going to say something and chickening out. I thought I could just move on. I mean, I survived, didn't I?'

Lotta shrugged. 'You did.'

'I've been secretly seeing a counsellor and feeling like crap. I should have just let on.'

It was Lotta's turn to lighten the mood. 'That's the last of your worries. Let me tell you, I've been so worried that you'd made a mistake in the proposal that I've been secretly binge-reading books into the early hours as a way to cope with what I thought might be going on with you. I have comfort-read a *lot* of books. One night I didn't go to sleep at all – I read through the night and then had to go to work.'

Jack's eyebrows shot up in mock horror. 'You mean to tell me you've been binge-reading, Lott? Who would ever believe that?'

'Guilty as charged.' Lotta smiled, pleased to see a glimmer of the old Jack returning. 'But seriously, we should talk about this properly.'

Jack nodded, his expression quickly sombre. 'Yeah, and also no. I think the counselling is doing me the world of good. It's almost like I want to keep it separate from us, if you see what I mean.'

Lotta leaned over and kissed his cheek. 'Happy to work with whatever you want to do, Just Jack. As long as you keep me in the loop. I don't want to go through that worry again. And I don't want to be so completely and utterly self-centred again that I don't see what's staring me in the face.'

Jack chuckled and made a little salute sign to the side of his head. 'Will do.'

'I already nearly lost you once.'

'You'll never lose me, Lotta as in hotter.'

As Lotta indicated and pulled into the road, she'd never been happier to hear someone say something in her life.

40

Lotta gazed around the lavish hotel suite and had to pinch herself as Liv buttoned up the back of her wedding dress. Everything around her was beautiful. An assortment of vases overflowing with flowers adorned the surfaces, the antique furnishings and brocade wallpaper made her feel as if she'd stepped back in time, and the light streaming in the window puddled on the floor beside the mirror as if she'd ordered it from the weather gods. Even the dust motes sparkled.

'This hotel is positively gorgeous,' Liv breathed as she secured the last pearl button on the back of Lotta's dress. 'The perfect start to our day. Just the right place for us to get ready for a wedding in a library. Where you, my friend, will be in your absolute element.'

'I will.'

'Just a reminder that it's not just about the books. You must pay attention to Jack, too.'

Lotta chuckled, running her hands over the skirt of the dress. 'Don't worry. I will.' She looked around the room. 'It's like something from a fairy tale, isn't it? I keep expecting to see butterflies fluttering about – it's that nice. It was such a good choice to stay here.'

Liv laughed, coming to stand before Lotta. 'You look beautiful. More than that, though, I've never seen you so completely and utterly happy.'

'Thank you. I feel it.' Lotta gazed at her reflection, thrilled with the dress. It was just what she'd wanted; simple and classy. 'It's everything I didn't know I wanted and more,' she said as there was a knock at the door.

Liv rushed to the door. 'Thank goodness, it must be the florist,' she said over her shoulder. As she opened the door to be greeted by mostly flowers, she gasped. 'Oh, my goodness. Wow!'

Lotta turned as Cath, the florist, walked in holding a huge bouquet of floppy pale pink heavily-scented roses. A woman in a floaty floral dress trooped in behind her, holding two flower crowns. 'Hi, how are you?' Cath said as she bustled in and did a double take at Lotta. 'Ooh, you look gorgeous.'

'Thank you,' Lotta said, blushing.

Cath looked Lotta up and down. 'Goodness, yes, I love it. Give me a twirl.'

Lotta turned around with a giggle. 'What do you think? As I said, it's very plain.'

'Very plain and *very* stunning. Absolutely perfect.' Cath held the bouquet in front of her and turned it to the left and right. 'I did have a few second thoughts that this bouquet was going to be too big. I thought it might overpower things, but you said you wanted big so I went big. Now, seeing the dress in the flesh, I know it's just right.'

'Yep. I thought so too,' Lotta added.

Cath gesticulated to the flower crowns where a plethora of roses was gathered onto a band. Instead of feathers like the green fascinator, pale pink rose petals stuck out into the air and danced on top of the flowers. 'We had some fun with these. That fascinator has a lot to answer for.'

Liv squealed. 'Ahh. It's all so lovely!' She pursed her lips and pinched the end of her nose. 'Oh my gosh, Lott. I'm a bit overwhelmed. I've literally been waiting for this moment for a long time. Years!'

Lotta put her hand up. 'No crying. I won't be able to stop. I haven't been waiting because I didn't think it was ever going to happen.'

Cath looked around at the hotel room as she put the bouquet down and took one of the crowns from her assistant. 'Okay, let me get this into your hair and we'll see how we get on.'

What felt like seconds later, the crown fascinators were in both Lotta's and Liv's hair.

Cath flourished her hands in front of her. 'Yes, tops you off nicely. A flower crown fit for a wedding in a library!'

Lotta touched the flowers on her head and peered in the mirror as the petals fluttered around her. Liv dabbed at her eyes. 'Best cousin bride I've ever seen.'

Lotta laughed, though she felt a swooshing of nerves as she looked at her reflection. It was really happening. She was really marrying Jack. Just as they were saying goodbye to Cath, Timmy came out of the lift and bustled down the corridor. His whole face looked in astonishment at Lotta and Liv. 'Looking good, darlings! Fabulous!'

'Ooh, look at you in your bespoke suit.' Liv chuckled. 'Good old Timmy, always to be counted on to look better than literally everyone else.'

'I aim to please.' Timmy winked.

'We are all dressed up to the nines!' Lotta chuckled.

'We are. Look at our beautiful Lotta,' Liv said, her eyes full of tears.

'I've been waiting a long, long, *long* time for this. Counting down the days,' Timmy said. 'I haven't slept a wink all week.'

'I just said the same.' Liv smiled. 'The day is finally here.'

Timmy touched the top of Lotta's fascinator. 'That is the icing on the cake.'

'Thanks. I actually feel amazing,' Lotta admitted as they walked into the room.

Timmy looked over to Lotta's white satin bridal bag on the table, walked over and tapped the top of it. 'Only one Kindle with you today?'

Liv shook her head. 'You haven't got your Kindle in there? Surely not?'

Lotta raised her eyebrows. 'Come on. Do you really think I wouldn't have my best friend with me for this?'

'I thought we were your best friends.'

'You're just behind my book friends.' Lotta laughed. 'Of which I have many. They have seen me through a few troubled times and back again.'

'Just like us, darling.' Timmy laughed.

'Yup. I have my oldest first-edition Kindle tucked in my bag to accompany me up the aisle. That thing has been through thick and thin and is still going strong. There is no way I was walking up the aisle without it.'

'Does Just Jack realise he's got the added bonus of marrying not just you but also a Kindle?'

'I think he's well aware of my book habits.'

'You had a Kindle in your hand when you met him, didn't you?'

'I certainly did. I started as I meant to go on,' Lotta joked.

Timmy threw his hands up. 'I love you, Lotta Button. You're such a little darling. And I am so, so, so happy. Like it's so good, I hardly know what to do with myself!'

Lotta smiled as her heart pulled on a sparkly white competition leotard covered in glittering jewels. The diamonds caught the light as her heart secured its handguards and rubbed chalk onto its hands. Time for the big guns. Time for Lotta Button to perform.

Lotta took a deep breath, feeling a jumbly gurgle of nerves. Exhilaration bubbled inside her as she glanced at her reflection one last time – the flower crown and the dress making her feel amazing. She took a deep breath, staring at her reflection. The satin gown, the soft pink roses in her hair, the petals dancing around her head. The simple look of happiness on her face. As she squinted at herself, she felt as if she were looking at both a stranger and someone she'd been waiting to meet, and *be,* for a very long time.

'Okay,' she announced as she picked up her bag and took the bouquet, trying to keep her voice calm. 'Let's get this show on the road. Let's get married in a library.'

Liv and Timmy exchanged excited smiles, their eyes glistening. 'Time to get to it!' Timmy cheered, grabbing Lotta's upper arm and giving it a reassuring squeeze. 'Let's go and make memories with a delightful grumpy man named Jack.'

'Ready?' Liv asked.

Lotta nodded, her pulse quivering as Timmy offered his arm with an exaggerated bow. 'May I have the pleasure, darling?'

Lotta giggled, slipping her arm through his. 'We're going to get some funny looks as we walk up the street.'

'I don't give a hoot.' Timmy trilled. 'Let them look. Let them fall down on the floor, green with envy. The best girl in the world is getting the wedding of her dreams.'

Once they stepped out of the hotel lobby, the fact that Lotta was getting married really dawned on her. The sun shone brilliantly, the sky seared a perfect blue, a smattering of wispy clouds floated by, and the buildings of Oxford seemed to whisper to Lotta as she walked to the library. It was as if everything had collided in a mishmash of English loveliness to create the most idyllic day for Lotta's wedding.

Lotta, Timmy, and Liv ambled along the cobbled streets, laughing and joking as Timmy couldn't stop gushing. Lotta held onto his arm in a daze, feeling a mixture of nerves, happiness and excitement surging around her body. She looked down at her dress as it swished elegantly as she walked, and the flowers filled her nose with an old rose scent. She'd never forget the smell as long as she lived.

As they passed the historic buildings, Liv also gushed. 'Just look at everything. It's like we're actually walking through a picture book. Now I get why you were so sold on this place, and we haven't even arrived at the library yet.'

Lotta beamed, her eyes taking in the surroundings. 'It's magical, isn't it? I couldn't have picked a better place to get married.'

Timmy nodded in agreement and swished his hand around grandly in front of them. 'Everything about today is perfect, darling. The location, the company, even the weather has shown up for us. Love it, love it, love it.'

Lotta's heart, in its tip-top competition leotard, puffed out its chest and doubled in size. Her voice caught. 'You two have been my rock through everything. Thank you.'

As they proceeded with their walk to the library, passersby stopped, smiled, and some offered their congratulations. Lotta felt as if she was floating on a fluffy cloud edged with pink and topped with happiness. 'I can't believe this is really actually totally happening,' she whispered to Liv and Timmy, her eyes full of emotion. 'Thank you both for being here with me.'

Liv squeezed Lotta's hand gently. 'Wouldn't have missed it for the world, Lott. You don't need to keep saying thank you.'

Timmy chimed in, his voice filled with fondness. 'And Jack is the luckiest bloke alive to be marrying you. Let us all remember that, shall we? Do you want a little marriage guidance tip from me?'

'Oh, go on then.' Lotta giggled. 'You twisted my arm.'

'Never let him forget it.' Timmy guffawed. 'I mean, like never.'

'Yes, best advice ever.' Liv agreed.

As the library came into view, Lotta took a deep breath, her heart thumping with anticipation. This was turning out to be a day like no other. As she gripped her flowers and felt her bag dangling beside her, she wanted it to last forever.

Approaching the doors to the small library, Lotta buzzed with anticipation. Timmy gave her arm a reassuring squeeze, and with a deep breath, they stood by the door. Everything in front of her was much better than she'd thought it was going to be; the floor-to-ceiling shelves filled with books, the high ceilings, the gathering of beautiful high-backed matte gold chairs swathed in white and clasped with huge bunches of the same floppy pink roses as Lotta's bouquet. Just as she'd requested, the heavy old shutters were closed, and hundreds of tealights were dotted in front of the books. The whole place had been transformed into a bookworm's wonderland.

Cath, the florist, had outdone herself. The bookshelves were entwined with roses, the scent of the flowers filling the air with a sweet scent that made Lotta's heart skip a beat. Large vintage jugs of the same floppy roses were strategically placed around the room, their soft pinkness contrasting beautifully against the old timeworn dark wood of the bookshelves. Trails of ivy hung delicately from the old chandeliers and the railing of the mezzanine overhead, and a white aisle carpet between the chairs was scattered with rose petals.

Lotta's breath hitched in her throat as she took it all in. The library, already her happy place, had been transformed. The perfect place for her to be wearing white. It was like standing at the entrance to a different world, a mix of books, prettiness, happiness and love. As she smiled down at Jack, all of it would remain etched in Lotta's memory, the place where there was no doubt whatsoever that she was loved.

'Blimey, Cath has really outdone herself,' Timmy murmured beside her, his voice filled with awe.

'She has,' Liv whispered, her eyes wide. 'I mean, I knew she was good when she somehow made the fascinator work, but this, this is… incredible.'

Lotta could only nod as she gazed into the flower-laden library. It couldn't have been any more perfect. She clutched Timmy's arm as the three of them stood in the hushed threshold, pausing momentarily. The air was thick with flowers, anticipation, and smiles. A heady combination Lotta loved. She felt the enormity of the moment sink into her bones. She was about to get married. To Jack. Here. Today.

As they started their walk down the aisle, Timmy leaned in and whispered, 'Darling, you are absolutely, positively, one hundred percent certain about this? Because if there are any gnawing doubts, now's the time to make a dash.'

Lotta looked up at him, her eyes wide in surprise. 'I've never been surer about anything in my life.'

'Good, just confirming for the people in the wings,' Timmy joked.

'I'm not going anywhere.'

'Good. Because, honestly, the sight of you making a run for it in that fascinator would probably give me a heart attack. Plus, this suit was more than my mortgage – I need to get my money's worth.'

A whisper-chuckle went between them, her nerves momentarily forgotten. 'Thank you, you two. For being here with me.'

Liv's response was soft. 'Not a problem, Lott.'

Timmy whispered again. 'You've got this, darling. That man there adores you.' His eyes misted over.

And with that, they continued their walk down the aisle, the scent of roses wafting around, and books completely surrounding them. This was where Lotta had always been meant to be. With Just Jack. Forever.

Lotta took one last deep breath, her heart pounding with a mix of nerves and elation. This was it – her very own happily ever after was about to begin. And she couldn't have been more ready.

As she took Jack's hand, Lotta's heart was now on the gymnasium floor for its final performance. Its pure white competition leotard dazzled under the spotlights as it presented and started to tumble across the floor. As she finished her vows, her heart went for the jugular, a double back salto tucked with a triple twist. It nailed the perfect landing. As it presented, it didn't really need to wait for the judges. It had scored the perfect ten. This was Lotta's moment, her final performance in a lifelong competition. Lotta Button, surrounded by books and with a fascinator on her head, had won. Her happily ever after, the big fat gold medal, and her Kindle, were all, quite nicely, nestled in the bag. She was never going to let go of it. Never in her life.

My next trilogy - The Old Ticket Office Darling Island.

My NEW novella Summer in the Pretty Beach Hills is at Amazon.

SUMMER IN THE PRETTY BEACH HILLS

A POLLY BABBINGTON NOVELLA.

Because summer in the Pretty Beach Hills is always a good idea. One day in the beautiful hills tucked safely behind Pretty Beach, a love story is about to occur…

Poppy cannot wait to escape on her annual jaunt to her holiday home in the hills of Pretty Beach, where she gets to enjoy every little thing the beautiful place has to offer. This year though, something fabulous is waiting for her. Something she very much didn't see coming.

Get ready to fall in love with the second in Polly's new series of novellas. In Summer in the Pretty Beach Hills, we meet Poppy and get to know more about the sweet little village near the sea. We explore the old cottages with their beautiful window boxes along the main street, pop into the corner shop to say hello, and delight in all the English summer feels.

Are you ready to escape to the Pretty Beach Hills with Polly? Pack up a picnic and a flask of tea. We are about to embark on a journey to your new happy place. A place where the sun is shining, the days are long, and love is in the air. You're going to fall head over heels as you're transported to another world.

A love story. A friendship. A slow amble down to the sea.

Order my novella Summer in the Pretty Beach Hills at Amazon.

THE OLD TICKET OFFICE
DARLING ISLAND

One long summer. One gorgeous old shop. One second chance at love.

Get ready to be swept away to Darling Island - the sparkling little place perched on the edge of the English coast where the old ferry crosses a glittering sea, sunshine shimmers, and love is most definitely in the air. From contemporary romance author, Polly Babbington comes the loveliest romantic treat to get lost in at any time of the year.

Emmy is all sorts of okay with her life, but that's about as good as it really gets. One day on a trip to Darling Island in search of the perfect birthday cake, her okay life takes a little turn in a way she most definitely hadn't seen coming.

As the sun shines and gorgeous old vintage trams rumble past, Emmy finds herself staring at a dilapidated old shop that has seen better days. The building, the setting and the Darling lifestyle tug at her heartstrings, and on an impulsive whim, she's sunk just about everything she has into a completely new way of life.

We follow along as Emmy not only dips her toe into a whole new world but peels back the layers of her heart, and Darling wraps her up in its charms.

Get ready to swoon as you fall deep down into Polly's world and Darling Island speaks to your heart. You will utterly love it.

The Old Ticket Office Darling Island.

READ MORE BY POLLY BABBINGTON

The Old Ticket Office Darling Island

Spring in the Pretty Beach Hills
    Summer in the Pretty Beach Hills

The Pretty Beach Thing
    The Pretty Beach Way
    The Pretty Beach Life

Something About Darling Island
    Just About Darling Island
    All About Christmas on Darling Island

The Coastguard's House Darling Island
    Summer on Darling Island
    Bliss on Darling Island

The Boat House Pretty Beach
    Summer Weddings at Pretty Beach
    Winter at Pretty Beach

A Pretty Beach Christmas
    A Pretty Beach Dream
    A Pretty Beach Wish

Secret Evenings in Pretty Beach
    Secret Places in Pretty Beach
    Secret Days in Pretty Beach

Lovely Little Things in Pretty Beach
    Beautiful Little Things in Pretty Beach
    Darling Little Things

The Old Sugar Wharf Pretty Beach
    Love at the Old Sugar Wharf Pretty Beach
    Snow Days at the Old Sugar Wharf Pretty Beach

Pretty Beach Posies
    Pretty Beach Blooms
    Pretty Beach Petals

OH SO POLLY

Words, quilts, tea and old houses…

My words began many moons ago in a corner of England, in a tiny bedroom in an even tinier little house. There was a very distinct lack of scribbling, but rather beautifully formed writing and many, many lists recorded in pretty fabric-covered notebooks stacked up under a bed.

A few years went by, babies were born, university joined, white dresses worn, a lovely fluffy little dog, tears rolled down cheeks, house moves were made, big fat smiles up to ears, a trillion cups of tea, a decanter or six full of pink gin, many a long walk. All those little things called life neatly logged in those beautiful little books tucked up neatly under the bed.

And then, as the babies toddled off to school, as if by magic, along came an opportunity and the little stories flew out of the books, found themselves a home online, where they've been growing sweetly ever since.

I write all my books from start to finish tucked up in our lovely old Edwardian house by the sea. Surrounded by pretty bits and bobs, whimsical fabrics, umpteen stacks of books, a plethora of lovely old things, gingham linen, great big fat white sofas, and a big old helping of nostalgia. There I spend my days spinning stories and drinking rather a lot of tea.

From the days of the floral notebooks, and an old cottage locked away from my small children in a minuscule study logging onto the world wide web, I've now moved house and those stories have evolved and also found a new home.

There is now an itty-bitty team of gorgeous gals who help me with my graphics and editing. They scheme and plan from their laptops, in far-flung corners of the land, to get those words from those notebooks onto the page, creating the magic of a Polly Bee book.

I really hope you enjoy getting lost in my world.

Love

Polly x

AUTHOR

Polly Babbington

In a little white Summer House at the back of the garden, under the shade of a huge old tree, Polly Babbington creates romantic feel-good stories, including The PRETTY BEACH series.

Polly went to college in the Garden of England and her writing career began by creating articles for magazines and publishing books online.

Polly loves to read in the cool of lazing in a hammock under an old fruit tree on a summertime morning or cosying up in the winter under a quilt by the fire.

She lives in delightful countryside near the sea, in a sweet little village complete with a gorgeous old cricket pitch, village green with a few lovely old pubs and writes cosy romance books about women whose life you sometimes wished was yours.

Follow Polly on Instagram, Facebook and TikTok @PollyBabbingtonWrites

PollyBabbington.com

Want more on Polly's world? Subscribe to Babbington Letters

Printed in Great Britain
by Amazon

39735284R00149